Other John Cuddy novels by Jeremiah Healy

Blunt Darts
The Staked Goat
So Like Sleep
Swan Dive
Yesterday's News
Right to Die
Shallow Graves

Published by POCKET BOOKS

Most Pocket Books are available at special quantity discounts for bulk purchases for sales promotions, premiums or fund raising. Special books or book excerpts can also be created to fit specific needs.

For details write the office of the Vice President of Special Markets, Pocket Books, 1230 Avenue of the Americas, New York, New York 10020.

Jeremiah Healy

Shallow Graves

POCKET BOOKS

New York   London   Toronto   Sydney   Tokyo   Singapore

For Jane Chelius

This book is a work of fiction. Names, characters, places, and incidents are either products of the author's imagination or are used fictitiously. Any resemblance to actual events or locales or persons, living or dead, is entirely coincidental.

POCKET BOOKS, a division of Simon & Schuster Inc.
1230 Avenue of the Americas, New York, NY 10020

ISBN: 0-671-70812-0

First Pocket Books paperback printing August 1993

10 9 8 7 6 5 4 3 2 1

POCKET and colophon are registered trademarks of Simon & Schuster Inc.

Cover art by Punz Wolff

Printed in the U.S.A.

1

A FUNNY FEELING, COMING AS A VISITOR TO AN OFFICE THAT ONCE was yours.

Harry Mullen cradled the telephone in its console and stood up. "Jeez, John Cuddy, it's been what . . . years, right?"

"Right, Harry."

I let go of his hand and fought the urge to wipe mine dry.

"You're looking real good, John."

I wish I could have said the same for him. In a word, Harry looked harried. Sloping shoulders over a donut of fat at the beltline, troughs under bloodshot eyes in a fleshy face. His teeth were yellowed from nicotine, like the keys of a neglected piano. Maybe two years younger than I was, he could have been mistaken for ten years older.

"I've been running, Harry."

"Running? You mean like jogging?"

"Right."

"What're you weighing these days?"

"About one ninety."

"On six three?"

1

"Not quite."

Mullen shook his head. "Next thing, you'll be telling me you did the marathon."

"As a matter of fact."

"You're kidding?"

"Just this last one."

"Jeez." Harry shook his head some more and sank back into my old swivel chair, the one with the frozen right front wheel. Moving forward, he scraped rather than skidded to my old desk and opened the red file folder on my old blotter. I noticed the laminate on the desk was starting to lift at the corner nearest the window. Mullen kept his telephone to the right and a trip-tych photo frame to the left. The frame held studio shots of his wife and two kids, one of them a boy of about eight who goofed his pose with no front teeth. I remembered keeping a vacation candid of Beth in the same place until she died. Then I moved it to the center.

The back of the visitor's chair was too steep, and I realized how uncomfortable people must have been when they had business with Head of Claims Investigation/Boston for Empire Insurance. From where Harry was sitting, he could just see the Prudential Insurance Tower, now mostly abandoned by that company. From where I was sitting, I could just see the Burger King on Boylston Street.

Mullen spoke without seeming to read from the file. "You know Phil's gone?"

"No, I didn't."

"Yeah. Early retirement, last—no, month before last."

"He earned it."

"Yeah. Head of Claims wears you down."

Phil had been Head of Claims/Boston in my time. One day Phil asked me to sign off on a jewelry theft west of the city that nobody on my staff had investigated. When I refused, two heavy hitters from Home Office shuttled up from New York to pressure me. One of them was Brad Winningham, the Head of Claims Investigation for the entire company. Winningham had that classic preppy look and manner, the kind of guy who tended

2

to use four syllables where one would do. When I still refused to sign off on the jewelry theft, I got a command invitation to see the Head of Region/Boston, who gave me a heartfelt hand-shake and a letter qualifying me for unemployment. The letter looked better than a lawsuit, and the government checks gave me the chance to go out on my own. The company at least had the decency to promote Harry into my old job. And my old office.

Mullen futzed with some of the documents in the file, his fingers trembling a little, making the papers crinkle till he no-ticed that I noticed and stopped. "So, John, you hear from any of the other guys?"

"From here, you mean?"

"Yeah."

"No. I made pretty much a clean break, Harry."

Mullen pursed his lips. "Meaning, how come I asked you to come in?"

"Crossed my mind."

"It's got nothing to do with anything while you were with the company, John."

"Good."

"In fact, it's a new claim entirely, and we'd like you to look into it for us. Your usual hourly or daily."

I shifted in my chair. "You want an outside private investi-gator looking into one of your claims?"

"You got it."

"Since when did Empire start using outside help?"

Harry grimaced. "Since they cut me down to five field agents."

"Five? From twenty-three?"

"And one of them's a gal just off maternity leave."

"What happened?"

"Long story. Some hotshots out of Home Office—New York-ers, think they're fucking gods—they get this brainstorm, they're going to change our computer system, company-wide. Great idea on paper, since we've always had kind of a roll-your-own approach to data processing around here."

"So?"

"So the company they buy the equipment from goes belly-up out in Silicon Valley, and now there's nobody who can keep the things on-line or find parts for them when they go down. It's not like you can just change a tube here and there, you know."

"Which means . . ."

"Which means that nobody can find anything because nobody can retrieve anything. The equipment breaks once, it's like the Arabs with their tanks, you just shoot the fucking thing and leave it in the desert to rot. I'm telling you, John, every department in the company, every regional office, has a bad case of the shorts. Most of the hard-copy paperwork's been shipped to New York, and we're down to only six floors here."

I hadn't checked the directory in the lobby. "I'm sorry, Harry."

"Yeah. Thanks." Mullen sank deeper into the chair, which balked as he pushed it back to open a drawer. He pulled out a towel and offered it to me. "John, do me a favor?"

"What, give you a rubdown?"

"No, no. Just run this under the door, like a draft protector."

I got up, took the towel, and wedged it under the door. A college freshman afraid the scent of marijuana would leak into the dormitory corridor. As I turned back around, Mullen was plugging in a small black appliance that had appeared at the center of his desk. The appliance had a front grille like an electric space heater but was no bigger than a clock radio. Harry flipped a switch on the side, which started a humming sound. Then he took out a pack of Marlboros and a lighter and fired up.

Mullen held the smoke inside him, like marijuana, then blew it into the grille on the little machine.

"Harry?"

"Yeah?"

"What the hell are you doing?"

"Another new policy. After they bought the computers they started worrying about some kind of disease you're supposed to get from being in front of the screens too long. Then *Ex*-pire

4

Insurance gets so damned worried about its internal liability in general that it makes all us coffin-nailers go outside the building to smoke."

I'd seen it in front of banks and other employers along the major streets. "You thought about quitting the habit?"

"No. Too late for me. And who's got time to make the trip every time I need one? But this little gizmo sucks it right up, so if I ration myself to eight, ten a day, I can get away with it."

"What happens if they catch you?"

"Three strikes and I'm out."

"Fired?"

"Uh-huh. Third violation and it's the axe."

Harry Mullen. Overweight and overwrought, worn down trying to do the job I left. Never a smoker, I thought about what the booze might have done to me by now if I'd stayed.

Sending my eyes toward the folder next to his black box, I said, "That the file you want me on?"

Mullen filled his lungs, nodded, and blew into the grille, spreading the stream of smoke around it like a suburbanite spray-painting patio furniture. "Model. The one got herself killed."

"When?"

"Week ago Friday."

"I was out of town."

"You wouldn't have heard much about it, anyway. Strangled in her apartment, looks like a burglary gone sour."

"We got the landlord?"

Harry took a small draw and held it. "No. We got the modeling agency. Key employee policy."

"Model as key employee, the owners of the agency as beneficiaries?"

"You got it."

"What's the face amount?"

Mullen pursed his lips again, then expelled the smoke into the grille. "Five hundred thousand."

Could have been worse. "We—Empire going to coordinate with the family on this?"

"Family?"

"Of the model. They're going to sue the landlord, right?"

"No." Harry finished the cigarette, which had burned down almost to his fingernails.

"How come?"

Mullen took a liter-sized Coke bottle from the cigarettes drawer, unscrewed the cap, and dropped the butt into a sludge of brown water and other filters bobbing near the bottom. "You see, John, the family is the landlord."

"She was renting from her family?"

Recapping the bottle, he put it away, but let his smoke-catcher hum a while longer. "Family realty trust." Harry slid a stapled document from the file over to me.

It was the application for insurance, completed by the "Lindqvist/Yulin Agency" as the applicant. The model's name was listed as "Dani, Mau Tim."

I said, "How do you pronounce the first two names?"

"I think it's '*Mahow* Tim.' "

I went back to the application. Her address was 10 Falmouth Street, Apartment #3, a zip code in the South End. The owner's line said "A and T Realty Trust." Next to "Relatives" and "Relationship" was "Vincent Dani/uncle and landlord."

I said, "What about the inspection report?"

Mullen took a breath that had nothing to do with his departed cigarette. "Wasn't any."

"On a half-million policy?"

"Jeez, John, I know you're right. Before we approved the application, there should have been a field agent out there, interviewing present employer, prior employer, neighbors, family—you name it and I'll agree with you. But we're so fucking pressed around here, have been for over a year, that nobody ever did it, all right?"

In the application packet, I turned to the medical exam of Mau Tim Dani, done by a nurse-practitioner. The dead woman was eighteen and a half at the time of the examination six months before. Next to race was a checkmark for "Other" and the handwritten word "Amerasian." Height five eight and a

6

half, weight one-fifteen, hair black, eyes violet. The rest suggested she enjoyed the kind of medical health you'd expect in a drug-free late teen.

I gave Harry back the application packet. "When did you hear from the beneficiaries?"

"Next day."

"Saturday?"

"No, I mean next business day. Called us that Monday, a week ago yesterday."

"Didn't waste much time grieving."

"Not only that."

"What?"

Mullen dipped into the file and came up with a pink message slip and a piece of stationery. "Guy telephones, then I get a hand-delivered letter yet."

"Belt and suspenders."

"And real anxious."

"What's this guy's name?"

"George Yulin. Types his title as 'Director' of the modeling agency."

"Types it."

"Yeah, like there's only the letterhead of the agency itself, no individual stationery for the bigshot."

"Who'd you have cover the funeral?"

"Nobody."

"Clip the obit?"

"No."

"Christ, Harry—"

"I know, I know, all right? But I already told you how short we've been."

I tried to take the edge out of my voice. "Okay. Do we know who's got the case at Homicide?"

"Yeah." Mullen dipped into the file again, came up with another pink message slip. "Lieutenant Houk, I think it says."

Uh-oh. "Let me see that."

I looked at somebody's poor penmanship. "That's Holt, Harry."

7

"Whatever."

"No, not whatever. We've got a problem."

"What?"

"Holt and I had a go-round last year. Still has a low opinion of me."

"What kind of go-round?"

"He thought I horned in on one of his cases."

"Yeah, but on this one, you got the right to horn in. I can give you a letter and all."

I shook my head and returned the slip. "Won't matter to Holt. He won't give me squat."

Now the pink paper trembled in Mullen's hand. "Jeez, John, can't you . . . like, apologize to the guy or something?"

I sat back without saying anything.

The slip trembled some more before he put it down. "What's the matter?"

"I'm just wondering."

"Wondering what?"

"You call me in for a heavy case when I didn't leave the company on exactly the best of terms. Then you want me to stay on the case after I tell you I may not be effective in dealing with the cop assigned to it. Something smell funny to you, Harry?"

Mullen took a breath and chewed the inside of his cheek, the way he did when he'd been a little shoddy in the old days. Then he came forward, working one hand in the other.

"Between you and me, John?"

"Everything has been so far."

"No, really. I mean it."

"Between you and me, Harry."

"The pressure . . ." Mullen's voice got a little scratchy, and he cleared his throat. "The pressure's worse than I've ever seen it. I don't know if the company's . . . I don't know if Empire's going to be okay with the economy and all, especially around here."

"Go on."

"Winningham . . . You see, this claim, the letter and all, came in when I was up in Portland. We got this new rule. Any claim with a face amount over three hundred thousand has to get reported to Home Office."

"So?"

"So Winningham down in New York gets wind of this one when we fax him Yulin's letter last week. Before he sends us the app', he calls me and says, 'Give this one to Cuddy.' "

"Winningham wanted me to have it?"

"Yeah."

"He give you a reason?"

"He said he felt bad about all the shit we heaped on you."

"Winningham said 'shit'?"

"Uh, no. No, what he said was 'indignities.' "

I pictured Winningham. Ivy League smile, razor-cut brown hair, shirt cuffs he'd shoot like a magician about to do a card trick.

"Harry, I'm not exactly convinced that the milk of human kindness is behind all this."

"That's what I said to the guy, John."

"What'd he say back?"

"Winningham said . . . Aw, shit, he said if I couldn't handle this, maybe I was getting a little light to be running a regional office."

I watched Harry Mullen chew on his cheek some more. Thought about how he backstopped me when I slid into the bottle over losing Beth, even drove or carried me home a couple of times. Thought about his wife and kids and how he'd look to another company at a job interview. Winningham was a son of a bitch, and I could see him canning Harry for this while saying it was because of other mistakes that probably had piled up since the cutbacks. On the other hand, it was possible that Winningham saw the handwriting on the wall for Empire, the preppy prince just feathering the private-sector nest he might have to fly toward himself.

Mullen said, "John, he thinks we owe you this one."

"He does."

"His exact words. 'Reparations, Harry. We need to effectuate reparations here.' "

Indignities, reparations, and effectuate. Four syllables, every one. Sounded like Brad Winningham, all right.

2

ON THE DESK IN FRONT OF LIEUTENANT HOLT AT HOMICIDE WERE A multipart form and a soggy paper plate with six congealing french fries. Around forty-five, Holt wore a short-sleeve white shirt and plain wool tie. His gray hair was snipped close, his skull like a round magnet that had picked up iron filings. The chin was square and the nose long, enough lines in his forehead for terrace farming. The portrait of a man who'd had a humorectomy.

Holt's right hand held a stubby pencil above a box on the form. He entered two numbers in the box, then used his left hand to reach for a treat. When the hand couldn't find the plate, his head rose. Holt pinched a fry just as he caught me standing in his doorway.

"Lieutenant."

"Christ on a crutch. Cuddy."

"Nice to be remembered."

"Not when it's me doing the remembering." Holt apparently forgot about his fry, still between thumb and forefinger. "The fuck do you want?"

11

"Can I come in and talk about it?"

"Tell me first. Then I decide whether you get to sit."

"I'm doing an outside investigation for Empire Insurance on one of their death claims."

"Empire?"

"Yeah. They had the model who was killed in her apartment."

"Danu . . . ?"

Holt seemed to suffer a brain cramp.

"Lieutenant, I think it was 'Dani.' Mau Tim Dani." I pronounced it the way Harry Mullen had.

Holt stopped for a minute, face unreadable. Then he dropped the fry and said, "Sure, Cuddy. Sure, I can spare a minute for that."

I took it I could come in and sit down. Holt used the time to tip back in his chair and fold his hands over his stomach. They had to stretch some to do it.

He said, "So what did Empire tell you?"

"Not much. She got strangled, apparently by a burglar, but the modeling agency that had the policy on her seems kind of quick on the trigger."

"And you'd like to see our jacket on it, right?"

"Right."

Holt stopped again, just short of smiling at me.

"Lieutenant?"

"I was thinking about last year, with that Marsh guy and the hooker at the Barry."

"You know I wasn't involved in that."

"How about what happened afterwards?"

"I was in jail, remember?"

"I remember a lot of things, Cuddy. And like I said, it's not so good for a guy in your line of work to have me remembering. But you've got to make a living, too, right?"

I wasn't following the way this was going. "So I can see the jacket?"

"Seems to me last time I showed you a little cooperation, it blew up in my fucking face."

12

I didn't need this. Then I thought about Mullen and his family and how much my old chief investigator needed my old job. "Lieutenant, all I'm asking for is a little help here."

"A little help? A little help, that I can give you."

Holt stood and crossed to a file cabinet, yanking one, then another folder out before deciding on a third. He returned to the desk and laid the file on it, but in front of his chair, not mine. Settling into his seat, he opened it, scanned a cover sheet, then looked up at me.

"Tell you what, Cuddy."

"What?"

"I'll feed it to you. Like they do with the little chunks of fish at the Aquarium."

"The Aquarium."

"Yeah. I'll toss you a little chunk, and then you make like a seal and catch it in the air and clap for yourself. What do you say?"

I drew in a long breath, thought again about Mullen's goofy kid with no teeth, and took out a pad and pen. "Fine."

"First off, the girl, she gets it on the top floor of a three-story in the South End. She's supposed to be going to a party downstairs, then they're going out afterwards somewhere."

"Who's hosting the party?"

"Another model, name of Sinead something or other." Holt pronounced the name the Irish way, Shuh-*nade*. Probably thanks to the rock singer. "Only after this Mau Tim doesn't show on time, they go looking and find her Dee-Oh-Ef."

"DOF?"

" 'Dead on floor.' "

Maybe the humorectomy didn't take. "Who's 'they'?"

"This Sinead character and two guys. One's a Jap, ad exec over on Newbury, first block and very upscale. The other's a black guy, photographer."

"Names?"

Holt seemed to think about that, then said, "Sure." Skipping ahead in the file, he said, "The Jap, Larry Shinkawa."

"That's S-H-I-N-K-A-W-A?"

"Right. The colored guy's Oscar Puriefoy."

"Can you spell that one for me?"

Holt did.

I said, "How about Sinead's last name?"

"She's with the same modeling agency as the dead girl. How many 'Sineads' can they have?"

Holt was enjoying this. I said, "Go on."

He read some more of the file. "Like I was saying, they go up to look for this Mau Tim and have to break down her door. They find the body crumped on the floor, nice shade of blue. This Shinkawa checks the fire escape."

"Fire escape?"

"Yeah. He figured that's how the perp got out of there."

"How'd the killer get in?"

Holt looked at me. "Same way, it's a Break and Entry." He went back into the folder. "Then this Puriefoy tries CPR on the girl, but her throat's crushed from the perp's hands, so that did about as much fucking good as an enema."

I looked at Holt, but he was still in the jacket. Homicide hardens you after a while, but this wasn't hardness or even gallows humor. This was Holt having fun with me in a way nobody should enjoy.

"Can you back up a little, Lieutenant?"

The face rose. "Huh?"

"Did the guy who checked the fire escape see anything?"

"No."

"We know who had keys to the place?"

"No. How come you ain't clapping, all these little chunks I'm throwing you?"

I took another breath. "The people downstairs at the party didn't hear any kind of struggle upstairs?"

"How the hell . . . Oh, I see what you mean. No, Cuddy, the girl was killed on the top floor of the house, and the party was on the first floor."

"Who lives on the second?"

"Nobody. Family just keeps it furnished, case somebody wants to stay over."

"The dead girl's family?"

Holt smiled. "Yeah."

"You talk with them?"

"Not much. Just with the uncle. Dani, Vincent."

The landlord name in the application for the policy. "How about mother and father?"

Holt's smile broadened. "I think I'll let you go for that on your own."

Swell. "When did all this happen?"

"Week ago Friday."

"Time of day?"

"The call to 911 was 7:45."

"Quarter to eight on a Friday night in April. Kind of an odd time for a B & E."

"Used to be. Now we get them during Thanksgiving fucking dinner."

"One of the chunks I'm supposed to catch wouldn't be any leads you've got?"

"No leads to throw, Cuddy. We got a dead girl and part of a necklace near the body."

"Necklace."

"Fancy fucking thing. Purple stones."

"Amethyst?"

"No. The uncle called it 'iolite.' "

"Never heard of it."

"Me neither. Looks like the girl maybe surprised the perp as he's going through the jewelry box. They fight over the necklace, and it breaks, him getting away with most of it and a couple of other things the uncle knew she used to have."

"How do I get the uncle?"

"Lawyer, downtown firm."

"Number?"

"Let your fingers do the walking."

Okay. "Anything from forensics?"

"The party animals, they pretty well wrecked the body position and all trying to bring the girl back to life." Holt skipped

15

ahead again to a photo envelope. "Here's a couple of pictures you might like to see."

He spun them to me like a man dealing poker. Both were eight-by-tens. The first showed part of a necklace against a hardwood floor background, peeking out from under the edge of a print futon couch. A large purple pendant and some purple stones above it, all set in what looked like gold. The gold appeared to lead to a more elaborate, but missing, neckpiece.

The second photo was of an Amerasian woman, taken from her feet back up toward the face. The hair on her head seemed stringy, maybe from being wet. The robe she was wearing was open, no panties or bra. Her skin tone was golden and perfectly consistent, no tan lines or blemishes. The only problem was the abrasions down toward the throat, where a smudgy blue spoiled the skin. Her eyes were only half-closed, the irises glazed in the giving over of vision from life to death.

Holt said, "Notice anything?"

"The medical examiner say whether these were cuts on the throat?"

"Yeah. M.E. thinks the perp had the necklace in his hand when he choked her. Notice anything else?"

"No sexual abuse."

"No."

Holt sounded impatient, like I was getting colder rather than warmer. It was hard to tell from the photos, but the application had listed her eye color.

I said, "They're the same."

Holt sat back again and smiled. "Spooky, isn't it? Her eyes and the necklace there, the same color."

The telephone company keeps track of all calls, even local ones, made from any address. "You have her phone records yet?"

"They're being sent."

"Ten days, you don't have them?"

Holt came forward, reaching across the desk to reclaim the photos. "What do you think, our boy stopped to call his momma, see if she needed anything from the store on the way home? We got no eyewitnesses on the perp and no hope of turning one. We find somebody dirty with the necklace, he's a done guy. Or, somebody pops a name at us, gives up the killer, we can lock it in with maybe a little pressure and a couple of statements. But otherwise, this one's a dream you can't remember once you wake up."

"I'd think you'd be showing a little more enthusiasm for a glamour killing like this."

"Cuddy, we've logged over fifty homicides in the city since January one, and we're not into May yet. Used to be, we'd have maybe a hundred in the whole Commonwealth the whole year. Enthusiasm's kind of tough to come by, these days."

Holt tipped back in his chair again. "Besides, now that you're on this, we can relax and watch you bring it home for us."

I thanked him and got up. He told me to be sure and have a nice day, now.

I went up the hall and around the corner to another office. Inside, I could see Robert Murphy wading through a file that had two inches on the Manhattan Yellow Pages. Black, burly, and blunt, he'd been promoted to lieutenant and assigned to Homicide some years ago when a biased city councillor mistook an Irish name for an Irish cop.

Murphy wore a long-sleeved blue shirt with a collar stay under a blue silk tie. Two fingers held his place at two different points in the file. "Gotcha."

"Lieutenant?"

Murphy looked up and down again. "Cuddy. Take a seat."

I closed the door and angled a chair toward him. "Am I interrupting anything?"

"Minor victory. One of maybe ten suspects in a drive-by tells the uniforms he was with a homeboy named Jomo when the shooting started. Only problem is, Jomo was enjoying the county's hospitality on Nassau Street at the time."

The new jail near the Registry of Motor Vehicles. "I haven't been there yet."

"You saw it, you wouldn't believe it. They got something

17

like 450 cells with computerized doors. The cells're in color-coded units for different kinds of offenders, with different-colored jump suits to match."

"*Alice Through the Looking Glass.*"

"Compared to Charles Street, anyway. New facility's got twenty beds for women, no more 'Susan-Saxe' cells in the bowels of the courthouse. Windows, recreation decks . . ."

"Jacuzzis."

"Next budget."

"Save me the trip to Florida for Spring Break."

Murphy stuck a couple of yellow Post-Its into the file as bookmarks. "You still looking a mite sickly."

"Thought I might try to hold the weight."

"You really run the marathon with that bullet wound?"

"Wasn't much of a wound."

"Isn't much of a brain, you ask me. The shit about that law professor all cleaned up?"

"As much as ever will be."

Murphy rocked back, slitting his eyes. "Doesn't seem like you and me have much to talk about, then."

"Less than that. I'm just here as a courtesy."

"Courtesy."

"Right."

"About exactly what are you being so polite?"

"I drew a case from my old employer."

"You had a real job once?"

"Insurance company. I worked there before you knew me."

"So?"

"It's a death claim."

"Homicide?"

"Right."

Murphy passed a hand over a stack of six or seven thinner files near the corner of his desk. "One of mine."

"No."

"No?"

"One of Holt's."

Murphy closed his eyes all the way. "The door's right behind you."

"There's something funny—"

"That little round thing, they call that a knob. It opens the door."

"Lieutenant—"

"Cuddy, maybe you're forgetting the last time I helped you out on one of Holt's cases. Ever see *True Grit?*"

"You a Glen Campbell fan, too?"

"I was thinking of the scene, the Duke warns the rat to get the hell out of the grain bag, but that rat, he just don't listen so good. You remember what caliber it was the Duke used to chastise him?"

"Like I said, just paying you the courtesy of letting you know."

"And I appreciate that, Cuddy, I really do. This job, you treasure every little courtesy comes your way."

I left before Murphy could wish me a nice day, too.

3

AFTER LEAVING POLICE HEADQUARTERS, I WALKED BACK TO MY OFFICE on Tremont Street. The few documents from Harry Mullen and my notes from Holt went into a case folder. I did two more hours of paperwork on other files, looking forward to seeing Nancy Meagher for her birthday dinner.

By the time I got to the entrance of the New Courthouse building, she was already down from the District Attorney's office and talking with a female Sheriff's Deputy at the metal detector. Nancy's suit was a nubby gray tweed with black and green specks over a ruffled white blouse. The deputy wore blue.

Seeing me, Nancy brought the strap of her briefcase onto her shoulder. "Thought I'd save you a trip up the elevator."

I said, "Mustn't seem too anxious for a date, counselor."

Nancy and the deputy rolled their eyes in unison. The deputy said, "When do you suppose men'll stop being such jerks?"

Nancy said, "The day genetic engineering becomes available for household use."

I stood a little straighter. "Could be that day has arrived. You're looking at the body of a twenty-year-old paratrooper."

SHALLOW GRAVES

The deputy said, "What're you gonna do, he asks for it back?"

Nancy was still howling as we went through the revolving door.

I said, "It wasn't that funny."

"Oh, John, it was priceless."

"It was a cheap shot. She can't be more than twenty-two herself."

"She's almost thirty, and you've been so cock-proud ever since you ran the marathon that I was beginning to wonder how to bring you back to earth."

"A few weeks of feeling like a young warrior doesn't seem so long."

"It does if you're 'dating' the warrior."

I decided to change the subject. "So, how was your day?"

Nancy shook her head. "The usual. I'm on a bank robbery. Pretrial, our boy moved to suppress an eyewitness ID from a photo array."

"Denied?"

"Yes. At trial, defendant renewed his motion, but the judge, bless her, refused to review her denial. At that point, our boy conceded identification and tried to make like he was the new Patty Hearst."

"I thought the Symbionese Liberation Army abolished their draft."

"Not to hear this guy. He actually took the stand, tried to persuade us he was kidnapped and forced to cooperate at gunpoint."

"Let me guess. His credibility was not without stain."

"Twelve priors, three for armed robbery, seven all told admissible under the prior conviction statute."

"You had that kind of ammunition and he still took the stand?"

"It was his only shot, John. If he's convicted of this one, he's going away forever."

"Jury get the case yet?"

"I finished my cross this afternoon. My guess is some wrangling over requests for jury instructions tomorrow, then closing

21

arguments and charge by lunchtime. Speaking of eating, where are you taking me tonight?"

We'd reached the Park Street corner of the Boston Common. I pointed diagonally across it, though even in bright daylight you couldn't have seen the building I meant.

Nancy said, "The *Ritz*?"

"You got it."

"John, it'll cost a fortune."

"You're each age only once."

She linked her arm in mine and looked up at me. Irish, freckled face. Wide-spaced blue eyes. High forehead with black, fine hair, parted on the right side, long enough to fall just so onto her shoulders. And a smile that took its time pushing up the corners of her mouth and dimpling her cheeks and finally flashing straight teeth under a nose that she'd punch you for calling perky.

Nancy said, "There are certain advantages to 'dating' successful, 'older' men."

"I'm not that old."

She balled her free hand into a fist, threw it straight into the air and said, "Airborne!"

Nancy was still laughing so hard, I thought they might not let us into the second-floor dining room.

At the table, the maître d' discreetly pulled out the birthday girl's chair and seated her. I tipped him a five for putting us at a window overlooking the Public Garden. The trees were a little too high to appreciate the flowers, but then it was early enough in the season that the beds weren't spectacular yet.

The waiter stepped over immediately for our drink orders, and Nancy said she'd rather have wine. The *sommelier* appeared with the wine list, which should have come in three volumes and an audiotape. I picked a price range in the red Bordeaux, and he made a suggestion that I accepted.

As the *sommelier* retreated, I said, "You know, I really don't mind the cracks about my physical condition."

"I know. Otherwise I wouldn't make them."

Nancy covered my right hand with both of hers, running the edge of a fingernail along the back of my knuckles. "I read somewhere that holding hands is pleasurable because of the nerve endings."

"Nerve endings."

"Right. For example, it feels good for me to do this."

"It does."

She turned my hand over. "But if I try your palm, it feels better, doesn't it?"

"Uh-huh."

"That's because there are more nerve endings there." The nail went to the pad of my middle finger. "It should feel even better now. Know why?"

"Still more nerve endings."

A nod before moving to the thumb pad. "And there are just bundles of the little devils here."

I cleared my throat. "Any more . . . bundles?"

"Yes, but unfortunately they're not yet accessible."

At which point, our wine arrived.

Halfway through the meal, a terrific rack of lamb for two, a pianist started playing, the kind of theme and variations that you recognize but have trouble placing.

Nancy stopped the wineglass halfway to her lips. " 'Phantom of the Opera'?"

"I think so."

She took a sip. "Growing up in Southie, did you ever think you'd eat here?"

"Same as you, Nance. I thought I'd work hard and do well and yeah, eventually eat somewhere outside of South Boston."

Nancy said, "Do you enjoy it?"

As the pianist segued into "Out of Africa," I looked around the room. Lofty ceiling, delicate molding, crystal chandeliers. Wall-tall windows with drapes that had to be gathered like the robes of an emperor. Enough tuxedos and evening gowns to prove that fifty-year-olds still held proms.

I came back to Nancy. "Yes, I enjoy it."

"As much as eating at a fish joint in Southie?"

"The same, I think. In Southie, the guy who brings the wine bottles twists off the tops. I'm not sure the enjoyment goes up just because the guy here pours a little into a silver spoon around his neck."

"I was impressed with how you handled that, by the way."

"The man knows his job. I should let him do it if it helps me."

"Speaking of jobs, what did you do today?"

That was the tough part of being with an assistant D.A. There were some things I couldn't talk about because of client confidentiality and other things I couldn't talk about because I might put Nancy in a conflict of interest. She wore the mark of one of those conflicts on her right shoulder, a little pleat of scar tissue over the hole a thirty-eight slug made when we first got involved.

The good part was that I could be vague without seeming rude. "I'm doing a death case for Empire."

"Empire? I thought they hated you."

"They do. It's a long, boring story."

"The death case. Here in Suffolk County?"

"Right."

Nancy nodded. She had her professional obligations, I had mine, and we both knew it was best not to mix them.

Going back to the lamb, I said, "You still on for the conference in Dallas?"

She smiled without showing teeth. "Convention. I confirmed it this morning."

"They still want you to talk?"

"Uh-huh. One of the panels at plenary session."

"What does 'plenary' mean?"

"Before the whole convention in the big auditorium."

"Quite a feather in the young prosecutor's cap."

"It'll hold me till you do."

By the time we were ready for dessert, the pianist had taken a break. Over the hushed talk and clinking of cutlery, I said, "You know, I thought about embarrassing you with a cake and singing."

24

Nancy looked up, horrified. "You didn't?"

"Picture it. The Great Nancy Meagher, the center of attention at her convention, unbearably self-conscious in the best hotel restaurant in Boston."

"That would be cruel, John."

"Cruelty has its place. Instead, though, how about a chocolate mousse torte?"

"You memorized the menu?"

"That one kind of jumped out at me."

Our waiter wheeled over the dessert cart anyway. Nancy picked a seven-layer walnut cake and a tea I couldn't pronounce. I went with the torte and the last of the wine.

Pointing my fork at her cake, I said, "There's still time to stick a candle in that."

She looked up. "Want a taste?"

We exchanged forkfuls, making appropriate "ummm" sounds.

The pianist came back on just as we were finishing. I said, "We could order some brandy, hear one more set?"

Nancy seemed to consider it as he began playing again. Then she frowned. "What is that?"

I looked at the piano, thinking it would help me. "Something with words, but . . ."

"A theme song, like from television."

"Yeah. Sure. 'The first mate and the skipper, too . . .' "

Nancy put a hand to her mouth. *"Gilligan's Island!"*

I said, "Maybe it is time for the check."

We walked up Commonwealth to Fairfield and then over to Beacon and the condominium I was renting from a doctor doing a two-year residency in Chicago. We got only as far as the parking lot because Nancy wanted to sleep home in South Boston to be fresh for battle the next morning. My silver Prelude, 'old' but reliable, took us to Southie, finding as always a spot on the street near her place.

I climbed the stairs behind Nancy. Drew Lynch, a cop whose parents owned the property, opened his door on the second floor, just to be sure that she was okay. As we reached her door on the third, I thought for a moment about the model in Holt's photo. Mau Tim Dani died in an apartment on the same floor in a probably similar building across town in the South End.

Nancy turned the key and pushed the door. A ball of fur swirled around her feet, biting me at the sock line of my shoes.

I said, "Can't you teach him not to do this?"

"He's an attack cat, John. Aren't you, Renfield?"

At the sound of her voice, Renfield backed off. A gray tiger, the yellow eyes seemed to move independently as he looked for any exposed flesh. Nancy had named him after the Englishman in *Dracula* who eats small mammals. A few months before, he'd been declawed up front and neutered, but at almost a year old, he was still a terror with his teeth and rear claws.

I said, "Do they make cat muzzles?"

Nancy swung her briefcase onto the kitchen table. "I don't know why you two don't get along better."

"He senses I'm a competitor for your affections."

"He's a eunuch now. Maybe I should take him for therapy."

I moved in behind her. "Depends on what affections he's competing for."

Nancy arched back into me just a little. "I think we left off with your thumb pad."

"Shall I start making the rest of me accessible?"

"No. It's my birthday, I get the bathroom first."

"And in the meantime?"

"You get Renfield. Try to tire him out so he doesn't bother us."

"You have any tranquilizer darts?"

Nancy moved into the bedroom and closed the door behind her.

I sat down on one of the kitchen chairs, unbuttoning my collar and tugging down my tie. Renfield hunkered onto his haunches, eyeing the end of my tie with bad intent.

I said, "Don't even think about it."

Renfield suddenly looked up and past me. I fell for it. As

soon as my head was turned, he was on my lap, the rear paws pedaling for purchase, the claws sinking through my suit and the teeth sinking through my tie.

I yelled and stood up, prying him off and dropping him from about waist height. He hit the floor on all fours, but cried out, slinking away and favoring his right hip in a limping circle.

Nancy's head and bra-strapped shoulders came around the bedroom door. "What was that?"

"I don't know. I just dropped him and—"

But she'd already spotted Renfield, now lurching near the pantry shelves, trying to scuttle under the lowest one. "Renfield? Renfield, what happened?"

"Nance, I told you. He—"

She was out in the kitchen now, trying to corner him gently. "Jesus Mary, John! He's just a little cat. What did you do to him?"

"Nothing. Like I said, he jumped on me and I dropped him."

"It looks like his leg is broken."

"It can't be. I just let him go from like here."

Nancy glanced at my hands in front of my belt, then finally got Renfield bracketed. He let her pick him up, a little at a time. Once in her arms, Renfield hissed at me.

"John, he's hurt."

"He probably just pulled something."

"Pulled something? The marathoner's a vet now?"

"Nancy, give me a break, okay? I dropped him from like three feet in the air, and he landed on all fours. He's a cat, he ought to be able to take that."

"Well, obviously he couldn't." She shifted him carefully to hold him more easily. "I should never have had him declawed."

"Nance, he was shredding your furniture. And spraying it, too. Were you not going to have him fixed now, either?"

That got me the steady, even voice. "It's my birthday, John. It's my birthday, and you crippled my kitty."

"Nancy, he's not crippled. His leg looks fine—"

"He was limping!"

"His leg seems okay. It's his hip, like it's out of joint, maybe."

"First he pulled something, now he's got a dislocated hip?"

I put up my hands. "Okay, okay. We'll take him to the vet's. Right now." I started digging in my pants for the car keys.

"No. No, let me call first."

I waited while Nancy, using just two fingers of one hand, found the animal hospital's number in her address book and dialed it. The half of the conversation I heard was: "My cat just fell from about three feet above the floor and . . . No, no, he didn't land on his back or head. He landed on his feet . . . No, it just seems to be his leg. Or hip, maybe . . . Well, I don't know if he's in pain. He's limping around and . . . No, he cried out once"—Nancy looking to me, me nodding to her—"but that's it. Now he's just hissing and . . . No, no, not at me. At—just hissing a little, now and then . . . You do? You're sure? Well, I guess that makes sense . . . Yes, yes, thank you. I appreciate . . . Right, right. Bye."

Nancy hung up the phone. "A family just arrived with a collie who'd been hit by a car. The vet's covering by herself, so she had to go."

"So should we bring Renfield in?"

"The vet said no. She wants me to wait until morning because he might just 'walk it off.' "

I thought about saying, "See?" Instead, I said, "That sounds like a good idea."

"She said to pay a lot of attention to him, to make sure he's comfortable. If he seems to be in constant pain, though, I should call her back."

I couldn't think of a good way to ask the next question, so I didn't. Nancy answered it for me by moving forward with the cat. Renfield growled, burrowing his head into her crossed arms.

"John, I really think he has to sleep with me tonight."

"I understand. I'll take off."

"No. No, could you stay here, on the couch? If he has to go in at three A.M., you could drive and I could hold him."

"Sure, Nance."

"I'm sorry about this."

"Same."

Nancy carried the cat into the bedroom. Over her shoulder, Renfield snarled at me, his two front teeth like the fangs of his namesake.

4

I THINK THE SOUND OF A VERY LIGHT RAIN WOKE ME UP. THE DIGITAL clock on Nancy's VCR said 8:20 A.M. Now 8:21. I sat up, my back creaking. The night before, I moved past her bedroom to the living room and tried the couch. Fine for sitting and cuddling, a tad short for sleeping. I'd taken the seat cushions off and spread them on the floor, covering myself with an afghan Nancy's mother had crocheted two years before she'd died. Even so, my kidneys felt as though someone had forgotten to hinge them.

I got up and put the couch back together, folding the afghan on an armrest. At the bedroom door, I knocked, got no answer, and knocked louder. Opening it, I saw a made bed. I didn't hear any water running in the bathroom, so I moved all the way back to the kitchen. There was a note propped up between the salt and pepper shakers:

John,
   I woke up early and took Renfield to the vet's. I looked in
on you but you were asleep.

I'm sorry you got the floor and I'm sorry I got mad at you.

Call me later,
Nancy

I read my kidneys the part about the floor, but they weren't much comforted. Raiding the refrigerator, I had a couple of English muffins and orange juice.

In the bathroom, the scent of Nancy's potpourri was zingy in the air. I weighed myself on her scales. It was an old building, and depending on where I put the scales, the needle moved a little more or a little less. I liked by the sink best, coming in at just under one ninety there.

I wanted to see the Dani woman's apartment house before talking with the people at the modeling agency. Given the time, I couldn't really go home, change, and run for a while first, so I decided to make a short visit instead.

"I got to Mrs. Feeney's just as she was putting the carnations out on the sidewalk."

But I get roses instead?

I straightened back up, almost using the headstone to steady myself against the stiffness. "Transference, Beth."

Fight with Nancy?

"Not exactly." I told her about Renfield.

So, the question is, did the cat jump or was he pushed?

"Not funny, kid."

I'm sorry, John, but if it was an accident, you can't let it get you down.

"I know."

The rain had turned to mist, the mist curtaining a rainbow that vaulted over Logan Airport across the harbor and down to the foot of her hillside, almost touching two men in a small boat, fishing. The convex edge of the rainbow was red, then yellow, and finally blue-green near the concave edge.

Is Renfield all that's distracting you, John?

I looked back from the rainbow. "No. Remember Harry Mullen?"

At Empire?

"Right."

Sure. Is he all right?

"Sort of." In a way I couldn't do with Nancy, I caught Beth up on the case so far.

And you smell a rat.

"I don't know. I can't see Harry suckering me, but Brad Winningham was never exactly my rabbi, and Holt should have told me to hit the pike."

Maybe you're looking for a reason not to take the job.

"Because I'm still bitter over what Empire did to me?"

A pause. And maybe over when they did it.

I thought back to Winningham coming into my office, now Harry's office, with the jewelry claim. Sign off or sign out. It was Christmas time, two months after a priest and I had buried Beth. My leaving the company, the boozing, a kid on a bike that I nearly turned into a hood ornament—

John?

"I'm okay. And you're probably right. I'll see you soon, huh?"

I'll be here.

We laughed together as the fishermen below us upped anchor and putted off. I wondered if they could see the rainbow. Or even feel it.

The apartment house at Number 10 Falmouth Street might still be taken for the single-family town house it probably once was, one of many in a part of the South End where the byways were named after towns on Cape Cod. From the front, the building itself was dull red brick, bowfront rather than bay windows on all three floors, trapezoid lintel blocks over each bowfront section. The front entrance was the height of a ten-step stoop above street level. The elevation of the entrance gave the basement a daylight effect, a separate smaller door leading into it. A low iron railing, painted black, enclosed the front of the house, separating it symbolically from the sidewalk. I say symbolically because there were no bars on the windows, not even across the openings at basement level.

The South End never quite caught on during the yuppie boom. Back Bay, where I lived in the doctor's condo, was the first to be renovated, followed by the waterfront around Faneuil Hall and then Beacon Hill below the State House. But there was always a damper on the South End. Too many drugs, too many fires, too many homeless long before they were everywhere. As a result, you had one block of rehabbed town houses straight out of *Mary Poppins* bordering another block of dehabbed crackhouses straight out of the South Bronx.

I opened the gate and climbed the steps. Four doorbell buttons, three of them labeled. The front door was locked, but from the handle it looked like a spring job, no bolt. Through a glass panel I could see it was the only secured entry, the staircase to the second floor lying behind an opened, inner door. Probably an internal buzzer system tied into the bell buttons. I was thinking that Empire should be glad it didn't have the landlord on this one when I remembered the building was owned by the dead woman's family.

I examined the bells. The top button was captioned "Dani, M. T." Expecting nothing, I tried it and got what I expected. Next was the unlabeled one. Nothing again. Next was "Fagan, S.," which I took to be "Sinead," the other model Holt had mentioned. Still nothing. The bottom button said "Super." A four-unit building probably didn't need its own superintendent, but landlords had a tendency to own several properties in the same neighborhood and to put the manager up in one of them. I pushed the bottom button and got nothing a fourth time.

I walked down to the super's separate entrance and knocked. No answer. I climbed back to sidewalk level and looked up at the building. No shade or drape moved abruptly. I went out the gate, then down the block and around to the alley behind the building.

A lot of South End houses have postage stamp backyards, with patios off the basement door. This block was more like

Back Bay, with the house almost abutting on the alley itself. No parking, maybe ten feet between where the fire escape's raised last flight would come down and where two big trash cans stood covered against the wall and near the back door.

The escape itself was black except for rust spots here and there. My eyes followed it up the rear wall. The raised last flight retracted to a landing outside the window on the elevated first floor. The escape then switchbacked to a landing at the second-floor window, a third flight ending in a landing outside the third-floor window. Mau Tim Dani's apartment. There were no bars on any of the back windows either. Christ, these folks were asking for it.

Somebody nine feet tall probably could reach and pull down the raised, last flight of fire escape. The green trash cans were ribbed plastic and looked sturdy enough to support my weight. I had just positioned the second can under the escape when the basement door opened.

A man dressed in droopy pants and a strappy T-shirt put one foot over the threshold, keeping the other inside the door. Maybe five six, he had the face of a pug from the club fights at union halls in Dorchester. Both eyebrows had divots missing, and the nose detoured more than once on its way to his mouth. The left ear was cauliflowered, the right loppy, like the Velveteen Rabbit. His hair was black, thinning unevenly at the crown, scruffy around the sides. Pushing fifty, his head flicked right, like he was ducking a punch, and he sniffed twice in quick succession through his nose.

"Whaddaya think you're doing?"

"You the superintendent?"

"Who wants to know?"

"John Cuddy." I reached into a pocket for my ID. "I tried the buzzer and knocked."

He brought the other foot outside and stood in front of me. I handed him the holder, open. He stretched out his arms and studied it.

"I'm a private investigator, Mr. . . . ?"

He looked up from the ID, then down again, although there was no picture on it to compare against me.

"Whaddaya want from me?"

I extended my hand for the holder, which he gave back carefully. "I represent the company that insured the life of the woman who died here."

"The . . . ?"

"She was a model. Mau Tim Dani?"

This time he winced before flick, sniff/sniff. "I don't know nothing about that. Nothing."

"That's okay. I'd appreciate your letting me see the apartment, though."

"What for?"

"She was killed there, Mr. . . . ."

"Don't mister me, pal. Okay?"

Not my best start ever. "Okay. You got a first name?"

"Yeah. Carmine."

"All right. Carmine—"

"But everybody calls me Ooch."

"Ooch?"

"Yeah. From when I was in the ring. The other guy'd hit me, everybody went 'Ooch! You see that shot?' "

I laughed politely. "You fight, you're going to get hit, right?"

"You can take it from me."

"So, can I get a look at the place?"

Flick, sniff/sniff. "No way."

"I have a letter here from the company."

"I don't know from no letter. The owners told me nobody gets in without they say it's okay."

"You let the police in, didn't you?"

"No. The others let them in. I wasn't here."

"Where were you?"

"Over to the gym. They was going to have a party up there." He gestured toward the elevated first floor. "They get loud, the music, you know? I get itchy, gets too loud down there." He gestured back toward the basement door.

"Where do you work out?"

"The Y. Over by Northeastern. Ain't too many real gyms left."

"What time you get over there?"

He shrugged. "I worked out, is all."

"Then came back here?"

"Uh-unh. Had a few beers along the way. Didn't want to get back till they was all out for dinner."

"I thought there was supposed to be a party?"

"Yeah, but Sinead, she said Tina and them were going out to eat after. So I could come back then, it wouldn't be loud no more."

"Tina?"

"Huh?"

"Who's Tina?"

"Tina's . . ." Flick, sniff/sniff. "Tina's dead."

"I thought her name was Mau Tim?"

"That's what she called herself, for the modeling and all."

"What was her real name?"

"Tina. Whaddaya, deaf or something?"

I smiled. "How can I get in touch with the owner?"

Ooch stopped. "I'll call them, let them know you were asking."

I reached into my side pocket, found a business card. "You can call me there. Leave a message if I'm not in."

Taking the card, Ooch said, "Right, right." Then he pointed with it. "You don't mind, you put those cans back where you found them."

"Sure." I started moving one of them.

"The city, they raise hell with me, those cans ain't right along the building 'cept for Tuesdays and Fridays."

I came back for the second can. "Trash days."

"Right."

I replaced the second can. "So, Tuesday and Friday mornings, you put the cans at the alley, the truck picks up the trash, and you put these cans back against the wall."

"Right, right."

"And you did that a week ago Friday, too."

"A course I did."

"And they were still against the wall after the police were here that night?"

"Yeah. I even checked, after they went." Flick, sniff/sniff. "Fucking cops, you can't trust them to do nothing right."

"When you checked the cans, did you find anything else back here?"

A blank expression. "Like what?"

"A rake, maybe?"

"A rake?" Ooch's eyes went around the bricked space of his and the adjoining buildings. "You see any lawns back here, pal?"

"How about a push broom, even a piece of rope with a hook or bar tied to it?"

"No. Whaddaya, crazy?"

I looked up the fire escape. "Too bad you weren't here."

"Huh?"

"Earlier that night, when Tina was killed. Too bad you weren't here. You might have stopped it."

A pained expression, like he hadn't thought about that before. Then flick, sniff/sniff. "I was here, none of this woulda happened to her."

Ooch got weepy. "I was here, I woulda killed the bum did this. Tina was a good girl."

He moved back into the doorway, drawing the strap of the T-shirt up to dry his eyes before closing the door behind him.

I stood in the alley for a while. Holt might have been lying to me back at Homicide. Or maybe he just didn't throw me a "little chunk" about what his people found behind the building.

Staring at the back wall of Number 10 Falmouth Street, I tried to figure out how a burglar could get up to Mau Tim Dani's apartment by the fire escape without using the cans, or a rake or something, to pull down that raised last flight.

5

I DROVE FROM THE SOUTH END TOWARD MY NEIGHBORHOOD. IN A parking lot on Newbury Street, a guy was maneuvering a large vehicle that had to be seen to be appreciated. Or believed. A brown, swaybacked tube of a cabin like a hot dog was laid partially inside a yellow chassis and frame like a bun. A meat company's name was printed on the side of the cabin. The passengers could see through Flash Gordon windows at the front and use a hatch where a panel truck's door would be. I tried not to embarrass the driver as I went by and headed the Prelude back to its space a few blocks away.

The address Harry Mullen gave me for the Lindqvist/Yulin Agency was on upper Newbury, but when I got to the numbered front door, there was no sign on the building that the agency was located inside. The outside door was unlocked, however, and the mailboxes in the foyer showed a listing for both the agency and a "LINDQVIST, E." on the next floor. I pressed the button by the agency name, and the inner door buzzed long enough to let me pass through it. I climbed stairs, one office

38

suite to a floor, until I reached the fourth level and a yellow six-panel with brass knob that had the agency name on a brass plate. I knocked and a male voice said to come in.

As I swung the door inward, I saw a man about my age and height in blue jeans, turtleneck, and a corduroy Norfolk jacket. He was good-looking in a college professor way, but with a weak chin and shaggy hair, as though he'd told the barber to give him a Beatles look, then said, what the hell, take off another two inches. The hair seemed black and silver, but more like each strand was half each color. He used a telephone receiver to beckon me into the reception area while his free hand reached for a loose-leaf binder on a shelf behind a desk.

The man was saying, "Right, Kyle. Trunks, athletic wear . . . Half day guaranteed at a thousand . . . No, *plus* agency fee. Any problem if it runs over? . . . Over half a day, what do you think? . . . Good, good . . . No, no your legs are fine. You get a chance, you might work on the upper body a little . . . No, generally it's fine, Kyle, you're in great shape, but for this one . . . Right, right, a swimwear catalog, not just a department store—what? . . . No, no tanner than you are now. Right, right."

I assumed I was watching George Yulin in action. I decided to wait until he got off the phone. The reception area had a love seat and two barrel chairs in complementary colors. I tried the love seat. On the beige walls were enlarged photos, all black and white, matted but not framed. A couple of advertisements were in stand-up cutouts, backed by cardboard. Most of the models shown were female, but three were male. One of the men flexed the kind of physique I might have had in college if I'd been eating complex carbohydrates instead of drinking them.

Behind the guy on the phone was a restored brick wall and some leafy plants. He fingered one of the leaves and seemed close to finishing the call when a female voice said, "Can I help you?"

I half turned and stood up. She was in the doorway to what looked like the front office. About five five without the two-inch heels, the woman had lush brown hair drawn back and down her neck. Maybe thirty-five, her face was a notch to the handsome side of pretty, with a perfect smile. The shoulders were a little broad for the body, and her breasts inside a turquoise dress were no more prominent than the pockets on a lumberjack's shirt.

"Are you Ms. Lindquist?"

"Lind-qvist," coming down on the "v," but still beaming the smile.

"Sorry. My name's John Cuddy. I wonder if I could talk with you for a while."

"About what?"

"I'm representing Empire Insurance on the claim you have on one of your models."

"The claim—Oh." The smile faded. "You mean Mau Tim, don't you."

Lindqvist pronounced it "*Mahow* Tim," just like Harry Mullen had. As I said "Yes," the man on the phone said, "Kyle . . . Kyle I have to hang up now," and put the receiver down.

He said, "Mau Tim's death was a terrible shock to all of us."

"Mr. Yulin?"

"Yes. Yes, George Yulin."

He came around the desk as Lindqvist came a step further into the reception area. I shook hands with him, then with Lindqvist.

Yulin said, "I have to admit, I'm impressed with your service."

"I'm sorry?"

"Coming to deal with us only a week after I made the call, I mean."

"I'm a private investigator, Mr. Yulin. I'm looking into Ms. Dani's death as part of processing your claim."

A different tone came into Lindqvist's voice. "I thought the police said she was killed by a burglar?"

"A policy this size, we do an independent investigation."

Lindqvist moved her tongue around inside her mouth. "Should we be calling our lawyers, Mr. Cuddy?"

"That's not up to me. I'm just here to ask you some questions, help the people I work for process your claim."

Yulin said, "What can there be to process? We had a policy for half a million dollars on the girl. She died, you pay, correct?"

"The company decides that after they get my report."

The telephone began bleating like a sheep. Then another line joined in, just out of phase with the first. Lindqvist made no move for either, Yulin jumping for both.

While her partner covered the calls, Lindqvist said to me, "If you want to confer with us, this isn't a terrific time. We're on the phone quite a lot during business hours."

Yulin hung up with identical promises to call back.

"That's okay. I'd rather talk to each of you separately anyway."

Lindqvist watched me while Yulin watched her. I was beginning to see why the agency was Lindqvist/Yulin rather than Yulin/Lindqvist.

She revived the smile. "Fine. Let's start with me. Come on in."

I followed her into the large front office. In addition to a desk with computer, calculator, and fax, there was a long conference table and six chairs in one corner. The office was decorated in blue and yellow: rug, walls, blinds, even furniture. The bay window behind the chair that Lindqvist took offered a 180-degree view of Newbury bustling with foot traffic below us.

As I chose a seat across the desk from her, Lindqvist said, "I've never been investigated before. How does it work?"

"I'm not investigating you, Ms. Lindqvist."

"Sure you are. And I can understand it. I just want to be helpful."

Sure you do. I took out my pad. "We can start with your first name."

"Erica. Full-blooded Swede, though you'd never know it to look at me." She pointed to an old sepia photo in a frame on the corner of her desk. It showed a man with a handlebar mustache and a little boy with a mop of pale hair, both in

41

homespun clothes. "That's my grandfather and his grandfather, Mr. Cuddy—by the way, is it all right if I call you 'John'?"

"If you'd like."

"Fine. Why don't you use 'Erica'? A little easier to say than the hard 'v.' "

"Okay," I said, kind of liking the way she'd taken charge of the conversation. Sometimes you learn more by letting the other side ask its own questions.

"Well, John, my grandfather was in retailing, but his grandfather was an immigrant from north of Stockholm. Came over on the boat and made his way west to Minnesota, even fought Indians, believe it or not. Funny, I never thought much about Indians in Minnesota, as opposed to maybe Montana or the Dakotas. But that's what he had to do, and quite a lot, too. You ever see *A New Land?*"

"No."

"It's a movie with Max von Sydow and Liv Ullman, all about that time. Terrific piece of work, but then I don't suppose you need my Swedish heritage for your report."

"Probably not. What I could use is some background on Mau Tim Dani."

"Background." Lindqvist shook her head. "That'll be tough."

"Why?"

"You know much about how the business works, John?"

"If you mean modeling, no."

"Actually, I meant agenting, but let me give you a little orientation about both. George and I run this agency. We're both called 'directors,' but basically that means we're both like vice-presidents when there's no one president."

"With you so far."

"I do the pitching, the rain-making, getting new accounts from ad agencies or the advertisers themselves. George does the booking, matching the right models for the right jobs. Sometimes it's like a little of both. An ad guy will see our book and say, 'How about Sandy on page ten, I like her. Can you send me her composite, maybe her mini-book?' "

"Now you've lost me."

"Okay. The composite, that's kind of like a brochure on the girl herself. Just a fold-over glossy piece, with a couple of photos of her, her measurements and specialties. The mini-book, that's a more substantial . . . scrapbook of her, kind of. Quite a lot of photos, some tear sheets."

The "quite a lot" seemed to be Lindqvist's catchphrase. "What are tear sheets?"

"Ads actually run in Sunday supplements or whatever. We tear them out, put them in the mini-book so the ad guy or the client can see she actually is a professional."

"You represent only female models?"

"Oh, no. We're a full-service agency here. Male/female, fashion, corporate. Print as well as runway."

"By runway . . . ?"

"Fashion shows for designers or boutiques. They'll hold them as a luncheon, invite the big-spenders off their mailing lists. We'll supply the girls, who show the clothes off on the runway, then walk through the crowd during lunch, let the ladies see how nice the merchandise looks up close on a beautiful girl."

"With the price tag still on?"

The beaming smile again. Like Nancy, a bright, direct woman who became more attractive the longer you talked to her.

"Actually, they do have the tags still on the garments. Part of the cachet of going to the luncheon is seeing how much looking great costs."

"Did Ms. Dani do many of those?"

The smile became wistful. "Mau Tim could have done just about anything she wanted, John. Elegant neck, generous mouth, perfect skin tone and bone structure. But most of all, those eyes. The most exotic girl I've ever seen."

"How did you come to represent her."

"The usual way. A scout."

"A talent scout?"

"A photographer who spotted her in a mall. Or maybe just on the street, I'm not sure. But he spotted her, asked her if she wanted to be a model."

"Sounds like kind of a pick-up line."

"I know, but it works. Especially on a fifteen-year-old."

"Fifteen?"

"Not Mau Tim. No, she was at least eighteen when she first came to us. But the prime age is fifteen to nineteen."

"Why so young?"

The good smile again. "Unfairness of nature, John. It's easy to use makeup to make the face look older. It's tough to use makeup to make the body look younger."

"So the career is over early?"

"Not for everybody. Some of the girls do fine into their mid-twenties. And after that we can use them as commercial models."

"As opposed to?"

"Oh, sorry. Commercial as opposed to fashion models. Mommies selling diapers or businesswomen selling computers rather than vamps in evening wear. Some even subspecialize as parts models."

"Parts of the body?"

"Right. Hand model, leg model, even foot model for shoe ads."

"Do you remember which photographer scouted Ms. Dani?"

"Sure. But you might make more headway if you called her 'Mau Tim.' That's how she was known in the business."

"Thanks. The scout?"

"Oh, right. It was Oz Puriefoy."

Oz. Short for Oscar Puriefoy, one of the men at the party.

Lindqvist looked at me strangely. "If you need to talk to Oz, George will have a number for him."

"Thanks. Did you ever meet any of Mau Tim's family?"

"Never did. That's what I meant about it being tough to give you any background on her. She was over eighteen when Oz sent over her test shots and she first signed on with us, so she didn't need parental permission."

"You ever speak to them by telephone?"

"Her parents, you mean?"

"Yes."

44

"No." Lindqvist seemed to think a moment, her eyes flitting left-right-left without focusing on anything. "No, I think the only person I ever talked to was an uncle. On the telephone. I think he owned the building she lived in."

"Vincent Dani?"

"Maybe. I know she changed her name."

"From 'Tina' to 'Mau Tim'?"

"No. No, originally it was even more ethnic—'Amatina,' that was it. I wanted to change it to 'Violeta,' for the eyes and all, but there was already a black model with a name like that. Then I think she checked on the Vietnamese word for 'violet,' and it turned out to be '*mau tim*,' which fit her beautifully."

"Do you know how I could reach her parents?"

"No, but their number might be in her file."

"Her file here?"

"Right. It would have places where we could reach her, that kind of thing. Might have some family stuff, but can't you just get that from the police?"

I thought about Holt. "Maybe, thanks. I take it you didn't go to the funeral, then."

"No. No, we didn't. I think George called the uncle, but he said—the uncle said that the family wanted to keep it closed. The funeral I mean, not the . . . well, maybe that, too. I've never . . . I've never seen anybody strangled before. I don't know what it does to . . . the features."

Lindqvist spoke more carefully than emotionally about it. Like she wanted to use the right words, not that she was upset by discussing violent death.

"Did Mau Tim ever talk with you about her personal life?"

"No. No, she really didn't, John. We talked a little once about what growing up in an ethnic Swedish family was like, but—you see, quite a lot of the girls see me as kind of a big sister."

"Somebody they can confide in?"

"Yes, but not Mau Tim."

"Independent?"

"More . . . insulated. I think growing up Amerasian must

have given her some problems. I don't mean while she was working. She could be dazzling on a shoot. I mean more that she kept her personal side to herself."

"Might she have confided more in your partner?"

"George?"

"Uh-huh."

"I doubt it. Maybe Sinead, though if you meet her, you'll never see why."

"She the model who was having the party?"

"Right. Sinead Fagan. George can give you her number, too. Only, don't release it, okay?"

"Release it?"

"Yes. Some of the girls use the agency as their number and address to screen out the creeps."

"Models get approached a lot?"

"You bet. Even agencies like this one have to avoid them."

"Like by no sign out front."

"Right. And by being on the fourth floor instead of street level. If they could spot us from the sidewalk, every pervert with an Instamatic would be in here, trying to hire 'nude models' for 'private photo sessions.' "

"Did Mau Tim ever have any problems with 'creeps,' Erica?"

"Not that I know of. I think she would have told me that."

I nodded. "Who decided to take out the policy on her?"

"We both did."

"You and Yulin."

"Yes."

"Whose idea was it to start with?"

Lindqvist watched me very carefully. "Should I be thinking about my lawyer now?"

"Same answer as before."

She paused. "It was George's idea."

"You have policies on any of your other models?"

"No. We thought about it on a guy a few years ago, but he moved to New York."

"And on to another agency?"

Another pause. "Yes."

"Any reason you applied for half a million?"

"It seemed like a good number at the time. Believe me, John, Mau Tim was a rising star about to become a superstar. There was nobody quite like her. Two years from now, that policy would have been for two million dollars and every model in the country would be showing up at test shoots with violet contact lenses."

"Would she still be worth that to you by then?"

"Mau Tim wasn't going anywhere."

My turn to pause. "I didn't mean to imply that she was. I just meant since Mau Tim was nineteen now, she'd be 'past-prime' in another two years."

Lindqvist brought out the good smile again. "You're very . . . accomplished at this, aren't you, John?"

"I've been doing it a long time. You get lucky."

"First, Mau Tim wasn't going to leave our agency. She'd heard quite a lot about how you have to go to New York to hit the megabucks, but she was loyal to us. Second, Mau Tim was an exception to the rule-of-nineteen. She would have been sensational for a long time to come."

"All right. Mind telling me where you were a week ago Friday?"

A darkening. "When Mau Tim was killed?"

"Yes."

The eyes flitted again. "Upstairs? Yes."

"Upstairs?"

"I have the penthouse unit in this building. I was catching up on some paperwork."

"Alone."

"Unfortunately."

"On a Friday night."

Lindqvist traced an index finger from her throat to her navel. "All dressed up and no place to go."

I shook my head. "Anything else you can think of?"

"Yes. Would you like to have dinner with me sometime?"

I folded my pad. "That's pretty fast."

"This business moves pretty fast, John." Her eyes went to

the ceiling. "The penthouse has a great deck. Barbecue for two?"

I stood. "Thanks, Erica, but I'm already taken."

The beaming smile. "The best always are, John. The trick is learning how to take them away."

6

GEORGE YULIN'S DOOR WAS HALF-OPEN. I RAPPED ON IT. HE LOOKED up and waved me in before I realized he was on the telephone.

His office was more modest than Erica Lindqvist's. The one window gave him a view of the alley and parking area of the buildings on the south side of Commonwealth Avenue. The "codirector's" guest furniture consisted of uncomfortable director's chairs. His desk had a fax, calculator, and computer also, but there were dozens of magazines strewn over it and the floor nearby, most of them with I guess a fifteen- to nineteen-year-old puckering for the cover.

Into the receiver, Yulin was saying, "Yes, Melanie, it's George . . . Well, I wouldn't have to be calling you if you checked in like you were supposed to, now would I? . . . Yes, well, we all have a rough night from time to time. The trick is not to let it ruin our days. Or our looks, right? . . . Yes, I've got something for you. Lingerie catalog, should be lots of—No, your hair is fine the way it is. Clean-shaven . . . Yes, of course 'down there, too.' How long have you been living off this dodge, Melanie? . . . Probably Wednesday next week, maybe into Thursday . . .

49

Yes, well, how's your period been the last three . . . All right, all right. If it isn't, call me at least twenty-four before the shoot, got it? . . . Yes, love you, too."

Yulin hung up. "The fucking *cunt!*"

I decided to play along. "One of your favorites?"

"You have no idea, Mr.—tell me, now that you've heard me use foul language, can we call each other by first names?"

Just like Lindqvist. "Sure, George."

"Well, John, models have egos the size of their bottoms rather than their brains. They love the glamour and the travel—when they work, that is, which might be only two or three days a week. They have time off like a stewardess and get paid like a company president. Plus all the stroking, the wining and dining, propositioned by every Platinum Card in sight. But no matter how many great spreads you get them, a lot of the girls are so unappreciative, so bitchy, it drives you up a wall."

"Was Mau Tim like that?"

"Mau Tim? Oh, right. No, no, she was pretty professional, actually. A good kid, if a little quiet."

"Erica led me to believe that Mau Tim was on the verge of stardom."

Yulin leaned back in his chair, combing the fingers of his right hand through the grizzly-bear hair over his ear. "Are we going to play lawyer/witness here, or can you just ask me questions?"

Maybe Yulin had a little more juice than I thought. "Erica said something about a file and a book you kept on Mau Tim?"

"Sure. Just a second."

Yulin left the office for maybe twenty seconds, coming back carrying a yellow suspended folder and a six-inch by nine-inch loose-leaf album. He handed me the folder and set the album on the desk near me. Then he pulled over another director's chair so we were sitting side by side.

"Why don't you just go through the file, John? I can give you a running commentary on it."

"Fine."

I opened the folder. There was a cover sheet with MAU TIM (DANI) and date of birth at the top.

Yulin said, "That's the casting card."

"How come her last name is in parentheses?"

"Because she goes by her first name professionally. A lot of the girls do."

"Why?"

"They think it's sexier. Also, it keeps the creeps from finding out who they are and where they live."

Lindqvist had already taken me down that road. I pointed to a smattering of telephone numbers, some of which had been lined through and others arrowed in. "What are all these?"

"The places we can reach her. Sorry, *could* reach her. Sometimes a job will crop up after a model's called in for the day."

"Why so many numbers?"

"Well, some are out of date. The ones with arrows are more recent."

"Can you tell me which numbers went with which times?"

Yulin craned over my arm. "That first number was her uncle's, I think. He's a lawyer, downtown. The second is Oz Puriefoy's. He's the photographer who scouted her." Yulin looked up at me. "Who sent her to us in the first place."

"Right. But they're scratched out."

"All that means is she got her own place."

"Meaning she used to live with her uncle, then with Puriefoy?"

Yulin gave me a knowing grin. "Mau Tim was the sort of girl who could probably live anywhere she wanted."

I said, "You know these numbers by heart?"

"Not anymore. Just the current ones. But you call them so many times, you remember which one was which, you know?"

I pointed back down to the card. "How about these two newer entries in the margin?"

"That one's the number at her apartment." Yulin dropped his voice. "Where she was killed."

"And the number in red?"

"That's Larry Shinkawa."

"The police said he was one of the men at the party."

"I'm not surprised. Mau Tim and Larry have been . . . They were a thing for some months before she died."

"He's in advertising, right?"

"An exec at one of the smaller agencies."

"Advertising agency?"

"Right. Berry/Ryder. Just down the street."

"Do you know how they met?"

Yulin gave me a funny look. "I introduced them, as a matter of fact. At a party we threw at the Cactus Club."

A trendy bar around the corner on Boylston Street. I went back to the card. Mau Tim's height, weight, bust, waist, hips, dress size, shoe size, and so on. I picked up from the file a black-and-white pamphlet the size of a big birthday card. It had a head-and-shoulders photo of Mau Tim on the cover, an elaborate necklace around her throat and her first name emblazoned at the bottom.

Yulin said, "That's a comp, for 'composite card.' "

"You sent this out as kind of a brochure for her?"

"Right." Yulin opened it up. Inside were two more photos of Mau Tim, one in evening wear, one in lingerie. On the back was a long shot of her in a wool dress and heels, boutique shopping bags in hand, apparently trying to flag a taxi. Alive, the most arresting woman I'd ever seen in two dimensions.

Yulin said, "Breathtaking, wasn't she?"

I looked at him.

He blinked and said, "The next thing in the file is—"

"Just a second. You have a color version of that photo on the front?"

"Probably in the mini-book. You want to go through it now?"

"In a minute." I turned the comp card sideways to pick up the names of the photographers given credit in the margins. "None of these was taken by this Puriefoy."

"Oh, no. No, she graduated from old Oz, if you get my drift."

"I'm not sure I do."

"Oz is a good photographer. With a good eye for talent, like

52

hitting on Mau Tim, for example. But he's not a great photographer. She got to be too good for him.''

"Can that happen with agencies like yours as well?"

Yulin clenched his jaw, then relaxed it quickly. "It can. But Mau Tim knew what we'd done for her. She wasn't going anywhere we didn't take her."

I looked back into the file. There were some advertisement photos from newspapers. Only a few months old, from the dates handwritten on them, but already yellowing. There were also some studio shots of Mau Tim, with Oz Puriefoy's name as photo credit.

"What are these?"

Yulin said, "Those are old shots that we rotated out of Mau Tim's mini-book. See what I mean about Oz's work?"

Mau Tim did look less sophisticated, less well turned in the face and hair. I couldn't have attributed that to the photographer as opposed to the model, but then, I wasn't in the business.

"I don't see any paycheck stubs or tax records in here."

"That's all on the computer now."

"What did Mau Tim pull down in a year?"

"I could look it up for you, but basically she went from a thousand a day to two within a few months. Lately we were getting twenty-five hundred guaranteed."

"A day."

"Right."

"From which your cut was?"

The jaw clenched again. "Twenty-five percent. Standard in the industry."

Six-twenty-five a day to Lindqvist/Yulin. "And how many days a week did Mau Tim work?"

"We could have gotten her six if she wanted, but usually four, sometimes five. You see, she could pose for one photographer during the day, another on a small job at night with a guaranteed half-day rate for the smaller job."

"So be conservative and call it two hundred days a year. That means she'd earn a hundred and a quarter a year for you in commissions."

Yulin lifted his chin a little. "No, John. *We* earned that money. By placing her in good shoots that paid top dollar for her."

"Had you placed her in a shoot that day?"

"That . . . ? Oh, you mean the day she died. No."

"You don't have to look it up?"

"No. I'm positive. She'd told me in no uncertain terms that Saturday was her birthday. She wasn't working Friday or the weekend."

"She call in that Friday?"

Yulin shut his eyes, then said, "Yes. As usual."

"Meaning?"

"Meaning midafternoon."

"Can you be more specific?"

"Two, three?"

"She seem worried to you?"

"No. We talked about a job two weeks down the line. In Jamaica for a casino. She seemed very up for it."

A knock at the door. Yulin said, "Yes?"

Erica Lindqvist stuck her head in. "I'm sorry to interrupt, George, but Larry Shin is on the phone from the airport, and I've got to run. Can you take it?"

"Certainly, Erica."

She nodded and left. Yulin had said "certainly" like a bank teller asked to count out a thousand dollars in singles.

The man stood. "Excuse me, John." He went behind his desk and picked up his telephone. By the time he pushed the button on the console, his voice had a "how can I serve" lilt to it.

"Larry! Great to hear from you, Chief. How goes it? . . . Right, right. Give me what you . . . Right, blonde and redhead. The blonde? . . . Young Christie Brinckley, sexy, lots of energy. Got it. The red? . . . Firm breasts, cup no bigger than 34C . . . No *taller* than five ten? . . . Oh, right, right. He's just barely six feet. Okay . . . What? Oh, shit no, Larry. We've got a drawerful of them. Any leg shots on the redhead? . . . No, that will narrow it a little, but let me see if the one I have in mind . . . Right, right. I will. Thanks, Larry."

Yulin hung up, took a breath, then came back to me.

I said, "Larry Shinkawa?"

"Yes. Yes, as a matter of fact."

I didn't say anything more. Yulin asked if there was anything else.

"The mini-book?"

"Oh, right." He retrieved the album from the desk and gave it to me, again taking the chair next to me.

I turned plastic sleeves of Mau Tim in swimwear, sportswear, and yachtwear. It was hard to just flip through them. There was something about each that really caught the eye, like fine paintings of the same subject by different artists. None by Puriefoy.

Then I hit the head-and-shoulders shot of Mau Tim and the necklace in full color. The purple stones lay perfectly symmetrically around the throat, the pendant weighing the least bit heavily toward the cleavage that the dressline suggested but the photo didn't show. Eyes and necklace glittered in whatever light the photographer had shone on her.

Yulin said, almost reverently, "That is a heart-stopper, isn't it?"

"Yes."

"The way I've described the shot to people, it's as if a man asked her to sleep with him, and she just decided to say yes."

I tried to picture the broken pendant from Holt's eight-by-ten of the crime scene. "You know anything about the necklace?"

"You mean the way the stones pick up her eyes?"

"I meant, do you know if the necklace was hers?"

"Oh. No, I don't. Probably hers or the photographer's. I don't think it was an ad shot."

"Meaning it wasn't some jewelry store's necklace."

"Or manufacturer's. Why, is it important?"

Yulin tried for open innocence, tried hard, but something made the corners of his mouth twitch just a little.

"You remember where you were a week ago Friday, George?"

"Well, let me see now . . ." The eyebrows knitted, giving the impression he hadn't thought about it until I'd just asked.

The brows cleared. "Yes. Yes, I went to an ad party after work. Just an hors d'oeuvres and cocktails sort of bash, but enough dinner for me. Then I made the rounds of a few bars I know. Then I decided to call it a night and headed home."

"When did you leave the party?"

"I don't know. It was winding down."

"Six, seven?"

"More like seven."

"And did you go drinking with someone?"

"My friend, I talk all day with people. I like to do my drinking anonymously. An atom in the mass society."

"Which bars did you hit?"

He named three, all of them madhouses on a Friday evening. An uncheckable alibi.

"And after the bars?"

"As I said. Home to Brookline."

"Your partner told me—"

"My what?"

"Erica."

"Oh. Yes?"

"Erica said some of the models confided in you two. Mau Tim ever do that?"

Yulin turned it over. "No. No, she was really . . . well, quiet, as I said before."

"You ever visit her apartment?"

"Never."

"Okay. You said Larry Shinkawa was her current boyfriend?"

"Right."

"And Oz Puriefoy before that?"

"Right, right."

"You know of any other boyfriends?"

Yulin preened his hair again. "No."

"She never mentioned anybody else to you?"

"No. As I said, she was real—oh, wait a minute. Yes. Yes, one other. Shawn somebody. She said he was her first."

56

"Her first?"

Yulin brought out another knowing grin, affecting a bad brogue. "He who managed to deflower the lass."

"Do you know if it was S-H-A-W-N or S-E-A-N?"

"Beats me. Probably just some Irish kid."

I gave Yulin a longer look this time.

He said, "Uh, no offense meant."

"None taken."

Yulin licked his lips anyway.

I said, "Erica seemed to think that Sinead Fagan might know more."

"Ah, the Marquesa of Medford."

Medford is a blue-collar town just outside Boston. Yulin pronounced the name like somebody growing up there would, *Meh*-fah. He seemed to like doing dialects.

"Remember what I said about unappreciative bitches, John?"

"Yes."

"A prime example. Though, with apologies to the ladies of the night, if Sinead weren't being paid for it, she'd probably still pose for free."

"Why is that?"

A shrug. "The glamour and the . . . bright lights?" Yulin smiled at his industry joke.

"You have a home number for Sinead?"

"Yes, but I'm not sure she's still living at the same place."

"Where Mau Tim was killed, you mean?"

"Right. I think she's moved in with Oz."

"Puriefoy's dating her, too?"

"No. He's dating her currently, though 'dating' might be an awfully chivalrous way to put it."

"Do models usually get involved with their photographers?"

"Some. However, in Sinead's case, it might just be that Oz is the first man she's known who hasn't thrown up on her."

"There any way I can see her today?"

"I doubt it. She's on a longish shoot."

"Where?"

"Nearby. But it's not a great idea to interrupt a model on a job."

I folded my pad. "The sooner I see her, the sooner Empire can decide whether you get paid on the policy."

George Yulin mulled that over for all of five seconds. Then he jotted an address on a slip of white paper while saying, "You might just catch her."

7

THE MUSIC WAS SO LOUD I COULD FEEL IT IN MY CHEST.

There had been no one in the waiting area of the photography studio a few blocks from Lindqvist/Yulin, and I could hear a driving beat from behind a closed, inner door. I opened the door and was hit by a rap-reggae hybrid from four floor speakers that topped off above my waist.

On the far side of the thirty-by-thirty room were four people. The two men wore black mock turtlenecks and black pants, the two women bikinis. The taller man played with his earring behind a long-lensed camera on a tripod, an identical camera lying on the crest of a stepladder beside him. The shorter man brushed the billowing hair of a statuesque blond woman who was physically perfect. Standing next to the blonde was a red-head who looked younger than the blonde but had a similar body. The redhead's hair was short and spiky, a cocklebur with a haughty face.

The women didn't seem to match, like somebody's older sister running into somebody else's younger sister at the beach, but maybe that was the effect they wanted. It took a minute for me to realize that I was standing in shadow, and probably the models couldn't see me through all the lights shining on them.

The redhead began pouting, hands on hips, a pair of sunglasses halfway down her nose, eyes searching out the photographer over the rims. Above the music, she shouted, "Chris, these shades are like weird."

The photographer spoke to his camera. "They look fine, Sinead."

"I feel like somebody's grandmother."

"Don't worry about it. They fit the scene, and nobody's looking at your eyes, anyway."

"They still feel weird."

George Yulin was right about Sinead Fagan's Medford accent. Weird came out "we-id," grandmother "gramuva."

The "scene" appeared to be a beach. There was a big striped umbrella guy-wired into the shallow sand, the background wall draped with a blue and white cloth that looked enough like sky and clouds to fool me, and I knew it was fake. The blonde patiently waited through the shorter man's fussing and Sinead's whining.

Chris the photographer said, "That looks fine, Bruce."

As the man with the brush moved back out of the scene, Chris said into the lens, "Sandy, hold where you are. Sinead, just a little to the right."

Sinead huffed out a breath and shifted left. "Awright?"

Bruce mouthed something into the photographer's ear and grinned mischievously.

Chris said, "Other way, Sinead."

"Other way what?"

"Move the other way, toward Sandy."

Sinead huffed again but moved the correct way.

"More."

Sinead nearly bumped into the other woman, Sinead's sunglasses slipping off her nose and into the sand below. Reaching for them, Sinead lost her balance, plopping into the sand behind them.

Sandy closed her eyes and broke her pose. The brush man burst out laughing. Chris raised his head from the camera and said, "Bruce, kill the music."

The shorter man went to the stereo on a side wall and suddenly the room grew still. It was as though the sound instead of the shadow had been covering my presence, because as suddenly everybody seemed aware I was there.

The photographer said, "Who are you?"

"John Cuddy. I'd like to talk to Ms. Fagan, if I could."

"Who?"

"That's me, Chris."

Sinead Fagan came off the set, one hand holding the sunglasses while the other whisked her bottom. Sand on her feet squinched a little on the linoleum floor. "What do you want?"

It came out "Wotchawan?" Posed and silent, she looked poised, mid-twenties. In motion and talking, just another gangly teenager.

I said, "I'd like to speak with you privately."

Before Fagan could answer, Chris said, "Tell you what, folks. Let's take fifteen, everybody shake out the bugs, okay?"

Sandy said, "Fine." Bruce looked like he wanted to laugh some more, but thought better of it. All three of them moved off toward a coffee machine on the opposite wall under a collage of giant lips.

Fagan watched me warily. Up close and out of the harsh lights, the makeup was heavy, covering a lot of freckles and a little too much sideburn edging close to her jawline.

I said, "My name's John Cuddy, Ms. Fagan. I'm a private investigator."

"No shit."

Fagan said the second word flatter than the first, as though she didn't believe me. I took out my ID folder, letting her mouth what she read on it.

"What's this for?"

"The death of Mau Tim Dani."

The face behind the makeup seemed to cave in, crumbling the caked-on powder. "I don't wanna talk about that."

"Ms. Fagan, it won't take long. We can talk here at your convenience, or in a conference room with lawyers and a stenographer. Up to you."

She thought it over, maybe struggling to remember if that's what happened on *L.A. Law*. "Let me get a robe, awright?"

Fagan walked, then trotted behind the set, returning wrapped in a short terry cloth, sash undone. And now wearing the sunglasses, something she probably thought of in front of the mirror, to hide her emotions from me.

I pulled up a couple of folded folding chairs and unfolded them. When we were settled, I said, "You and Mau Tim were friends."

"Yeah."

"You lived in the same apartment house."

"Yeah. You know the answers to all these, how come you gotta ask them?"

Defiant, not flirty. "I'm trying to make this as easy for you as I can."

"Big of you."

"Also, when I get information from one person, I check it with another. That way, I can tell when somebody's lying to me, setting themselves up for perjury down the line."

Perjury seemed to soak in. Fagan said, "Ask."

"You were having a party for Mau Tim that night."

"Right."

"Do you know where she was before the party that day?"

"Up in her bathroom, taking a shower."

"Before that."

"I dunno. On a shoot somewheres, probably."

"Where?"

"I dunno. She did quite a lot of shoots."

Quite a lot. "George Yulin said she wasn't working that day. Called in, but wasn't on a job."

"Then I dunno."

"How did you and Mau Tim come to live in the same building?"

62

"She was living there, there was this other apartment open, so she says do I want it and I says yeah."

"I understand her family owns the building."

Fagan stopped. Then, "Far as I know. I just give Ooch the rent money, he sends it in."

"The super."

"Yeah."

"You pay him in cash?"

"That's the deal. What the fuck does this have to do with Mau Tim?"

"Okay. That night—the night she was killed, when did you last see her?"

"I didn't."

"Didn't see her?"

"No."

"Did you talk with her?"

"I called Mau when I got in. She said she'd be coming down for the party later, was there anything I needed."

"When was this?"

"When I got home."

"When was that?"

"I dunno. It was a nice warm day out, so I walked."

"Approximately."

"I dunno. Five, five-thirty, maybe."

"What did you tell her?"

"Tell her?"

I began to empathize with Chris the photographer. "When she asked you if you needed anything, what did you tell her?"

"Oh, I says no, it's your fucking birthday, for chrissakes."

"What did she say?"

Another stop. "Not much. She had to call some people, maybe."

"Who?"

"I dunno."

I didn't see Holt giving me a look at the telephone company's

63

local line records when he did get them. "What did you do after you hung up with Mau Tim?"

"I took a shower, trimmed my nails, turned on the stereo. What the fuck—"

"Did you talk to her after that?"

"No."

"Did you hear anything from her apartment?"

"We're like a floor apart. You can't hear nothing except the water."

"The water?"

"The water in the pipes. Mau Tim took a shower, I'd hear it in my kitchen pipes."

"And did you hear that?"

"Sure. I was in my kitchen, I can hear the water through the pipes."

"That night?"

"Yeah, that night."

"When?"

Fagan huffed. "I dunno what fucking time. Look, I don't keep looking at my watch, you know?"

"Okay. At some point, you hear the water in the pipes."

"Right. I'm in my kitchen, getting things ready for the party, and I hear the water and then Oz comes in."

"Oscar Puriefoy."

"Yeah. Oz."

"And he comes into your apartment?"

"Yeah."

I thought about the raised last flight of the fire escape. "He's got a key?"

The stop again. "No. No, he don't."

"Then how did he get in?"

"How do you think? He rang me from outside, and I opened the door for him."

"Go on."

"Awright, so Oz is in my apartment, right? So I says to him, go get us some wine, I forgot."

"You forgot the wine for the party."

"Yeah."

"How old are you, Ms. Fagan?"

A stop. "Nineteen."

Underage to buy the wine even if she hadn't "forgotten" it. "Then what?"

"Then Oz goes out and—"

"Wait a second. Is the water still running?"

"The water?"

"From upstairs through the pipes in your kitchen."

"I think so. It was just like, water, awright? Besides, I had quite a lot to do."

Lindqvist's influence again. "So Puriefoy goes out for wine."

"Right."

"And you give him your key?"

"No. No, he don't have no key, understand?"

"Okay. How long is he gone?"

"I dunno."

"Can you estimate?"

"Ten, fifteen minutes maybe."

"Then what?"

"He comes back."

"And you let him in and all."

"Right."

"What happened then?"

"Oz is in the kitchen, opening the wine, and then Larry Shin comes by."

"Larry Shinkawa?"

"Yeah."

"He rings the bell—"

"—and I let him in."

"Shinkawa was invited to the party."

"Sure. Him and Mau was going out."

"That night?"

"No, no. We was all going out after. They was, like, 'dating,' you know?"

Fagan said the word like I might have heard it back when I was young. I wondered when it had turned sour. "Who else was coming to the party?"

The stop. "That was it."

"Nobody else was invited?"

"Well, this other guy was invited, but he couldn't come."

"What other guy?"

"This other model."

"His name?"

"Quinn."

"First name?"

"That is his first name. Quinn Cotter."

"Where does he live?"

"I dunno."

"How'd you invite him?"

"Saw him on a shoot. Why?"

I no longer even remotely envied Chris the photographer. "This Cotter work for Lindqvist/Yulin, too?"

"Yeah."

"Why didn't Cotter come to the party?"

"I dunno. Ask him."

"All right. How about a guy named Shawn?"

"Shawn?"

"Yes. I'm not sure which spelling."

"What do you mean?"

Fagan seemed blank, and for just a second I wasn't sure she knew what 'spelling' meant. "Did you ever hear Mau Tim talk about a Shawn?"

"No."

"Somebody said he was her first boyfriend."

"News to me."

"All right. You, Puriefoy, and now Shinkawa are in your apartment. Then what?"

"Larry Shin says, where's Mau Tim, and I says she musta just got outta the shower, and he says, let's go up and surprise her."

"Did you?"

"Uh-unh. He did, not me."

"Puriefoy?"

"No, him neither. Just Larry Shin."

"Then what?"

"Larry Shin goes up, awright, and like two seconds later he's down the stairs, saying that Mau Tim ain't answering."

"You remember what he said?"

"No, just like he was knocking and hollering for her, and she didn't answer him."

"What did you do?"

Chris the photographer called over. "Sinead?"

"Right." She stood up. "That's it."

"Wait. What did you and Puriefoy do?"

"I don't wanna talk about that, awright?"

I didn't want to see this woman again if I could help it. "Did you ever talk with Mau Tim about anything that was bothering her?"

"No."

"How about going to New York?"

The stop. "Everybody talks about going to New York. It don't mean nothing."

Chris said, "Sinead, how about it?"

"Awright, awright." Her sunglasses slipped as she looked down at me. "That's all I can tell you."

"Sinead, you seem to have been her best friend. Is there anything else she talked about with you? Boyfriends, family, anything?"

Fagan righted the glasses. Very evenly, she said, "We didn't talk about family, awright?"

Sinead trotted off to rejoin the others at the beach.

I TREATED MYSELF TO LUNCH AT THE HARVARD BOOKSTORE CAFE, A place where you can think about eating while browsing or think about browsing while eating. A friend of mine named Moncef designed the menu there. He and his wife Donna used to own L'Espalier, the best restaurant in the city. A few years ago, they pulled up stakes and moved to Virginia, to raise their family in a calmer environment. Moncef still comes up to Boston once in a while, and he was there that day. We shot the breeze for half an hour over a plate of perfectly stir-fried turkey and vegetables.

To walk off lunch, I crossed the Public Garden and the Common to my office on Tremont. I'm in an old building, and my door on the third floor has a pebbled-glass top with "John Francis Cuddy, Confidential Investigations" stenciled on it. Behind the door is a desk, a desk chair, and two client chairs. Two windows overlook the Park Street Subway Station, and my license hangs from a wall I painted myself to save a few bucks on the monthly rent. The rest of the office could be carted off in the front basket of a bicycle.

I was upstairs for five minutes and in my desk chair four when there was a knock on the door. "It's open."

A guy came in wearing a knee-length leather coat over a navy blue suit. In his mid-forties, he was five seven and pushing two hundred pounds. A comb had recently slicked his black hair to the sides in a Teen Angel look. The face was pudgy, the complexion reminding me of an all-weather radial. A toothpick stuck out from one corner of his mouth, the corner curling in a half-smile.

He said, "How ya doin'," as a statement rather than a question and then settled into one of my client's chairs, the leather coat squeaking against the wood.

I said, "You want to take your coat off?"

"We ain't gonna be staying that long."

"So maybe I should put my coat on."

"You don't want to catch cold on the way to the car."

"Where are we heading, we aren't going to be here that long?"

"Some friends of mine, they want to have a little talk with you."

"And if I don't exactly feel like going with you?"

A shrug so small the coat gave just one tiny squeak. "I leave, come back with two associates, and then we go see my friends."

"And if two more aren't enough?"

The only part of his expression that changed was the toothpick. It rolled to the other corner of his mouth. "Then I come back with four more. Sooner or later, you have that talk with my friends."

"I step on some toes somewhere?"

"I don't know. I'm just transportation."

If he were just "transportation," he'd be leaning against a car downstairs, and somebody else would be talking with me. I thought over what I'd been doing the last couple of weeks and came up with only one possibility.

I said, "Where are we going?"

"You find out when we get there."

I shook my head very slowly. That brought a good smile.

"Hey-ey-ey," he said, dragging out the syllable. "Look, we was gonna clip you, we wouldn't send somebody you don't know, would we?"

"You would if you don't have anybody I know."

"You raise a good point." He sat back into the chair, folding his hands over his stomach, lifting his shoulders once and letting them sag into the chair, a symphony of squeaks from the coat.

When I didn't say anything, he waited thirty seconds or so, then said, "You come now, we beat the afternoon rush."

"These days, there's always traffic."

He rolled the toothpick back to where it started, then used the thumb and forefinger of his left hand to pull back the lapels of his coat and jacket. Letting me see he wasn't reaching for anything lethal. He pulled out a long wallet from the inside pocket of the jacket, extracted a plastic card, and sent it across the desk to me.

"My license. A picture of me and everything."

I looked at the driver's license. It seemed legitimate. Social Security number, date of birth. The photo was recent, the expiration date four birthdays away. The address was in the North End, Boston's Italian-American section.

I read off, "Zuppone, Primo T."

"Yeah, only you gotta pronounce it 'Zoo-*po*-ny.' "

"Primo, how many of these do you have?"

The small shrug again. "Six, seven. But that there's the real one."

I couldn't help but grin at him. "People underestimate you a lot, Primo?"

That got the half-smile. "Just once, usually."

"Primo, what's the license number on your car?"

"That ain't on there."

"I know. I want the plate of the car we're going for a ride in."

He rattled it off, no more hesitation.

"I'm going to make some calls, Primo. Then I'll decide whether we're taking a ride."

Zuppone and his coat made themselves more comfortable in the chair.

I dialed the Boston police, making a point to ask for "Homicide" and "Lieutenant Robert Murphy" instead of Holt. Murphy wasn't in, so I left Harry Mullen's name and telephone number at Empire, then Zuppone's name, address, and plate number. Then I called my answering service and left the same information with them.

When I hung up, Zuppone said, "You want to call your friend, the assistant D.A., we got time."

I spoke to the half-smile. "That's okay. She needs you, she'll find you."

Zuppone said, "You carrying?"

"At least one."

He said, "Okay. Let's go."

I said, "What if I'd said no?"

"What, about carrying?"

"Yeah."

The leather squeaked its last as he got up. "I wouldn't have believed you."

"This road's a fucking disgrace, ain't it?"

We were driving out of the city on the Southeast Expressway, more typically known as the Distressway. Originally named after Boston mayor "Honey Fitz" Fitzgerald, his famous descendants should be ashamed of its current condition.

Zuppone continued. "I was one of the Kennedy kids there, I'd kick in a coupla bucks from the trust fund, get these potholes fixed."

The holes were more like craters, but Zuppone's Lincoln Continental ate them up, just a slight "whump" noise from the tires.

"We were in my Prelude, our heads'd be through the moon roof by now."

Zuppone rolled the toothpick. "Never could see them foreign jobs, myself. Uncle of mine had a Lincoln back in the fifties, and I always promised myself one." He caressed the wheel lovingly. "And the stereo system's dynamite. Watch."

Or listen. When we'd gotten in the car, his starting the engine brought some soft, solo piano music. Now Zuppone pressed a few buttons that made the sound bounce all over the cabin, front to back and side to side.

I said, "That a radio station?"

"Uh-unh. Tape, but it's a homemade jobbie, forty-five minutes a side, so you don't have to change it so often."

"Easy listening."

Zuppone glanced at me, to see if I were kidding. "George Winston."

"Never heard of him."

"Guy records for Windham Hill, New Age stuff."

"Hot tubs and healing crystals?"

"I gotta tell you, I don't know from nothing about the philosophy side of the shit. I just know, I put in the tape, and I feel good, you know?"

We rode for a while, Zuppone taking the Route 3 prong instead of 128. The traffic petered out, but he kept the Lincoln at a steady fifty-five, the tires barely slapping the junctions of the asphalt in a way you felt rather than heard over the music. The leather upholstery was the same color as Primo's coat and supple to the point of buttery. But a cold softness, not the way I'd want my last car ride to feel.

Zuppone picked up the telephone nestled between us and hit a button. After no more than one ring, he said, "It's Primo . . . Yeah . . . Ten minutes . . . Right."

He hung up, looked at me. "You were in Vietnam, right?"

I said, "Right."

"One of the people you're going to meet, he was there, too. Let him talk about it, he wants to, but don't like . . . encourage him, okay?"

My turn to look at Zuppone. "Okay."

He noticed me looking and shrugged. "You made it easy on me, coming along. I make it easy on you. One hand and the other, you know?"

"Can you tell me where we're heading?"

The toothpick changed sides again. "You ain't figured it out yet?"

I thought back to Sinead Fagan being emphatic about not discussing "family" with Mau Tim Dani. "I figure the super at an apartment building this morning called the owners, and now I'm going to meet them."

Zuppone nodded. "You're close."

We left Route 3 and started winding through suburban intersections with three gas stations and a convenience store on the corners. After a couple of turns, the retail areas gave way to narrow streets with small homes, which in turn gave way to wide streets with large homes. One of the wide streets matured into a boulevard, the center strip less impressive than Commonwealth Avenue in Boston, but with big shade trees far enough south and close enough to the ocean to be showing the full leaf stage of spring.

Zuppone eased the Lincoln into a long driveway that curved gracefully past high hedges toward a white Greek Revival mansion, fluted pillars supporting the roof over the main entrance. He parked behind a Mercedes and a Volvo, the piano music dying abruptly as he turned off the engine, the air vibrating inside the car.

Primo got out before I did, the door thunking solidly against the frame as he closed it. He made sure I was still with him, then walked up the flagstone path to the side entrance. He rang the bell but pulled open the door without waiting for anyone to say or do anything.

I followed him through and into a huge kitchen, the pans all copper and polished. They hung from rings in their handles over tiles the color of dried blood. The tiles covered the work areas of the counters as well as the floor.

As Zuppone stepped behind me to close the door, probably the tallest Vietnamese woman I'd ever seen stood up from a stool. There was a cigarette burning in a crystal ashtray in front of her, at least half a dozen smoked ones in the base of the tray.

The woman self-consciously touched her hair, swept up in a bun with jewelry combs. Her cheekbones were high, her lipstick light. She wore a *bao dai*, the traditional long, slitted dress of her country, but the slit was conservative and the dress itself was black, not a gay print. A mother in mourning.

She said, "My husband and the brother of my husband are in the den."

As we went by her, I said, "I'm sorry for your loss."

The woman dropped her gaze toward her feet. Her eyes started to close, but the left lid went only halfway down as the right closed completely. As she looked back up, I realized the left eye was gone, the brown and white egg in its socket a beautifully wrought piece of glass.

I felt a chill as Zuppone led the way through the first floor of the house.

From across the den, they looked like twins standing in front of adjoining mirrors at the fun house. One was stocky, with coarse black hair in clots that didn't stay put. His jaw seemed about one generation removed from cracking bones around a cooking fire. He wore a shirt and tie, but the tie's knot was wrenched almost halfway down his chest, and the sleeves were turned up twice, revealing forearms thatched with black hair. As he drained a glass of what looked like Scotch, he made you think of why Webster put the word "guzzle" in the dictionary.

The other guy was slim and five inches taller, maybe six one. The tide on his hair was going out, front to back. His features were more delicate, like the altar boy who goes on to play guard for the CYO basketball team. I guessed the suit to be in the seven-hundred range at Brooks Brothers, a Repp tie still knotted tightly at the collar. There was no drink in his hand or anywhere nearby.

As Zuppone and I got closer, I realized the stocky one was about my age, the slim one a little younger despite the hairline.

The stocky one said, "This him, Primo?"

"Yes, Mr. Danucci."

I thought, Jesus Christ.

The stocky one put down his glass. "The name registers with you, don't it."

My eyes went to the slim one. He seemed mildly amused but not inclined to show it much.

The stocky one said, "Look at me, Cuddy."

I did. "I thought you'd be older."

The slim one said, "You're thinking of our father."

I said, "Tommy Danucci was your father?"

The stocky one said, "*Is* our father."

Tommy Danucci. Tommy the Temper. One of the mob bosses you heard about but never saw, directing things quietly from the backroom instead of splashing across the front page. I remembered whiffs of him coming up during the media coverage of the Angiulo cases, but I thought he'd died in the mid-eighties.

The slim one said, "I think you're entitled to an introduction, Mr. Cuddy. This is my brother, Joseph Danucci. My name is Vincent Dani."

I said to Dani, "You were Mau Tim's—"

"Tina!" thundered Danucci. "My daughter's name was Tina! Use it."

Nobody said anything until Primo said, "Boss, can I freshen that up for you?"

Danucci was breathing through his mouth. The sound was like a hurricane blowing through a lantern. It wasn't hard to see which gene he got from Tommy the Temper. "Yeah. Yeah, Primo. Thanks."

"Chivas?"

"No. The Johnny Black tonight."

Zuppone crossed to the wet bar in a corner of the room. The paneled walls were covered with framed prints of different Boston athletes. Dom DiMaggio and Rico Petrocelli from the Red Sox, Gino Cappelletti from the Patriots, Phil Esposito from the Bruins. It took a minute to realize they all had Italian surnames.

Danucci accepted his drink and downed half of it. He ran the back of his hand across his mouth, then ran his palm over his head, scattering the clots of hair into a different pattern.

He said, "I'm not dealing real well with this shit," and inhaled the rest of his drink.

This time Primo didn't offer to get another.

Around the empty glass, Danucci said, "I want to talk with the guy alone a couple of minutes."

His brother said, "Joey?"

"I'll be okay, Vinnie. You guys try the TV or something, huh?"

Vincent Dani looked at Primo, who looked at me. Then Primo said, "Right, boss," and left the room, Dani taking two short steps, then striding out behind him.

Joseph Danucci said to me, "Take a seat, Cuddy."

I tried one of several leather easy chairs across from the leather couch. All the cowhide, including the tufting on the bar and stools, was royal blue, held in place by brass tacks.

Danucci circled over to the bar, setting his glass on it. "Get you something?"

It was a little early, but I said, "Beer, if you have it."

He disappeared behind the bar. "What I don't got, you don't need." His voice echoed a little as he spoke into what sounded like a refrigerator.

Using a church key, Danucci opened the bottle of Sam Adams the way a busy bartender would, the top arcing through the air like a tossed coin.

He brought the bottle over to me. "Primo said you were in the 'Nam."

Danucci pronounced it to rhyme with "Mom." As he moved back to the bar, I thought about what Zuppone had told me in the car.

I said, "One tour."

"When?"

"Late sixties."

Danucci poured himself more Scotch. "Where?"

"Mostly Saigon."

He started to raise his glass, then said, "Tet?"

"Yeah."

Danucci swigged two fingers of the Johnny Walker. " 'Who owns the night?' "

" 'The night belongs to the 101st Airborne.' "

He watched me. "You were a Screaming Eagle?"

"No. Ran into them from time to time."

"What outfit you with?"

"Military Police."

Danucci came around the bar. "Fucking Mike-Papa?"

"That's right."

"Ever out in the boonies?"

"Once in a while."

Danucci started pacing back and forth. "Yeah, well I fucking lived in the boonies, man, seventy into seventy-one. I never minded so much the assaults, even on a Huey going down into a hot LZ. And on search-and-destroy, you got so you could see the booby traps, especially old ones. At least you were doing something, going after Charlie where he lived. What I couldn't take was standing down on a firebase some fucking general named after a mission from World War II, guarding some fucking artillery against Charlie probing us at night."

My host kept pacing. "Sweating on top of some fucking bunker because it was crawling with rats inside. Waiting. All the time just waiting for Charlie to hit. You can hear a lot further at night than you can see."

Danucci stopped in front of me. "Know what was the worst part?"

Without thinking, I said, "The rain."

This time Danucci stared at me. That cold, dead-eyed stare Tom Berenger captured so well in *Platoon*. "Fucking A. That rain starts, you couldn't hear nothing moving, nothing. It started to rain, didn't matter I wasn't pulling guard duty, I couldn't sleep."

The palm went through the hair again. "Like now."

I knew he wasn't referring to the weather.

Danucci emptied his glass, then brought it down hard on the bar. "Tina was my daughter, Cuddy. We had our problems, she was always more her mother's daughter than her father's, but that happens, right?''

He didn't seem to need my answer.

''Girl hits a certain age, she's got to rebel. Okay, fine. She goes off on her own. Fuck, we did the same thing when we were eighteen, right? Only I made sure she was safe, get me? Primo, he checked out the modeling agency. No porno, no kinky shit. She flopped at my brother's apartment a while, then into a family building, my cousin Ooch there in the basement. Guy was a tiger in the ring, Cuddy. One fight he had, undercard in the early sixties, he takes enough punches the first two rounds to kill a horse, then knocks the guy out middle of the third. Know what I do now?''

I didn't like Danucci being so erratic, jumping from one topic to the next. I'd seen grief like that in Vietnam, the kind of strobe-light emotion that turned into violence. Easily.

The cold stare. ''I said, know what I do now?''

''No, I don't.''

''I build strip malls. Not strip joints. The little eight- or ten-store things, with maybe an anchor like a supermarket or a discount house one end. Lay down an apron of asphalt, paint some white lines, you got yourself the American Dream. One-stop shopping. All the guys ten years ago put up the highrise office buildings, they're in bankruptcy court now, twenty guys' hands in their pockets. Me, I never had a mall go bad. Never, not one. Hard times, they might not make me a fortune, but every week, every year, people got to buy food and clothes, Cuddy, and they stop at my malls to do it.''

For something to do, I drank a little beer.

''That's where I am, I get the call. I'm in a meeting, we just came back from the site, a new one down near Philly. It was a tough deal to put together, and I was doing it, getting it through this guy's skull that it's going forward, no matter what he thinks. I'm in this meeting, I still have my hard hat with me, and this guy's secretary comes in and he fucking near bites her head off. She's probably been there three hours on her own time by then, but she looks kind of sick and says to me, 'Mr. Danucci, it's your brother on the phone.' And so I say, 'I'll call him back,' and the guy starts to chew out his secretary some more, and she says, 'I think it's very important.' I got to remember that girl, she stood up without letting on. Doing her job. I tell the guy who's ragging her to shut the fuck up, I can take the call. So here I am, in this conference room with a view of some dirty river they got down there, and my brother Vinnie tells me over the telephone that my Tina is dead.''

Danucci squeezed his eyes shut. He reached over the bar, grabbed the Scotch bottle itself and just slugged from it until I thought he'd drown. Then he kept hold of the bottle by its neck and coughed once.

"I took that hard hat, Cuddy, and I tried to throw it through the window. The glass didn't give, so I tried it with the phone. Then the guy I'm with figures he's next, he don't get me a seat on the first plane."

Danucci drew a breath, the hard, roaring kind he'd taken earlier. "You were a cop, right?"

"Just in the Army."

"Same difference. You know what the cops in Boston think about this?"

I pictured Holt, smugly feeding me little chunks like a seal. Keeping me from seeing the file and the name "Danucci" appearing somewhere in it, maybe all over it.

Joseph Danucci said, "They think, 'What do you know, there is a fucking God.' They think, 'We been trying to crucify Tommy the Temper for sixty fucking years for twenty different rackets, and we couldn't, and now his granddaughter's a corpse, and we don't got to do shit about it.' ''

This wasn't the time to bait him.

Danucci said, "They think it's like 'poetic justice,' Cuddy. The *capo*'s grand-kid gets strangled by some fucking junkie cat burglar."

He took another drink, less now that the level in the bottle was lower. Subconsciously, he seemed to want it to last, though

I bet myself there was a case of it in a closet somewhere nearby.

Danucci gestured toward the door. "Primo says you're working for some insurance outfit?"

"I'm private. The modeling agency your daughter worked with took out a policy on her to protect themselves. The company asked me to look into things."

Danucci's nostrils flared. "Oh, you're gonna look into things, all right."

He took a step toward me. Pretty steady for the booze he'd put away. I didn't get up.

"You're gonna find out who aced my daughter, pal."

I didn't say anything.

Another step. "And when you do, you're going to tell me. You're going to fill out whatever fucking forms the company makes you do, and you're going to shrug your fucking shoulders when the cops come around asking questions."

A third step. "But you're going to tell me who aced my Tina."

I said, "No."

Danucci telegraphed the swing of the bottle by a full second. I was up and blocking the sweep of his right arm with my left, the bottle flying and smacking into a leather chair before it boloed to a stop, some Scotch gurgling onto the leather cushion.

Danucci's breathing was almost deafening. "You . . . You . . ."

Then he turned away, starting for the bar before sinking into a chair without a bottle on it. He rubbed his face with his hands, then clasped them in front of him, a soldier assuming an unfamiliar stance in a chapel. "Should have been the happiest day of my life, Cuddy. I talked to my father that morning. The Order of the Cross, like a Holy Name Society thing, it was making him president or whatever. All his life, Pop wanted that. To have some kind of . . . recognition besides the rackets. The next night, Claudette and me were going in town, have dinner with Tina for her birthday, stay over at the South End house. My brother—Vinnie?—he did such a good job representing my company, they made him a partner at this old-line law firm in Boston wouldn't have let him take out the garbage twenty years ago. The business was going good, like the deal in Philly coming together. It was like everything was coming together. Sinatra in the song, 'a very good year,' you know? Then that phone call, looking at the filthy river from this guy's office. . . ."

I went over to the chair with the Johnny Walker Black, picking up the bottle and setting it on the counter of the bar.

Behind me, Danucci said, "Our ways, they don't work so good for this kind of thing, Cuddy. Somebody gets hit, you can usually trace it back up the line, figure out who ordered the contract. Something like this, this . . . random kind of thing, we got feelers out on the street. But they should have turned something by now, and they haven't given us shit."

I said, "I'm not going to give you a name so you can kill the guy."

Danucci looked up at me now, the dead-eyed stare, his tugged-down tie the only part of him moving. "What, you think, you give the name to the cops and they lock him up, he's some kind of safe from us?"

"I might not get that far. My job is to be sure the people at the agency didn't have her killed to collect on the policy. I decide they didn't, I can stop."

Danucci thought about that. "We pay you to keep going."

"No."

"You see *The Godfather?*"

"Yes."

"That Coppola, he got a lot of it right. Not everything, but a lot. We pay you with your life."

An offer I couldn't refuse. "I already have my life."

"Not if I decide otherwise."

"You decide otherwise, send two of your best. They don't come back when you expect them, don't call anybody, don't even pack. Just run for your life."

Danucci grinned, the big jaw jutting. Not a pretty sight. "You don't scare, huh?"

"I scare. I just don't change my mind."

Danucci sat there, maybe thinking what he was going to say next, maybe deciding which two of his best he was going to send. Maybe just remembering his daughter.

Finally, he said, "You find out who killed Tina, you tell the cops?"

"Probably."

"Then we can compromise here. You don't got to tell me the guy's name, but you stay on the thing till you find the cocksucker who done this. Then you give him up to the cops. We'll take it from there."

"And if I don't stay on the case?"

The grin again. "Life is sweet, Cuddy. Do yourself a favor, taste it a little longer."

When I didn't say anything more, Danucci said, "Okay, we got a deal, and you got our cooperation. One hundred percent. Anything you need, Primo'll be right there."

"I work alone."

"Fine. You need something, you give him a call."

Danucci seemed calm, almost rational. I tried to figure how much of what I'd seen with the bottle was an act. I thought, not much. He just went in and out like that. At least over his daughter's murder.

"I don't expect to be calling him."

Danucci went to the desk and used a pen to scribble some lines on a business card. Standing tall, his hair was about level with my chin. "This is Primo's apartment number, best way to reach him. This one's my home number here, you need it."

I took the card.

"You want to see the place in the South End?"

"It would help."

"I'll call Ooch right now."

"It won't be tonight."

"Fine. Whenever. What else you need?"

"I'd like to talk with your wife and your brother."

"Claudette and Vinnie? Why?"

"They knew your daughter. I didn't."

"You think it'll help, okay. When?"

"Now would be good."

Joseph Danucci nodded once, the developer who could be decisive. "You got it."

9

SHE WAS DEFINITELY THE TALLEST VIETNAMESE WOMAN I HAD EVER seen.

At least five and a half feet in just slippers like a ballerina, Joseph Danucci's wife must have seemed a giant in her home country. She came into the den haltingly, taking a step before returning to the door and closing it, as though she were the guest in my home and wanted to make a good impression.

She stopped a body length away from me. "I am Claudette Danucci. My husband say I speak with you."

The good eye wandered a little over me, the glass eye steady, its lid coming down only halfway as she blinked.

"Again, Mrs. Danucci, I'm sorry about your daughter."

A brief nod. "You will drink?"

I'd pitched the beer. "No. Thank you."

"You will sit?"

I took the unstained chair. Danucci lowered herself into the couch as though a glass of water were balanced on her head. If Mau Tim had half her mother's grace, I could understand her success as anything, model included.

83

"Mrs. Danucci, I'm investigating the death of your daughter for an insurance company."

Another brief nod.

"It would help me if you could tell me something about her."

She waited a moment. "I could tell you many things about her. I could tell you her first word to me when she is one year. I could tell you how many time I brush her hair when she is five year. I could tell you how there is a knife in my heart because I must think of these things to tell you them."

I dropped my head.

Her voice changed. "I am ashame, Mr. Cuddy."

I looked back up at Claudette Danucci. A large tear glided down along her nose from the good eye, nothing from the glass one.

"I am ashame because I embarrass the man my husband tell me will find the killer of my child."

"Mrs. Danucci, you have every right to be upset."

She turned her face, both eyes fixing on me. "You were in Vietnam?"

"Yes."

"In Vietnam, the life of a woman is her children. I can have one child only, and now she is take from me."

I decided to go with her. "You met your husband in Vietnam?"

"Yes. I was . . . You know what 'tea girl' mean?"

"I do." It was slang for a bar girl who got GIs to buy her drinks, usually iced tea masquerading as liquor.

"When my husband meet me, I am tea girl. Do you know why I am tea girl?"

"Mrs. Danucci, you don't—"

"I am tea girl because I am rape by your black soldiers. I am good Catholic girl, Mr. Cuddy. I hear stories from the French time, about the Morocco black French. They rape and kill peasant girls in the village. Stories say, that not happen in the city, but it happen to me. I am too tall for Vietnam man. I think, I find America man to love me. America black soldiers find me."

"I'm sorry."

84

"No. I want to tell you these things. You will see. I am tea girl because my family not want me after the America black soldiers have me. I am lucky. I am pretty and I am different because I am tall. I not have to eat rats or snakes, to steal to live. I get many gift from PX. I have many America white soldiers. I get *ma tuu*, the marijuana, to help forget.

"Then I meet my husband. He is different. He want to buy dinner, not drink. He bring me flowers to my apartment. He is honorable man, my husband. He walk with me in the streets. The old women say things in Vietnam words, names they have for the America invaders and women like me with them. My husband know these things, and still he walk with me.

"One day, I find out, I am pregnant. With my daughter. The other tea girls, they say, 'Claudette, you take this herb, it make the baby go away quick. Quick, before the America soldier see the baby inside you.' I do not want abortion, Mr. Cuddy. I want the baby of the man I want to be my husband. You know what happen to the children of America soldier and Vietnam woman in Vietnam?"

I'd seen the kids wandering Saigon, though there weren't so many of them when I was there. Stringy, sallow girls with blue eyes that didn't slant quite right. Husky, mocha boys with broad noses and ripply hair. Ostracized, even beaten or stoned by the relatively homogeneous Vietnamese.

"The children of the mothers who stay in Vietnam, they have nothing. The America soldiers are fathers but not husbands. They come to Vietnam and leave, but the mothers stay and the children stay and they have nothing.

"But my husband find out I am pregnant, he is happy. He say, 'I will marry you, Claudette. I will take you back to The World in the plane.' The other girls, they say, 'Claudette, all the soldiers say that, so you will still *bum-bum* with them until near time baby come.' But my husband is different. He find out I am pregnant, he take me out to big dinner. Celebration. We coming home to my apartment, we see two QC."

"QC" was short for "*Quan Canh*," the South Vietnamese military police.

"My husband, he want to tell them how he is happy. They curse at him in Vietnam words. He know some words, he hear other girls use. He get mad, he punch one QC. The other hit him with stick and break stick. I scream and use my"—her hands fluttered up—"nails to scratch his face. QC use his stick that is broke to hit me in face. My . . ." This time her hand fluttered toward her glass eye, but stopped and came back to her lap. "They run away from us. I get other America soldier to stop, get ambulance, to get . . ."

She stopped, took a breath. "I am in hospital. I do not lose my baby, but my eye is . . . gone. Not in my head. My husband come see me. He have bandage around his head, and he cry. My husband cry for my eye, Mr. Cuddy. He is honorable man, and he 'sponsor' me. I must see government officials, Vietnam men and America men, every day for many day. I must give some money, then same ones more money. But I get out, my daughter still inside me. I come to The World. And you know what I find?"

"No."

"I find The World is strange place. In Vietnam, new wife go to house of the mother of her husband and work for mother. Work hard. What the mother want new wife to do, new wife must do, no questions. Here, the father of my husband is not please with new Vietnam wife. The friends of my husband not please with new Vietnam wife. But the mother of my husband is a beautiful woman. I have so little English, I say to her, 'What need you done?' She say, 'You talk like I do, I first come to America. You pregnant, Claudette. You . . . eye. You sit. I work for you.' I love my husband, and I love the mother of my husband, who make me call her 'Amatina.' Her name from Italy. So when my daughter is born, and she has the beautiful eyes, the violet eyes, we give her name 'Amatina,' too."

Claudette Danucci swallowed with difficulty. "We call my daughter 'Tina,' because the mother of my husband say she cannot tell who we want when we call 'Amatina.' The mother of my husband teach me the things of Italy my husband like. In Vietnam, I learn to cook with mint and basil, cilantro and *nuoc mam* from the fish. From Amatina, I learn to cook with mozzarella and oregano, but also the fish, the anchovy, they use too. From Amatina, I learn to behave for the father of my husband, and even he start to like Vietnam wife of his son. And daughter of his son, with the eyes of his wife from Italy. Six, seven year ago, when Amatina . . . get sick, my daughter and me, we take care of her here, in this house. When Amatina . . . die, we take care of the father of my husband, who has the heart attack in his house and cannot care for himself. We are family, Mr. Cuddy. Like in Vietnam, I teach my daughter respect for the family of her father."

"Even though her father's family was a crime family."

Claudette Danucci fired up. "What is crime, Mr. Cuddy? What is crime when you are rape by America 'protectors' and beat by your own police and rob by your own government? What is crime when your whole country is victim?"

I didn't have an answer for her. "When did your daughter move to Boston?"

She lost the fire. "Year ago."

"Why?"

"She . . ." Danucci stopped, thought, and started again. "She want to be model in pictures. Many people in Boston tell her she is beautiful for model."

"How did you feel about that?"

"I did not like it. A daughter stay with her family until she find a husband. That is still the best way."

"How did your husband feel?"

"He did not like it, too. The city is . . . not safe, he say."

"Your daughter stayed for a while with her uncle?"

"Yes, but then my husband say, 'Tina, you must stay in the house of my father on Falmouth Street. Cousin Ooch, he protect you there.' "

"Tina agreed to that?"

"Yes. She even say that is better. Vincent apartment is not so large, and in Falmouth Street she can live for no money."

George Yulin had said Mau Tim had lived for a while with Oscar Puriefoy, too, but after Claudette Danucci's experience with black soldiers, I wasn't about to bring it up. "When did your daughter change her name?"

The good eye wandered, the glass one staying fixed on my left shoulder. "She all the time ask me about Vietnam. About what we do there, names we have for things. She asked me Vietnam word for 'violet,' for her eyes. I tell her *'mau tim.'* "

Everyone else so far had pronounced it *"mahow* tim." Danucci said it more like "maw *teem.*"

"When my daughter was little girl, I would call her mau tim when only she and me there because my husband want her to be all-America. Then she ask me last year, Vietnam word for model, but she already know it is 'mau' because she say, she look it up in dictionary. It is same word, but say different."

Claudette Danucci looked up at me. "She decide to use that name, not Amatina or Tina. My husband not like this, too."

"Why did she change her last name to Dani?"

The good eye closed, the glass one's lid again only halfway down. "I think she want to . . . break away. In Vietnam, when girl decide to leave village to go to city, her mother say, 'That is my Saigon daughter.' My daughter want to break away from family, live alone in city."

"The way her uncle did?"

Both eyes opened. "The brother of my husband is a lawyer. He decide his name to be different for business."

"Mrs. Danucci, I'm sorry to have to ask you these—"

"Ask."

"Did your daughter ever mention someone named Shawn to you?"

"Shawn?"

"Yes. Maybe a boyfriend from school?"

"No. My husband very strict with our daughter when she live here."

"How about after that?"

"After?"

"Did you speak with your daughter much after she moved to Boston?"

"Yes. I talk with her on telephone all the time. I see her sometime for lunch when I drive to Boston."

"Did she mention any boyfriends then?"

The head lifted. "No."

"Did she seem happy to you?"

Reluctantly, I thought, Claudette Danucci said, "Yes. Pretty happy."

"She enjoyed modeling?"

"She say, 'It is boring. You must hold things and stand stupid.' But yes, she most of time like the things she do, the people she know, her friends."

"Did she seem happy at the agency?"

Claudette Danucci cocked her head.

"I mean, was she satisfied with Lindqvist and Yulin representing her?"

"Oh." Danucci seemed to think about it. "She say, people tell her she must go to New York for modeling."

"Visit there, or live there?"

It was obviously a question Danucci had already thought about. "Live, I think."

"Did your daughter talk with you about that?"

"No. But I think . . ."

"Yes?"

"I think maybe she decide to go there."

"To New York?"

"Yes."

"Why?"

"Because on phone . . ." For the first time, the good eye completely filled, and she reached into the cuff of her dress for a hankie. She sobbed very quietly into the cloth for a moment, then wiped that eye. The glass one stayed at half-mast, the more hardened mourner at a funeral.

"I am sorry, Mr. Cuddy."

"I understand."

"The day . . . the day she die, we talk on phone. She seem excited."

"What did you talk about?"

"The trip of her father to Philadelphia, the dinner my husband and I take her to the next night in Boston. She was very busy on a . . . shoot somewhere that week, so I must catch her up on all family things. She tell me she have something exciting to say at dinner. Something she decide to do."

"Move to New York?"

The hand fluttered. "I am afraid yes."

"Afraid?"

"The dinner is suppose to be happy time. A birthday for our daughter and her father and me. I do not want her to . . . destroy the happy time with her . . . news."

Suddenly fierce, Claudette Danucci passed the hankerchief across her face. "Mr. Cuddy, in Vietnam, I am call '*Viet Kieu*' because I am Vietnam woman who come here to America. In Vietnam, the children eat sand to fill their belly with something. In Vietnam I cannot hope to work in a house one-half beautiful like the one I live in here with my husband. I have beautiful car my husband give me. I have five hundred dollar to spend on beautiful handbag that maybe go with three dress I wear. Five hundred dollar, a whole family live for year in Vietnam. Whole family, wait in Vietnam office, sleep on floor, on dirt outside, for month, two month, to come here to America."

Her voice surged. "I tell you these things so you will understand, Mr. Cuddy. I see hard things in my life. But nothing so hard like when I sit in my living room and the telephone ring and the brother of my husband from Boston tell me my daughter is dead. I give up all I have, I give my other eye, for my daughter to live again. Do you understand this?"

She was riveting, the good eye on me and the glass eye on me, too. "Yes."

"When I sleep, I dream. Before my daughter die, if I dream of things in Vietnam, bad things, hard things, I dream of these things in Vietnam words. When I dream of things here, in America, good things, beautiful things, I dream in America words. Now my daughter is dead, and I dream in Vietnam words, all things in Vietnam words."

"I—"

"You promise me, Mr. Cuddy. You find the one kill my daughter."

"Mrs. Danucci—"

"You find him, you tell me."

"Mrs.—"

"You promise!"

I promised.

10

THERE WAS AN AWKWARD MOMENT AS CLAUDETTE DANUCCI STOOD
and moved toward the door to the den. Awkward, because
Vincent Dani had knocked and then come in without waiting
for an answer, saying "Claudette?" His brother's wife just shook
her head, stumbling a little as she passed. Dani gripped her at
the shoulders, steadying her. His hands lingered a beat longer
than necessary, his eyes a beat longer than that as she patted
his left hand and went out the door, shutting it gently behind
her.

Turning to me, Dani had the look of a cat caught drooling
at the family canary. He stiffened, saying, "If I were you, Mr.
Cuddy, I would not upset my brother's wife."

I was thinking, funny how "upset" almost rhymed with
"covet."

Dani came all the way into the room, taking the part of the
couch that his sister-in-law had used, then shifting his rump a
little, perhaps in reaction to her residual warmth on the seat.
"My brother said you'd like to speak to each of us?"

"I would, thanks. What law firm are you with, Mr. Dani?"

"Winant, Terwiliger, and Stevens."

Joseph Danucci had said that his brother had made partner at an old-line firm. "Old-line" didn't quite do Winant, et al., justice. A hundred and fifty years in Boston, principal tenant of a harborside skyscraper, the firm was one of the five premier hives for attorneys in the city.

"How long have you been with them?"

"Since law school."

"Which was?"

"Eight years ago." Dani crossed his legs. "Is this line of questioning headed somewhere, Mr. Cuddy?"

"I don't know. I guess I was wondering why your brother decided to join the family business and you didn't."

Dani bridled. "My brother has an 'i' at the end of his last name and pictures of Italian-American athletes in his den and that makes him Mafia, right?"

"Your brother's the son of Tommy Danucci and sends a guy like Primo to see me, there's a presumption."

Dani's lips auditioned a smile. "Primo said you'd had a year of law school."

I was impressed. "Primo found out a lot in the time he had."

"Primo's what my father would call a 'situation guy.' "

"Maybe he ought to be doing this instead of me."

"No. No, you send in somebody like Primo to assess things, report back. He lacks what my father would call 'ambition.' "

"Takes some ambition to aim at Winant, Terwiliger as a target and hit the bull's-eye."

Dani's lips found the smirk line and held it. "I thought you were looking into my niece's death."

"I am. What can you tell me about it?"

"Nothing beyond a profile of the man who did it."

"I'm listening."

"Young, poor, probably on drugs, and not well versed in the lore of organized crime."

Dani seemed awfully cool about Mau Tim's death. Almost detached. "Why is that?"

"Hitting a building that's 'connected,' Mr. Cuddy."

"I thought you were one of the trustees, counselor."

"I am."

"And you filled out the property report."

"Yes."

"I'm wondering about the necklace."

"The necklace?"

"The purple one. Made out of iolite?"

Dani maintained the even expression. "And gold. What about it?"

"Where'd it come from?"

Dani watched me for a moment. "It was a gift."

"From?"

"After my mother died, my father had a bad spell, Mr. Cuddy. Heart attack, morose. I'd never . . . nobody had ever seen him like that. Tommy the Temper in a state of weakness."

"And?"

"And my brother made him comfortable here. I couldn't do that much . . . I was living in a one-bedroom apartment in Cambridge, and my father needed round-the-clock care but didn't want nurses and so on. Claudette was like a slave to him."

"Which changed his mind about her?"

Dani's face stayed neutral. "What do you mean?"

"I was under the impression he wasn't too pleased about his son's war bride."

Dani sat back, weighing something. "My father saw Joey following him into the business. Claudette . . . clouded that."

"How?"

"Mr. Cuddy, my brother loves Claudette. Once my brother gives his love for something, there's no holding back, no . . . tempering of the emotion. He loved her, he married her, he was staying with her. Beyond that, there are some things you really don't want to go into here."

"Why not?"

"Let me make it clearer: there are some things you should butt out of."

94

More the ring of the streets than the boardrooms. "Okay. Fair to say that Claudette's helping your father changed his mind about her?"

Dani said, "Yes."

"Then how come the necklace went to his granddaughter?"

"Mau Tim helped, too. Before and after school."

I was thinking that Vincent Dani used her professional name instead of "Tina," when he continued. "Also, my father gave that necklace to my mother on their twenty-fifth anniversary. It matched the color of her eyes." Dani bit his lip for a moment. "You've noticed Claudette's . . . eye?"

"Yes."

"Well, my father obviously couldn't give a gift with that . . . connotation to Claudette. Through some quirk of the gene pool, Mau Tim's eyes were exactly the color of my mother's. And the necklace was also, I think, like a peace offering. A symbolic way of welcoming them into the family."

"When they weren't originally."

"Look, I told you to butt—"

"Okay, okay. You listed the necklace as missing in the property report."

"Why wouldn't I?"

"It just seems like the kind of thing the son of Tommy Danucci might leave out to keep him from becoming involved in it."

The lips seemed to be the only part of Dani's face that reacted in any way. This time they lost their color. "I put the necklace in the report in the hope that it might lead the police to the killer before my brother's contacts found him."

"Your brother seems to think that police custody isn't exactly absolute sanctuary."

"If the police arrest the perpetrator, he has a chance. If my brother . . ."

Dani didn't go on. I said, "Did you know anything about your niece's life in modeling?"

He sat back. "Not much. She'd call me from time to time, we'd talk or have lunch."

95

"I thought she lived with you for a while?"

"Briefly. About a year ago, when Mau Tim first came to Boston. But I think she found that . . . confining."

"How do you mean?"

"Well, I put in rather long hours at the firm. When I get home from work, I tend to stay there. I don't have a great deal of time for social engagements."

"Did you know much about Mau Tim's social life?"

"No."

"Boyfriends?"

"No," again, a little more pointedly.

"I was under the impression that she might have lived with a photographer for a while before moving to Falmouth Street."

Dani's lips narrowed. "That is another thing I wouldn't mention to my brother, Mr. Cuddy."

"All right. How about her life in the Falmouth Street apartment?"

"Mau Tim was young and attractive. I assume that once she had her own place, she was . . . active."

"I notice you call your niece 'Mau Tim.' "

"That was the name she wanted to call herself. I respected her wishes."

"Why did she change her last name to yours?"

"You have a problem with people changing their names, Mr. Cuddy?"

"No."

"I didn't Anglicize mine, you know. I kept the ethnicity, just changed the . . . recognition factor for professional reasons."

"That your niece's reasoning as well?"

"I assume so."

"She never told you?"

"Mau Tim was at the age where people rebel against family. I was the one in the family who broke away, who did something different. She wanted to do the same. I changed my name, she changed hers to my new one. Simple."

Maybe. "How is it you came to be trustee of the building?"

"Limit the liability. It's done all the time."

"That's the reason for putting the building into a realty trust, Mr. Dani. What was the reason you're the front man?"

Dani's lips narrowed again. "My mother asked me to."

"The 'A and T' stands for?"

" 'The Amatina and Thomas Danucci Realty Trust.' "

"And your mother asked you to be trustee?"

"My father wanted to buy another building. They already owned a number of properties in the North End. My mother thought it would be a good idea to have some things in different parts of the city. So, my father bought the place on Falmouth Street."

"With you as trustee."

"Correct."

"How long ago was this?"

"Six, perhaps seven years."

He reminded me of something Claudette Danucci had mentioned. "Just before your mother died."

"Yes."

"I thought you said before that you kind of broke away from the family by going to law school."

"Look, Mr. Cuddy—"

"I'm just wondering, why did you decide to be a trustee of a family building when you'd already broken away?"

"Not that it's any of your business, but my mother asked me, and as a son I was happy to do it for her. She wasn't too well. . . . By then, my mother had an idea she was going to die, and she thought my being a trustee of the building would bring my father and me a little closer."

"Did it?"

"I've told you twice there are some things you shouldn't look into, Mr. Cuddy. Let me give you an answer that might save you some pain later on. My brother and I get along fine. Despite what you think, he runs a legitimate business enterprise and I represent him legally on it. My father and I are oil and water. Have been for a long time, no hope of reconciliation. That's family business, not yours, and if I were you, I'd stay out of it."

When a lawyer like Vincent Dani tells me some things aren't my business, and especially when he tells me three times, I wonder why he explains things at all. "After your mother died, how come you stayed on?"

"What?"

"After your mother died, why didn't you resign as trustee of the building?"

"Because she'd wanted me to serve. Besides, it always seemed like a sleeping dog."

"Until now."

Dani's lips glared at me and left the room.

"THIS ONE HERE'S CALLED SHADOWFAX."

The music came over the Lincoln's stereo system in a series of sounds, each from a different instrument until all had blended into chords I'd never heard before and couldn't even characterize. There was something about it that made you want to merge into the upholstery. Then I thought that might be why Zuppone was playing it for me.

I said, "How come you're not checking to see if we're being followed?"

Primo turned to me, then glanced at all the mirrors to be sure he was still aware of his car's position on the highway back to Boston. "Who'd be tailing us?"

"The FBI?"

That got a grunt. "The Feebs, I'll tell you something, they signed off on us a long time ago. Oh, they still root around, accountants and tax guys mostly. But once that task force busted the Angiulos and got their citations and all, they started looking for other fish to fry. Besides, they can't push their luck too far, asking for too many taps or warrants. Sooner or later, some

99

judge starts adding up how many times he signed his name and starts thinking, 'Hey-ey-ey, no more for a while, okay?' Naw, the Feebs, they ain't a factor anymore.''

"What is a factor?"

The toothpick rolled from port to starboard. "What do you mean, Cuddy?"

"Before you picked me up this afternoon, you checked me out pretty thoroughly. In the week since Mau Tim died, you've been doing the same thing with the people in her life, right?"

A sleepy smile. "Coupla guys said you was pretty smart."

"What did you find out?"

Zuppone thought for a minute. "I didn't do nothing like you're gonna do. Go talk to everybody, I mean. I checked a few things here, a few things there. Spread the word."

"About the necklace."

"Yeah. Somebody tries to fence it, we get a call."

"But no calls yet."

"Right."

"Kind of a long time for a junkie to sit on a piece of jewelry."

"Kind of."

I stretched my neck against the headrest. "Somebody told me tonight you're a situation guy."

"Somebody was right."

"What does a situation guy do?"

"What it sounds like. I go in, look around, let people know what's what."

"You checked out the modeling agency before Mau Tim went to work there."

"Yeah, but lemme give you a tip, Cuddy."

"Sure."

"You're around the family, her name wasn't 'Mau Tim.' It was 'Tina,' right?"

"Thanks."

"Don't mention it."

Zuppone put on his turn signal and pulled out into the fast lane to go around a garbage truck. As soon as we were by it, he used the signal again and tiptoed back into the middle lane, reducing his speed.

"You're a careful guy, Primo."

"Pays to be."

"About the modeling agency?"

"Yeah?"

"What was your read of the situation?"

Another migration of the toothpick. "Year ago they were clean. Otherwise, the family don't let Tina work for them, I don't care what she wants to do."

"How could the family stop her?"

"Simple. I pay a visit to the agency, and they all of a sudden decide to call her and say, 'Sorry. Turns out, we don't need you after all.' "

"What did you think of the people there?"

"I didn't talk to them direct-like."

"What did you find out about them?"

"The first name—Lind-something?"

"Lindqvist."

"Yeah, that's how somebody told me she says it. How do you spell that?"

I went through it.

"That's not the usual thing, right? I mean, usually you put the 'u' after the 'q,' right?"

"Usually in English. I don't know much about Swedish."

"Swedish, huh? She don't look good enough to be what I'd call Swedish."

"I thought you didn't talk to them."

The half-smile. "I sat in my car outside there a coupla days. Watching the door, making sure it looked legit. Kinda surprised me how tall and plain the model broads were. Out of their war paint, I mean."

"What about Lindqvist?"

"I got the impression she was the pants, with the guy— Yulin?"

"Right."

"With the guy Yulin kind of a second banana."

"That's how I read it, too." I stopped. "If it turns out one of them killed Tina, where does that leave you?"

"Fucked, if I should of seen it." Zuppone pushed a button on his armrest that lowered his window. He spit the toothpick into the night air. "Kind of the pot calling the kettle black, ain't it?"

"What is?"

"What you're thinking. Guy like me calling Yulin a 'second banana.' "

"I hadn't thought about it."

"Yeah, well, I am a second banana, Cuddy. I'm a guy used to not do so good in school there. You know why?"

"No."

"I got dyslexia. You know, I see '24' like it's '42' or 'art' like it's 'rat.' "

"Makes the studying tough."

"Yeah. Only Sister Angelica back in the third grade there didn't call it dyslexia."

"What did she call it?"

"Being stupid. But, turns out, I'm not so stupid once I'm out of the books. Real world, I do okay because I ain't got no ambitions."

"Run that by me again?"

"Ambitions. Like to be something I ain't. I'm good at situations, sizing things up, sizing people up. I'm not looking to run anything. Last thing you want to be in this business is the guy somebody in charge of an operation sees when he looks over his shoulder, get me?"

"I think so. It doesn't bother you, the organization you size things up for?"

Zuppone looked my way sharply this time, having to swerve just a bit to get back in lane. He eased five miles per hour off the speedometer. "You're a college man, right?"

"Uh-huh."

"Holy Cross, a guy said."

"That's right."

"Then you go in the Army, make—what, captain?"

"Eventually."

"Guy like you, a corporation welcomes you with open arms. You got a résumé reads like a guy they want to hire."

"I see your point."

"Good. 'Cause this is the only corporation that thinks my résumé is just fine. It ends after seventh grade, they don't think that's funny. I can't spell for shit, they don't think that's stupid. I go into a thing, I scope it out, I get back to them with what's what. That's what they care about."

"How about their views on capital punishment?"

"Whacking a guy out, you mean."

"That's right."

"We don't whack nobody without a good reason for it. These new gangs, the Jamaicans—or the fucking Dominicans?—they're animals. They do a drive-by, waste a fucking street corner full of fucking people, get the one they want. I never heard a one of our contracts wasn't specific, I never heard a hitter did anybody more'n he was told to. I tell you something else, too. You ever see an execution?"

"A hit?"

"No, I mean a government one. Like gas or the chair."

"No."

"Well, let me tell you. One of our associates, he got himself in a fight down in the Land of Grits. Shivved some redneck was trying to wrap a tire iron around his head, but that's not how the witnesses saw it. Anyway, the jury decides to puff him, then it takes nine years, nine fucking *years* for the courts to decide, does he go or not. Finally, they decide he goes, and somebody's got to travel down there, kind of get him through it, you know?"

"I think so."

"Well, it turns out I'm it, so I fly down there and rent a car and drive through some of the worst places I ever seen. Shit, the shacks with real tarpaper, outhouses, makes the worst block in Roxbury there look like Beacon fucking Hill. Anyways, I get to the prison early, I pay my respects to our guy. He's in this room, it's maybe eight by ten, with a stainless steel sink and john below it and one fucking bunk. The thing that got me is the colors, though. The bars are powder blue, powder fucking blue like some broad's bedroom, and the bulls are the same way, looking like maybe they got bleached out of the Navy or something. And our guy, he's in this orange jump suit, only he's sweating so bad, he's gotta change his jump suit twice in the hour I'm with him.

"He gets to me, Cuddy. He asks, can I stay for the show? He says it'd mean a lot to him, knowing there was somebody there he knew. So I tell him, sure I'll stay for it. Christ, like the guy's last request, you know? Then the bulls tell me, I got to go to the viewing room so our guy can get prepped. I say okay, and they put me in this place, looks like something outta a fifties horror movie. Like I'm in living color but seeing all this in just black and white? Well, I sit down on a folding chair, maybe ten other people around me, and they're all making small talk about the weather and the crops and some high school fucking football team ain't won a game yet and I'm the only one in the room can say a sentence in like less than five minutes.

"Then through the glass we see the bulls come in, and everybody sits down. The bulls work the door with this wheel on it, like in a submarine, but it's not my guy's time yet, they're just testing the fucking gas chamber. And get this, right? We're in the Old South, so what do they use to test it with? They use this little black rabbit, black as a jigaboo. It's in a cage like a milk crate, and they put it in the chair. Then they clear out and drop the pill or whatever, and there's a little cloud, like somebody's grabbing a smoke under the seat. And this rabbit starts twitching, then hops hard around the crate, so hard you figure he's breaking bones, fracturing his fucking skull banging it into the top of the cage.

"Well, I'll tell you something, Cuddy. I had to get out of there. I had to get out. I'm a made fucking member of our organization, and I couldn't take what one of our governments does to a guy. You want to croak somebody for what they did? Fine. They know going in they fuck up, you're going to croak them, fine. They do something real fucking bad, like plank your sister, then you torture them a little. Maybe cut off their fucking wang and stick it in their fucking mouth, that's fine too. Everybody understands why it happened. But for chrissake, don't keep a guy on ice for nine fucking years and feed him and play with his fucking mind over it. Do him, then move the fuck on."

The music ended. Zuppone took a breath, then said, "Let's try a little Wim Mertens, lighten things up."

He popped in a new tape. This was mostly piano, but not entirely, and was the best I'd heard in the car. Solid but varied, eerie but thoughtful.

I said, "I like that."

"You serious?"

"I'm serious."

"It's yours."

"Primo, don't—"

"No. Really. I got a dozen of them. They ain't so easy to find, this way you'll have it."

"Thank you."

We were within sight of the Pru and the Hancock, the lights from the smaller buildings downtown giving a halo to the horizon. "Primo, did you know Tina that well?"

A shrug. "I seen her from time to time. She was younger, I'd give her rides here and there."

"Talk to her much?"

"Naw. It was just like, 'Uncle Primo, please take me to the mall, please?' Like that."

"*Uncle* Primo?"

"Yeah." The half-smile. "I'm not really family, but her mother, she's a real stickler for respect to elders. So Tina'd call me 'Uncle Primo' instead of 'Mr. Zuppone,' you know?"

"What do you know about her life since?"

The smile winked out. "Just what I told you. She was a daughter and a model and now she's dead."

"Anything about boyfriends, enemies?"

"No. She was outta the house down there and into the South End for—what, like a year?"

"I think so."

"Girl that age, Cuddy, a year's like a fucking century to you and me."

I waited a minute, trying to figure a back way to asking where Zuppone was when Mau Tim was killed. "How did you hear she was dead?"

"I was out, running around for this gentleman I know. Got the word her mother'd called with the news."

"Who was the gentleman?"

Just the half-smile. "No big secret, Cuddy. I was grocery shopping."

"On a Friday night?"

"I go to the Star over by Fenway Park. The college kids, they got partying on their minds. So long as the Sox are playing on the road, it ain't too crowded."

Fenway Park was less than a mile from the apartment building on Falmouth Street. "You drive all the way across town from the North End to go food shopping?"

Zuppone caressed the steering wheel, the way he had on the drive south. "They got good parking, nice wide spaces. I buy the big items, the heavy stuff there, then shop the specialty stores back in the neighborhood."

Speaking of neighborhoods, we were approaching the Chinatown exit.

I said, "This time of night, probably Kneeland would be the fastest way back to my place."

Zuppone went by the turnoff and down into the tunnel without slowing. "We ain't finished with your visiting yet."

The lights inside the tunnel shimmered briefly across the hood and windshield. Then we were out and heading up on the Central Artery toward the Boston Garden/North End exit. Zuppone picked up the telephone, hit the number "one," and

waited. Then, "It's Primo . . . Yes, Mister— . . . Less than that
. . . Right."

I moved my tongue around in my mouth. There wasn't much
doubt who we were seeing next. "Should I be getting worried,
Primo?"

The turn and half-smile. "Hey-ey-ey, enjoy the music, huh?"

12

WE INCHED DOWN A NORTH END STREET NO BROADER THAN THE alleys in other parts of the city. Cars were parked up and onto the sidewalk but didn't sport any orange tickets beneath their windshield wipers. Zuppone pulled the Lincoln past a driveway that was barely a curb cut, then used the power steering to back into it. I figured I'd wait for him to get out first.

Primo turned off the ignition and shifted sidesaddle in his seat. He nodded toward a nondescript doorway with a small aluminum awning. The door led into one of the buildings off the driveway. "I think it's just gonna be you and me and this other gentleman upstairs, but he's got like a rule of the house."

"Which is?"

"Guests, they got to check their guns at the door."

I looked at him.

"Hey-ey-ey, Cuddy, we're gonna clip you, we let you take it inside, then we hit you over the fucking head, take it away from you."

"I don't like the number of times you've told me how I don't have to worry about getting killed just yet."

"You have my personal word, you got nothing to worry about up there. The gentleman wants you out, it ain't gonna be in his living room, right?"

I took the Smith & Wesson Chief's Special from the holster over my right buttock, swinging out the cylinder and unloading it. I put the bullets in my right jacket pocket and extended the weapon to Zuppone, cylinder still out.

He looked hurt. "What, you think we'd whack you with your own piece?"

"It's been tried before."

Primo took my weapon, closed the cylinder back into the frame gently, the way you're supposed to, and slid the revolver into the pocket of his leather coat.

I let him lead me from the car to the doorway, sounds of a radio station coming down from a third-story window in another building. On the outside sills and fire escape landings, large terra-cotta flowerpots squatted, new blossoms on the plants. The air was full of that warm, heavy smell of Italian cooking, the spices you knew by scent if not by name. I wondered if any were the ones that Claudette Danucci had learned to use.

Zuppone didn't have to use a key on the metal fire door. Inside the doorway, the building took on a different character. Another dingy brick four-story from the outside, the interior staircase led up a half flight of stairs to a majestic door, mahogany from where I stood. The runner on the staircase was a Persian that looked brand new and a thousand years old, all at the same time.

Primo led the way up the steps, knocking on the wooden door in a staccato sequence I thought might be code. This time he waited to enter. Within ten seconds, I heard the sound of a bolt and chain from the other side.

The man opening the door was somewhere between seventy and eighty. Five ten, he seemed thin but wiry beneath the block-patch sweater, creased wool slacks, and spit-shined loafers. The hair was white, a pronounced widow's peak, but just a bit long over the ears and combed back. He was clean-shaven, the skin still pretty taut except at the throat, where it dangled a little against the cords of his neck. His eyes were gray but unclouded, like two baby spots positioned to highlight the long, hooked nose. The eyes of an old man who still didn't really expect to die in bed.

Our host said, "Mr. Detective. Thomas Danucci. You're welcome in my home."

There was still an edge of accent on some of the words. Danucci gave no indication he intended to shake hands with me or Zuppone. We walked into a minimalist foyer, where Primo took my trenchcoat and hung it and his leather coat in a closet. Then we followed Danucci into a maximalist living room. Pedestal furniture that looked like it could support an elephant. Persian and Indian rugs that dwarfed the staircase runner. Oil paintings of Madonna and Child, the Gift of the Magi, and other biblical scenes in museum mountings with tiny lamps that reminded me of the old man's eyes. Molding around the intersection of wall and ceiling mimicked a bouquet of roses, a motif repeated every linear foot.

Danucci motioned in a master of ceremonies way at the dining room, endowed with pieces from the same massive period and illuminated by an icicle chandelier. There were more religious paintings around the walls, punctuated with a low cabinet against one wall and a tall china cabinet against another. The tall cabinet had glass panes and interior shelving that supported ornate serving platters and a large rosewood case. I counted chairs for ten but settings for only two, the head of the table and the chair to its left. The plates were pewter or silver, with similar chalices where you'd expect wineglasses.

Danucci said, "Primo tells me my family, they kept you from your dinner. How's about you join me in mine, eh?"

"Thank you."

The old man said, "Primo."

Zuppone pulled out the side chair for me. I sat in it, the cushion soft, the wood carving digging into the back of my knees. Then Zuppone pulled out the head chair, with its armrests and higher back, the head of a raging lion at the top above the back cushion. Danucci sat in it, lowering himself carefully with his palms on the chiseled claws that made up the ends of the chair's arms. He hunched forward as Zuppone pushed the chair and him in toward the table.

Danucci pinged the chalice in front of him. "White or red?"

"Whatever you recommend."

A pleased smile. "I like a man knows how to be a good guest." He said, "Primo," then a string of Italian.

Zuppone crossed to the low cabinet, taking a cut crystal decanter from it. Lifting the crystal stopper gently, he crossed back to me, pouring ruby-colored wine into my chalice, jewels embedded in geometric patterns on both its bowl and stem. When Primo finished with me, he did the same for Danucci.

The old man raised his chalice, closed his eyes, and intoned something that sounded more like Latin from the Old Mass than Italian from the old country.

Danucci opened his eyes. "That was, 'With thanks to God and to good health.' You get a little older, you go back to the things from when you're a kid. Even start believing in them again, eh?"

He gave a curt nod, and we drank together. The wine was spectacular, a mix of a dozen flavors that tumbled around the mouth before finishing with a dying fireworks glow at the back of the tongue.

I said, "The best."

Danucci said, "It is."

This time he just looked at Zuppone, who nodded and headed toward a door that turned out to be the kitchen.

"I gotta say, I'm lucky, Mr. Detective. I can still enjoy the wine and the food. I just gotta drink and eat a little early. Otherwise, I taste the spices a second time in my sleep, you know?"

"Actually, I'm not a detective, Mr. Danucci."

He didn't say anything.

"Detectives are on police forces. I'm just a private investigator."

The blood rose up his neck, stopping just as it flushed his

jaw but not his cheeks. Very quietly, Danucci said, "I'm an old man, Mr. Detective. Indulge me, eh?"

I decided I would not much like Tommy the Temper to get mad at me.

Zuppone came back in with a course of sausage and pasta in small bowls, one for each of us.

Danucci said, "I cook for myself, now. My Amatina was alive, I never thought about it. But I talked with her friends, they told me some of her secrets in the kitchen. I tried this and that, found a couple that reminded me of her."

I sampled the sausage first. Sweet, delicate. Then the pasta. Like cotton candy melting in the mouth.

I said, "Your daughter-in-law told me she learned a lot from your wife."

Danucci paused, his fork not quite lifted clear of his bowl, then put it back down. He paused again, then drank the rest of the wine in his chalice, Primo refilling without needing to be prompted.

When Zuppone had set the decanter back on the counter, Danucci said, "You and me, we don't know how to talk to each other, do we?"

I stopped eating.

"What I'm saying here, you don't want to say nothing wrong, you don't want to offend me you don't have to, but you just don't know what's what, am I right?"

"That's right."

"Can't blame you, Mr. Detective. I was in your shoes, I wouldn't know what the fuck's going on, either. Enjoy your dinner, the hospitality of my table. You don't got nothing to worry about. You might be the only detective in the city got nothing to worry about. Let me talk to you some, you don't even got to worry about answering, eh?"

"All right."

Danucci did another curt nod, but more to himself than a signal to Zuppone.

"Here's the way it is. Twenny years ago, my son comes back from the war, he has this—what I thought at the time, this pregnant squaw, only she's Oriental. He has this Oriental with him, he says to us, 'This is my wife.' Just like that, no letter, no phone call, just cold fucking conks us with it. My Amatina, she's a saint, she says to him, 'Joey, your wife is my daughter,' like that. I can't see it, I can't see the mixing of the blood, what it'd do to Joey's prospects. In the business, I mean. Our business.

"What I'm doing here, Mr. Detective, I'm collecting the story—no, fuck, that's not it. Primo?"

"Like 'collapsing the story,' Mr. Danucci?"

"Right, right. Like making a long story short. Well, six, seven years ago, my Amatina gets sick, Mr. Detective, bad sick, never-get-better sick." Danucci reached for the wine glass. "Primo says you lost your wife young."

"Primo's right."

"I don't know what that must be like. Losing your wife before you have the life that gives you memories. But I know what it's like to lose her after the memories, after all the things you done together, you thought you'd be talking about them forever. So, anyway, my son, he comes back from the war with this wife and then she has the baby, and you only got to take one look . . ."

Danucci's voice caught. I glanced at Zuppone, who just watched the man, no expression. I looked back to Danucci and waited him out.

"You only got to take one look at Tina, you see the eyes. My Amatina's eyes. I don't know how it's possible, but there they are. So I don't accept that too good. And the child grows up in my son's house as my granddaughter, the best because my Amatina, she's so in love with the grandchild, her only one, you see what I'm saying here? Tina gets everything, but me, I'm *siciliano*, eh? I can't accept her."

"Then my Amatina, she gets sick. And the 'Oriental,' the one I thought was a 'pregnant squaw,' she takes my wife into her home, because Claudette says, 'It is not right for the mother of my husband to be in the hands of strangers.' This woman, she lost an eye because of fighting for my son in some fucking chinktown over there, she lost an eye and she still acts like a daughter to my Amatina. There were times, I gotta tell you, there were times I could barely stand to be in the same room with my wife, Mr. Detective. Times the look on her face, or the smell . . . But Claudette, she was always there for her, and then Tina, too. Tina loved her *nana*—my Amatina. Loved her like an Italian girl would. They did everything they could, make her comfortable. Then, when my wife . . . after the funeral, I'm walking back up the stairs down there, where you just come up. If Primo here isn't with me, I'm dead, because I have a heart attack, it feels like five fucking linebackers, they're driving a battering ram through my chest. Primo, he calls my doctor —we call him Doctor T, he's kind of on retainer to us, but he's so famous now, he don't want everybody to know that. Anyway, Primo gets me to the hospital, and Doctor T and the others, they do their thing and I'm still alive, but I can't do nothing, nothing for myself. And the 'Oriental,' she's just got my Amatina out of her house, and she takes me in. Primo looks after things here, but Claudette and Tina, every day they take care of me down at Joey's house when I can't fucking lift my head or . . . clean myself up."

Danucci looked at me, the eyes blazing. "Then she grows into a beautiful young lady, my Tina Amatina, and some fucking louse, some fucking lowlife colored drug fucker kills her. My son Joey, he's out of town, so her mother, she has to call me. And ever since, it's like a blister on my heart. Every hour I think about it, and it's like you rubbing that blister, it don't get better. The best ones, Mr. Detective, we bury the best ones in shallow graves, shallow fucking graves. So you go ahead. You ask your questions, and I'll answer them."

The old man gave that curt nod again, then went back to his fork.

Primo said, "Mr. Danucci, let me warm that up a little for you?"

Danucci started to shake his head, then pushed the bowl three inches toward Zuppone, who scooped it up gracefully, did the same with mine, and hustled into the kitchen.

I said, "Your granddaughter give you any idea there was any problem in her life?"

"Problem? No. She kind of broke away from the family, year, year and a half ago. Go out on her own, be a model or some kinda shit. Just her age, every kid goes through that. But I'll tell you something, she still remembered to call me. She needed something, she didn't want to ask my son for, she asked me."

Danucci's hand doted on the stem of the goblet. "You know, she talked to me the day she died?"

"You saw her?"

"No. Just on the telephone. She called me, told me how happy she was about going to some party, about me and the Order of the Cross and all."

His son had mentioned it. "You're some kind of officer in it?"

Danucci looked at me sharply. "Not some kind of. I'm gonna be the next president, you hear that? Thomas Danucci, Tommy the Temper Danucci, he's gonna be number one in the most honored Italian Catholic society there is for laymen."

Danucci swung his head around the room. "You're wondering, even with all the paintings, the icons, you're wondering how come they let a guy like me in period, am I right?"

"That's what I was wondering."

Danucci softened the look a little. "You're okay, Mr. Detective. You get asked a question, you answer it." The rhythm of his speech changed. "When my Amatina got sick, I started to get the religion again. It happen to you, with your wife?"

I started to say no, then Zuppone came back in with our bowls. After he served us, I said, "Not so much."

"Well, you were young. I was—this was six years ago, I was coming up against seventy. The Office—that's what we call it, you know?"

I wasn't sure how much of this I wanted to hear. "It?"

Danucci attacked his food. "Come on, Mr. Detective, don't disappoint, eh? The organization. Here in Boston, we call it the

Office. In Chicago, they called it the Outfit. Till everybody got bit with the RICO shit. You know what that means?"

"I know it stands for 'Racketeer' something or other."

"Well, let me tell you, so you'll know. It stands for 'Racketeer Influenced and Corrupt Organizations.' That's what they called it down in Washington. Sound like a good name for a law to you?"

"Kind of cumbersome."

"Yeah, cumbersome. So they decide they're gonna shorten it, call it by the letters, the initials. Fucking coincidence, guess what they spell?"

Danucci looked at me like he expected an answer.

I said, "RICO."

"That's right. RICO. Like the name of that guy Edward G. played in the Bogey movie. The one in the hurricane."

"Key Largo."

"Yeah, *Key Largo.* Only you get the idea, maybe they thought of using 'RICO' first, then come up with the words to fit later. RICO, it's got that nice 'wop' sound to it. Give the boys at the station a good laugh, they pull in a friend of ours, they get to say to him, 'You're under arrest for RICO, Rico.' Fucking assholes."

Danucci finished his course, then took some wine. Primo cleared the bowls and disappeared into the kitchen.

"So, like I said, I got religion again after my Amatina got sick, and I started getting back to the church. Not since I'm eleven I go to Mass, but I start now every day, every fucking morning. My heart attack, that took me out of the loop. The rest of the Office—my friends, they understood, no problem, but I couldn't do nothing from that bed. Just as well, tell you the truth. Wasn't much after that, story broke that the Feebs, they had the Angiulos bugged over on Prince Street, they got them all, big falls."

Danucci leaned into the table but more in my direction. "I tell you something else, so you'll know. Almost sixty years in the business, sixty fucking years, I never once got arrested. I'm not talking convicted, I mean not even arrested. You know why? I copied this man, I fucking idolized him, Mr. Detective. You ever heard the name, Filippo Buccola?"

"No."

"You should read more. Buccola was a man, you saw him in the street, you woulda said, 'there goes a doctor,' or 'there goes a lawyer.' Guy wore little wire glasses and a bow tie. And he was a gentleman. He was the *capo* before Ray Senior down in Rhody. And he knew when to get out. He moved back to Sicily, he lived to be a hundred and one, Mr. Detective. He let me in on a secret. There are three things you gotta have, be a success in this business. You gotta have heart, you gotta have brains, and you gotta have ambition."

Primo brought in another course, this one veal in a wine sauce. Halfway through, I'd eaten more calories than I usually throw down in a week.

Danucci rested his fork. "You know, in the old days, you had a problem with some people, you could talk to them, eh? You couldn't settle it, sometimes you had them play a little Guts."

I said "Guts?" before I thought to keep my mouth shut.

"Yeah. Some of the old guys, they had these chrome revolvers, custom-made by gunsmiths back in Italy. A lot of guys had a pair of them, used to keep them in a box." Danucci gestured at the glass cabinet behind him. "Like my Amatina's jewelry box up on the shelf there. A couple of your boys had a problem and they come to you with it, couldn't talk it out, you took these revolvers. You put one bullet in each cylinder, then you put a spin on the fucking thing and closed it."

"Like Russian roulette?"

"Yeah, yeah. Like that. Then you gave one gun to each guy, they're standing maybe ten, twelve feet apart, and they point their pieces at each other. And the only other guy involved would be you, doing the calling. When you called out 'One,' they each got to pull the trigger once. Nobody's gun went off, you let them think a little, then said, 'Two.' Nobody got shot, you let them think a little more. I tell you, Mr. Detective, a lot of problems got settled, before they let you get to three."

I said, "Any chance one of your people could be involved in Tina's death?"

Emphatic shake of the head. "No way. No fucking way. Family's off limits. We're *siciliani*, not like the fucking Camorra back in *Napoli*, wasting little kids on street corners. The colored do that over the drugs here, not us. Besides, I got a son in the business. Somebody wants to send me a message, they go after him."

"How about somebody who's after your son?"

"Same thing. They'd come after me, they got balls for brains. Anyway, I can see you don't understand. They want to send a message, they don't break in like some fucking sneak thief. They send a clear fucking message, they want to send one."

"Could the necklace be a message?"

The blood rose right past the jaw and cheeks, the vein at the temple pounding as he worked on his food and swallowed hard. "That necklace was my gift to my Amatina. Her gift to me was her eyes and her love, Mr. Detective. My gift to her was that necklace. One of a kind item, stones had to come from Madagascar, down by Africa there. With the gold and the craftsmanship went into it, that necklace cost more to make than this fucking house cost to build. But after my Amatina died, I gave it to Tina, for nursing my wife and me. To show her she was really part of the family, mixed fucking blood, she was still my blood. The necklace shows up on the street, we go back up the line, snatch the guy and spend some time with him."

"Maybe the guy who has it knows it's too hot to peddle."

"Guy breaks into houses, especially one of *my* houses, he's a junkie, a fucking crackhead got shit for brains. He don't know enough not to hit a connected property, he don't know enough to check out a piece of merchandise before he fences it."

"It's been over a week. Kind of a long time for somebody to sit on it."

Danucci gave me a long look. "Sometimes you got to be patient, Mr. Detective." The old man glanced at Zuppone, who left us without a word to go into the kitchen.

Danucci squared around, his fingers playing with the goblet

in front of him. "You remember what I told you before, about what you got to have to make it in this business?"

"Brains, heart, and ambition."

"You met my son Joey tonight. What do you think of him?"

I didn't like this. "What do you mean?"

The spotlight look came into the old man's eyes. "You know what I mean."

I took a sip of wine. "Heart and ambition to spare. Enough brains to do fine, moneywise."

"Moneywise. Let me tell you something, Mr. Detective. There's only two ways to make money in this world. One, you steal it from somebody. Two, you inherit it from somebody who already stole it from somebody else."

Danucci's brow went toward the kitchen door. "So, how about Primo?"

I put down the goblet. "Brains and heart, but no ambition."

Danucci closed his eyes and smiled a little. "Primo, Primo. He's got what it takes, but he don't want it. I can't understand that, Mr. Detective. He don't want nothing past the leather coat and the Lincoln car and that elevator shit he puts on the radio."

The eyes suddenly opened again, the spots stronger than before. "And what about Mr. Vincent Dani, Esquire?"

"Brains and ambition, but no heart."

The eyes reached laser level. "You know what burns me about the fucking lawyers with their fucking RICO laws, looking down their noses at guys like me? What I offer, Mr. Detective, is protection. Protection so's a guy can turn a profit. You tell me, what do lawyers offer? I'll tell you. They offer protection, same as me. I keep somebody from getting ripped off by a coupla guys with guns in their hands and nothing between the ears. The lawyers, they keep somebody from getting ripped off by guys with pens in their hands and plenty between the ears. We both take our cuts off the top, the lawyers and me, and we ain't so different you'd notice it."

Except for the body count. I said, "Mr. Danucci—"

"Mr. Vincent Dani, Esquire. He never told you that, did he?"

"What he told me, Mr. Danucci, was that you two were like

oil and water. I imagine he was telling me that while Primo was on the car phone, giving you his read of me as a situation."

Danucci weighed things. He took a slug of wine, then replaced the chalice with delicacy on the tablecloth. "You learned a lot of things in a little time, Mr. Detective. You want to go through the apartment house over on Falmouth?"

"Eventually. I think I'd rather talk to everybody else first, then go through it with their stories in mind."

Danucci looked up at me with sad, tired eyes. "You got brains, Mr. Detective. My son Joey, he don't got real brains, but he's got real heart, maybe too much heart. He's the kind, he might do something rash. Joey's got too long a life ahead of him for that. You find the guy did this, you come to me first, eh?"

Tommy the Temper Danucci gave his abrupt nod, like I would do what he wanted whether I promised him or not.

120

13

WHEN PRIMO ZUPPONE DROPPED ME OFF AT THE CONDO, HE REMEMbered to give me both my gun and the Wim Mertens tape. I put the cassette into a pocket of my raincoat.

Upstairs, there were two messages on my telephone machine. The same two were on my office answering service when I checked in with it. The first was from Harry Mullen, asking me to call him about the Dani case. I decided to handle that instead with a face-to-face, the next morning at his office. The other message was from Nancy, asking me to call her at home.

"Hello?"

"Nance, it's John."

"Oh, John." A gap, as though I'd woken her up. "Can you come over?"

"Now?"

"Please."

"Sure. Anything the—"

"When you get here."

"Twenty minutes."

There was something in her voice, something I didn't recognize right away. Then I remembered her note between the salt and pepper that morning. She was taking Renfield to the vet's, and I was supposed to have called her. Shit.

I made the drive shaving five minutes off the twenty.

Nancy met me at the downstairs door to her building. She was wearing an old New England School of Law sweatshirt, jeans, and no makeup. Unless you counted the red nose.

Nancy Meagher, Assistant District Attorney for the County of Suffolk, Commonwealth of Massachusetts, was stiff as a fish.

She said, "Don't say anything. Just c'mon up."

I followed her, bracing myself at each step to break her fall if she went over backwards. As we passed the Lynches' landing, Drew and I exchanged nods. On the third floor, Nancy had to grope through the pockets of her jeans before finding the key to her place.

The kitchen table was cleared except for a single short tumbler and a half-empty liter of Stolichnaya. I suppose you could have said the bottle was half-full, but things didn't look that optimistic.

"Nance—"

Her right hand rose in a stop sign, then flapped down to her side. She crossed to the sink, steadying herself with her left palm on the porcelain while reaching up to the cabinet for another glass. After two tries, she managed to snag one.

Nancy crossed back, put the new tumbler on the table, and poured three fingers of rough justice into each glass before handing me the new one. "I don't want to be the only in-need-brit . . . in-*e*-briate in this conversation."

I accepted the glass, thinking that was the tone I hadn't recognized in her voice over the phone. I'd seen her drinking before, but never drunk.

She downed half her booze, took a breath, and downed the rest.

I just nipped at mine, covering the tumbler with my hand to mask how much was left. "What do you say we go into the living room and talk about it?"

Nancy turned, taking the bottle by the neck and caroming

past me toward the front of the apartment. At the couch, she yanked two cushions onto the floor, plunking herself into one of them. I took the other.

She started to pour herself another drink, stopped, and set the bottle and glass heavily on the rug. "I'm gonna be real sick, right?"

"If that bottle started the evening intact."

A nod. "When?"

"You eat anything?"

A shake.

"Then pretty soon and pretty bad."

"Before that happens . . ." She suppressed a belch. ". . . I have something to say. Renfield's gonna be okay. It's gonna take a while, but he's gonna be okay."

"Nancy, I'm sorry—"

The stop sign again. "Wasn't you. Wasn't your fault, I mean. And wasn't his hip, either. The vet said he has a congenial . . . congenital problem with his back legs. I can't remember the science name, but it's like his kneecaps aren't in the right place, so he has to have an operation to put them back. Where they should be. So it wasn't your fault. It would have happened sometime, when he jumped off a chair or down a step or . . ." She waved the last phrase away.

"If Renfield's going to be okay, then why the bottle?"

Nancy flapped both hands in her lap. "They called me at the office and told me he should have the operation or else be . . . put to sleep, and I guess I just realized how . . . fragile everything could be. When I'm with you, I'm fine. When you're not here, and Renfield is, I'm fine. But when I got home tonight, and he wasn't here, and no word back from you, I just realized how lonely it was to be alone."

"Nance—"

The stop sign came up halfway. "John, this isn't easy for me. I'm trying to tell you something, okay?"

"Okay."

"When I first started seeing you, I said to myself, 'Girl, this could be the one.' But then I realized that you have your life, and your job, and that's fine. That's fine, really, because I have my life and my job, too." Her right hand slashed through the air. "Even steven. But I just realized tonight that the main reason I got Renfield from the animal shelter in the first place is that . . ."

Something churned inside her, and I started hoping that this wasn't going to be a much longer speech.

". . . is that I needed company when we weren't together. Once I got used to having you around, I needed somebody around when you weren't."

"Like Renfield."

Nancy pointed at me. "Exactly."

"When can you pick him up?"

"That's the other thing. They have to keep him till Friday afternoon. 'Cause of the anestex . . . anesthesia. They have to keep an eye on him when he wakes up. But I have to leave for Dallas that morning for my talk, and I can't . . ."

Her voice quavered, and I got up on my knees and hugged her. "I can pick him up, no sweat."

She started to cry quietly. "But I can't even be—"

"Nancy, don't worry, okay? I'll pick him up, and he'll be fine."

She nodded into my shoulder, and I felt something else move inside her.

"Nance, why don't we get you into the bathroom?"

"Good . . . idea."

We just made it.

Nancy got out of bed Thursday morning on the strength of a quart of ice water and three Excedrin. After I dropped her at the courthouse, I drove to the condo space and decided to run to clear my own head toward seeing Harry Mullen.

It had been a few weeks since I'd done the Boston marathon, but most of the ill effects were gone. My right toenail, which had turned black, began growing out instead of falling off. My side, where I'd taken a bullet in the little pocket of fat above the hip bone, healed over nicely, just a livid mark on the love handle.

I still had the endurance the training had given me, but I expected that would evaporate over the next few months. In just a cotton turtleneck and shorts, I crossed Storrow Drive on the Fairfield Street pedestrian ramp, heading upriver on the macadam path. They were still repairing the Mass Ave Bridge, the orange cement trucks looking like ladybugs on a branch. It seemed as though they'd been repairing the bridge since I'd started high school.

Nearing Boston University, I passed over the painted outlines of several bodies, limbs akimbo. I think the outlines were supposed to represent some people killed during a coup in Chile. The paint certainly wasn't the work of a crime scene techie. The police use removable tape or washable chalk so as not to terrify the tourists any longer than necessary.

I made the turn for home at the Harvard Square bridge, thinking that it had been my first training run for the marathon and remembering how much trouble I'd had with it five months earlier. Then my mind shifted to confronting Harry Mullen over what he'd gotten me into, and I picked up my pace considerably on the way back.

He looked miserable even before he saw me in his doorway.

"Jeez, John, nobody told me you were here."

I gestured behind me. "There was nobody out here to ask. Where's the staff?"

Mullen motioned me in. He pulled a cigarette pack from his shirt pocket, and I reflexively closed the door.

Harry lit up without handing me a towel or setting up his electronic box. There was even an ashtray on his desk, five dead butts already in it. "You got my message on your tape there?"

"I got it. Of course, the Danuccis delivered their message a little sooner."

Mullen flinched, took a deep drag, and blew it out like a fire-eater. "I want to explain this, John."

"I want to hear it."

Harry waited for me to take the visitor's chair. No more comfortable than last time.

He said, "First, I swear to you, I didn't know a thing about the Danucci side of it."

"Bullshit, Harry."

"No, honest to God. Yulin's call and letter came in while I was out of the office. Because the policy's half a million, the claim went down to New York before we even started on it up here." Mullen took another hard drag. "And your friend Brad Winningham spotted the Dani name."

"How did he do that?"

"He knew somebody went to law school with the girl's uncle. I guess everybody at the school knew about the guy changing his name because of the family connection."

"Look, Harry, why didn't you tip me to this when I came to see you Tuesday afternoon?"

"Because I didn't know, John. I swear."

"How come you didn't know then but you did know by last night?"

"Yesterday afternoon, I—Jeez, John. Let me go back, go through it from the top, okay?"

I exhaled. "Okay."

Mullen mashed out the cigarette. "The claim comes in with the Dani name on it, nothing about 'Danucci.' It gets sent to New York. Winningham sees it, makes the connection, then tells me over the phone to assign the investigation to you. Get me?"

"You gave it to me without knowing about the Danuccis being involved."

"Right, right. I get the call from Winningham, I figure, he's trying to be a nice guy for once. I owed you, John. What you taught me here, what you said for me when they booted you out. I figured this'd be a good way to pay you back a little."

"So you didn't look the gift horse in the mouth."

"Right."

"So what happened to change things?"

Mullen closed his eyes and chewed the inside of his cheek. Then he seemed to talk to the desk. "Winningham called me yesterday. Said he was going on vacation. Said he wanted to tie up a few loose ends first."

"Like me."

Harry looked up. "Yeah. Yeah, like you. He asks me, 'You give that case to Cuddy yet?' and I say, 'Yes, Mr. Winningham.' And he says, 'He working on it yet?' And I say, 'You bet he is.' And then he says, 'You hear back from him yet?' and I go, 'No, Mr. Winningham, but I just gave him the file yesterday.' And the shit says, 'Well, don't hold your breath, Mullen.' And I stop. Then I say, 'What do you mean?' And he says, 'You ever heard of the Danucci family?' And I say, 'Like in the mob stories, you mean?' And Winningham just laughs, John. The son of a bitch just laughs at me."

I watched Mullen. "He told you not to tell me, right?"

Harry looked away, out his window toward the Burger King. "Yeah, but fuck him."

I watched my old friend some more, tried not to see his little kid with the goofy smile.

Harry said, "Besides, another month, it won't mean anything anyway."

"Why not?"

Mullen stabbed at the pack of Marlboros. "Another month, I'm gone."

"They caught you?"

He looked at me like I wasn't speaking the mother tongue. "What?"

I inclined my head toward the ashtray. "The company policy on smoking. They caught you?"

"Oh." Harry acted like he wanted to laugh, but just couldn't find the right muscles. "No. Jeez, that's right. I was so worried about that the last time I saw you. No, John. They're folding us up."

"They're what?"

"They're closing the office. That was one of the other 'loose ends' Winningham wanted to tie up before he hit the beach.

Seems some MBAs didn't have anything better to do down in New York, they punched me and my people into the computer and found out they could save a dime, folding us up and doing all the regional investigating with free-lancers out of Boston or Portland or Providence."

"You're kidding?"

Mullen's face told me he wasn't. "So, you want to punt this Dani/Danucci thing, it doesn't matter. You want to stay with it, I'll let you know when to start sending your reports to New York."

I let out a breath and sat back in the chair as Harry lit his cigarette. I couldn't see how leaving the case for Empire would take me out of Mau Tim's death as far as the Danuccis were concerned. At Homicide, Holt wouldn't be any help, and Murphy couldn't be any help. Right now, being with Empire was a justification, maybe even a buffer.

Then I noticed the little kid in the photo again. "Harry, what are you going to do?"

He blew smoke from his nostrils. "Check with some guys I know, dust off the résumé." He tried to smile. "They still call it that, right?"

"I'll keep my ears open for you."

"Thanks, John."

"I hear about something, I'll let you know."

"Good, thanks."

As we stood and shook hands, I couldn't decide whose hail words sounded more hollow.

I had left the Prelude in the condo space for my walk over to Empire. After seeing Harry Mullen, I walked back to the condo and tried to call Brad Winningham in New York. His secretary advised me he would not be available for a week. I told her I'd like to see him then and she told me that he'd be very busy upon his return. I said that was all right, I'd be happy even if I had to wait to see him. When she asked for my name, I told her "John F. Danucci." She said she'd put me in the book but couldn't promise anything. I told her I was sure that Mr. Winningham would think that she'd done the right thing.

I went down to my car and headed toward the *Boston Herald*, one of the two big newspapers in town. I wanted more background information on the Danucci angle, and there was one reporter I was pretty sure could help me.

"You notice it, don't you?"

I said, "Notice what, Mo?"

"Notice what. Notice what's different."

I looked around Mo Katzen's office. The old typewriter was still on the stand next to his desk, Mo detesting the concept of computerization. The avalanche of papers, both documents and sandwich covers, was still on top of his desk. Mo himself sat behind the desk, wavy white hair on his head and a dead cigar in his mouth. He still wore the vest and pants of a three-piece suit, the jacket to which I'd never seen on him in all the years I'd known him.

No visible changes. "Sorry, Mo."

"Christ, some detective you are. This." He reached up to his left ear and pulled out a tiny, flesh-colored lump of plastic. "This little bugger."

I took the other chair. "A hearing aid?"

"Finally. Can you believe it? A few years past my prime, and I got to wear one of these things."

Mo's prime may have passed recently, but he was never going to see seventy again. "How long have you had it?"

"Couple weeks now. My wife and I are at this banquet thing back in March, and we're sitting around this big round table, like for poker. This guy I never met before is asking me some kind of cockamamy question from across the table and I'm answering him and then my wife starts elbowing me in the ribs, telling me I'm 'not replying in the context of the question.' Can you believe that?"

"Hard to believe about you, Mo."

"Damn straight. Anyway, this happens like two or three more

times in the course of the evening, and my wife is just about to file papers on me, so I tell her, 'All right already, I'll go see my doctor.' And she tells me, 'You need an audiologist.' And —I gotta admit—I say 'A what?' And she smiles this superior smile of hers, and she doesn't have to tell me 'I told you so' before she makes an appointment for me.

"So, all right, I go to this audiologist guy. Only instead of an office like a doctor, it looks like an appliance store. But, she made the appointment, I go in anyway. The guy asks me some questions, takes some kind of a 'reading' he calls it, then pokes around in my ears with this thing, looks like a miner's pick with a light on it. He says to me, 'Well, Mr. Katzen, no trouble with your wax,' like I've been to the dentist and he tells me I've been flossing right. So then he puts me in this sound booth with keys, but not like a piano."

"Like a recording studio, Mo."

"What?"

"Like—"

"Just a second." Mo put the aid back into his ear. "Like a . . . ?"

"Like a recording studio?"

"Yeah, yeah. Like that. Except instead of earphones, I'm wearing this stethoscope thing. And he beeps me up and over the cowshed, both ears. Then he says I hear the low tones okay, but not the high ones. So now I get to sit in this chair and he pours a moulage of like wax in my ear, with a wick in it. He lets the wax harden, which is not the greatest feeling in the world, I'll tell you.

"Then, maybe ten minutes later, he pulls the wax plug out of my ear by the wick. Then he puts it on the side to harden some more while he asks me questions. He tells me he'll mail the little plug out to some company and my aid will come back in like three to six weeks."

"So now you have a custom-made hearing aid."

"Yeah. Only they don't tell you some things. Like the little bugger's custom-made for only one ear, not the other. My case, it's the left, but guess what?"

"What, Mo?"

"My left is the ear I use for answering the phone. Guess what else."

This could take a while. "What, Mo?"

"The thing's murder if you put the receiver to that ear. The habit of a lifetime, John, and I'm supposed to change it now?"

"That's a tough one, Mo."

"Huh. Tell me about it. Another thing. The little bugger costs like a thousand dollars, and I'm not completely covered by insurance."

"How come?"

"Because it's not from an accident. Can you believe that? I tell the guy, 'What, you can't see your way clear to reimburse me for all the years I've been on this planet?'"

"I'll bet that shut him up."

"Yeah. Yeah, it did. I got to admit, though, it is a clever piece of machinery. I mean, it's got this little wheel, you can adjust it for noise, even while you're wearing it. The audiologist says to me, 'Mr. Katzen, you can even turn it off completely, should say a motorcycle start up next to you.' And I say to him, 'Doctor'—I don't know, is he a doctor, but I figure, it doesn't hurt to be polite, right?—'Doctor, I'm not sure how to tell you this, but my *Wild One* days are behind me, you know?'"

"Good comeback, Mo. I—"

"So then he tells me the battery lasts six months and the aid itself is built for a lifetime. He says, 'It's got the Manhattan Project in it.' And I say, 'Great, my age, I have to have an atomic bomb in my ear,' and he says, 'No, Mr. Katzen, the Manhattan *Circuit*,' and that's when I realize, John, I got to have the thing."

"I think you're right, Mo. Listen, I wonder if—"

"'Course, the little bugger does have its drawbacks. I told you about the phone business?"

"Yes, Mo."

"Well, it's no picnic riding in the car, either. Oh, it closes out the engine noise just fine, but you put the directional signal on? Because it's inside the cabin with you, the thing sounds like a Mongol gong. Also, if it falls out or you can't remember

131

where you put it, there's a homing device inside, makes this sound to let you know where it is. But, surprise, surprise, guess what?"

"You can't hear it."

"On the button, John. On the button. You need a hearing aid to start with, how're you supposed to find the little bugger from a homing sound you can't hear without the little bugger in your ear?"

"Speaking of finding things, Mo."

"What?"

"I said, speaking—"

"I heard you, John. You're sitting not four feet away from me, right?"

"Right, Mo."

"No need to repeat things, right?"

"Right, Mo."

"So, what'd you come over here for. Spit it out."

I took a breath. "I'm working on a case. It involves somebody I'd like to talk with you about."

"Who?"

"Thomas Danucci."

"Thomas . . . Tommy the Temper?"

"Yes."

Mo shook his head, fired up the dead cigar with a war memorial lighter. "John"—puff—"I don't think"—puff-puff—"working on a case"—puff-puff-puff—"involving Tommy Danucci is such a great idea."

"I'm inclined to agree with you. But I'm already in it, and for a lot of reasons, it's easier to keep going than to bail out."

"Your decision." Mo blew a smoke ring. "Tommy Danucci, Tommy Danucci. One of the last of the old ones, John. The ones who made their bones before the war—W W II, I mean. He stayed in the background, always the gentleman, I heard. Like he ran one of those Renaissance city-states with the Borgias and whatever."

"Do you know much about his family?"

"You mean his relatives or his organization?"

"Good point. Start with his organization."

"He came up through the Buccola crowd, late thirties. Heard a little bit about him, here and there during the war. Loan-sharking, barbooth games, something with the Teamsters. Nothing unusual. Then around the early sixties, he really hit his stride with the sharking. You were still in school then, John, but Boston started getting a reputation."

"What kind of reputation?"

"As a place where deadbeats got beat dead."

"Catchy."

"Yeah, I'm sure Tommy intended it that way. He wasn't all that big, but boy he was tough. And blind to the pain if he was in a fight. I have this friend who's Italian—grew up with me in Chelsea. My friend says he saw the Temper take a knife in the shoulder from a deadbeat when Tommy was doing some collection work in the old days. Knife and all, my friend says Tommy was able to punch the guy senseless."

"Danucci still in the rackets?"

Mo shucked some ash from the cigar. "Who can say? Those guys, I assume they got the equivalent of profit-sharing after they retire, even if they're not still active. Seems to me I heard Tommy had a heart attack a few years back, not much since."

"How about his relatives?"

"Tommy married a little late as I recall. Beauty from the old country, real ethnic name. Couple of sons, but I think one went to Vietnam like you, and the other . . . I don't know, doctor or lawyer, maybe?"

So far things checked out pretty well. "There's an obituary I'd like to see, if I could."

"Obit?" Mo's brow furrowed. "John, the hell you got yourself into here?"

"Between us?"

"You mean off the record?"

"I mean between us, Mo."

A glacial sigh. "Okay. My word on it."

I told him about what happened with Mau Tim Dani when I was out of town.

Mo fumed. "Well, I'll tell you, John, I wasn't the fuck out of town and I don't remember anything about it. Hold on a second." He picked up his phone, pushed a button, and hit three numbers. Then he cursed, pushed another button, and hit three more. He rasped at whoever answered, and whoever answered read him something. Mo asked whether there were any accompanying pieces, and he cursed some more, then hung up without saying thank you.

"Well, John. It seems your Mau Tim Dani died on a Friday night, and being only murder number forty-seven in a year that ought to break the record set last year, which should surprise nobody, there was a story without a victim's name in the Saturday paper. A follow-up with 'Dani' but not 'Danucci' got pushed to page sixteen of Sunday's, and then nothing but 'Dani' in the obit. Nobody else ran this, print or broadcast?"

"I don't know."

Mo sucked on the resumed-dead stogie. "It's possible Tommy still has enough juice to get people to sit on something like this, John. I wouldn't have bet on it, this day and age, but it's just barely possible. So I have some advice, you can take it from a man needs a hearing aid in his head."

"Say it, Mo."

"Tread softly, John. Muffle the drums and tread very, very softly through the jungle."

"What are you doing back here?"

"Nice to see you, too, Lieutenant."

"Cuddy, what?"

"I was driving home and a parking space opened up across the street. I figured it might be an omen."

Robert Murphy reached for a sheaf of phone messages on the corner of his desk and started riffling through them. Finding the one he was looking for, he held it up to the light from the window behind him. "Says here, 'John Cuddy called. He is going for a ride with Primo Zuppone.' "

"He likes you to pronounce it 'Zoo-*po*-ny.' "

134

"You take a ride with a wiseguy, you're lucky the M.E. didn't have to pronounce you."

"How did you know he was connected?"

"His name's cropped up over the years."

"In what kinds of cases?"

"Various gentlemen we've pulled out of the harbor."

Lovely. "I thought maybe you looked him up special."

Murphy made the phone message waffle in the air. "Account of this?"

"Made me feel safer, thinking you were watching out for me."

"Cuddy, the fuck you into?"

"I can't tell you."

He put down the slip of paper. "Why not?"

"The other name there."

Murphy looked back at the phone message. "Harry Mullen?"

"Right."

"Who's Mullen?"

"He's with the insurance company I used to work for."

A memory worked its way across Murphy's forehead and jumped for its life. "Not Holt's case."

"That's why I can't tell you."

Murphy closed his eyes. "Get out."

"If Holt screws up, I want you to haunt him for me."

"Cuddy, you screw up with the Danucci family, you'll be able to haunt him yourself. Now—"

I got out.

14

OSCAR PURIEFOY'S ADDRESS ON BOYLSTON WAS PAST MASS AVE, almost to the Fenway. Inside the glass entrance door, a mailbox on the wall had its lock staved in and his name over it. I climbed four flights of stairs past a palm reader, a discount travel agency, a total health consultant, and a CPA before I reached Puriefoy's studio door. I knocked, and a deep bass voice said, "Yeah?"

Inside the room, a teddy-bear black man was on his knees, bending over a set of toy railroad cars on a black velvet blanket. The cars were made from blocks and dowls of wood, all enameled in primary colors. The man consulted what looked like a polaroid photo, then used the thumb on his large hand to nudge the caboose a quarter of an inch.

There were bright umbrella lights over the cars and a camera on a tripod, but from there any comparison to the studio where I'd met Sinead Fagan was unflattering. Puriefoy's place was maybe four hundred square feet, with only a door to a half bath and no windows. Exposed pipes wended through the original stamped tin ceiling, which itself looked fifty years the worse for wear. The wallpaper curled over the chipped and gouged wainscoting, painted an uneven white. A couple of plastic chairs and two TV trays were the furnishings.

"Help you with something?"

The voice really was sonorous, like a Shakespearean actor. His complexion ran to medium brown. Puriefoy was mostly bald, with a beard that seemed to ride up and over his ears into the fringe of hair remaining on his head. He wore hiking khakis with button pockets on the thighs and an old chamois shirt, stained down the front like a mechanic's overalls.

I said, "My name's John Cuddy. I'm a private investigator."

Puriefoy made a face as he stood up, rising to about six feet. "You got some ID?"

Taking out my leather folder, I walked over to him.

He examined it, shook his head, and handed it back to me. "I can't help you."

"You haven't heard what I'm here for."

"Don't matter." He turned back to the train set. "I don't know anything about it."

"I'm looking into the death of Mau Tim Dani, and I'm guessing Sinead Fagan already told you I spoke to her about it."

His head came up as he stopped and turned to me again. "She said you were working for some insurance outfit."

"That's right."

"Why?"

"Why insurance, you mean?"

"Yeah. Her family, they own the building. Who's getting sued?"

"Nobody yet. Everybody helps me, maybe nobody will."

A cynical scowl. "Yeah. Right."

"I understand you were the one who scouted her."

Puriefoy looked like he was trying to decide which would be less trouble, to throw me out or talk with me and get it over with. Then he said, "How long you gonna be?"

I dropped my head toward the train. "Tell your models to take their lunch break."

A laugh. "I'll tell you, man, these here be a lot easier to work with than the prima donnas in this trade."

"How so?"

"Aw, these girls, they hook up with an agency, they figure they're movie stars. They get to wear hot clothes, go to big parties, everybody coming on to them. Then they find out modeling's just standing around for an hour, hour and a half, same leg set, same perfume or wine or whatever the fuck product in their hand. They cop an attitude, you know?"

"Was Mau Tim like that?"

A more cautious look. "They're all like that. This strictly product work, like I'm doing here? This is easy money. You do good work, it shows. How your work looks don't depend on some model's got a hair across her ass, you know?"

"How did you discover her?"

Puriefoy took a deep breath, went over to a chair, and slumped into it. "You want to sit?"

"Thanks, no."

Puriefoy rolled his shoulders, then crossed his arms, feet flat on the floor. "Mau Tim—she was calling herself 'Tina' then, by the way—Mau Tim I spotted in a café over in Copley Place. She had this bag from Neiman's next to her, and she was checking it, maybe figuring somebody'd try and walk with it. I watch her, eating this croissant. She takes a little nibble, like a rabbit, you know? Then she sends out her tongue after the little bits around her lips. Man, I watch her for like a minute, I know she's a natural. You know about scouting, you know what a natural is?"

"Naturally photogenic?"

"Yeah, but more than that. See, Mau Tim, she was perfect being herself. Like they used to say about that actor dude, Spencer Tracy. I mean, you don't have to pose a girl like that, you don't have to like *direct* her, you just tell her the theme for the shoot, and she does it and you click away at her. They say somebody with grace, it shows when they move? With Mau Tim, it showed even when she didn't move. It showed through the lens and on the paper. I printed a galley sheet for her test shots, I couldn't decide which ones ought to go in her mini-book, they were all that good."

I thought the mini-book decision was up to the agents. "You sent her over to Lindqvist/Yulin?"

The photographer pulled back a little. "Yeah. Why?"

"Just checking something. Why that agency?"

A shrug. "They were a little hungry. They did okay by a sister I sent them, got her good fashion bits, even a couple of runways for the lah-di-dah boutiques. See, Mau Tim was exotic, man. She needed a little bringing along before she hit the big time, and I figured Erica could do that."

"But not George?"

"George? Man, George is like a booker, not a creative guy. Erica's got the vision, George's got the rolodex, you know?"

"According to Yulin's rolodex, you and Mau Tim were pretty good friends."

Puriefoy pulled back a little more. "You could say that."

"Lovers?"

"The fuck difference does it make?"

"I have to follow through on anything that might help me find out who killed her."

"Who killed her? The fuck you talking about? I was there, man. Some burglar done it."

"Back up a step, all right? Mau Tim lived with you for a while?"

Puriefoy waited a moment before answering. "Yeah. She was overage, man, her decision to check out on the family. Only I didn't know about . . . her *family*, you know?"

"She didn't tell you she was connected?"

"Shit, no. I walk over to her—at that café with the croissant?—and I say, 'Hey, lovely lady, you a model?' And she says, 'No,' but not like 'Get-the-fuck-lost' no, just kind of a 'not yet.' And I like her more as a natural, and she tells me her name is Tina and we go around on that for a while, and pretty soon we're back at my place for a little sweetness in the dark."

"Where's your place?"

"Apartment, over in JP."

Jamaica Plain, the farthest west of the Boston neighborhoods. "How soon after that did she move in with you?"

"Like a week, maybe two. Didn't tell me her last name that first time. But when she did, she said it was 'Dani,' and I should start calling her 'Mau Tim,' on account of that was her name in Vietnamese, only not exactly."

"What do you mean?"

"Well, it wasn't her name, translated like. It was more a description." Puriefoy closed his eyes. "It meant like, 'purple flower,' or something. For her eyes. She was always doing that."

"Doing what?"

"Making up names for things. She was at my place one night, and we're watching one of the *Star Wars* videos, I forget which one. But when that Darth Vader comes on the screen, she— you know whose voice they used for him?"

"James Earl Jones."

Puriefoy looked disappointed, like I'd spoiled a punch line. "Yeah, old James Earl with that voice comes up from his high tops somewhere. Well, we're watching the screen, and in walks the guy all dressed in that black outfit, and Mau Tim jumps on me and says 'Your voice is just like his, and you're a big brute, too. I'll call you Grute Vader from now on.' "

"Why 'Grute' Vader?"

"Account of it rhymed with 'brute,' maybe. But it could have meant something in Vietnamese, too. Mau, she was into that kind of thing."

"What kind of thing?"

"People's backgrounds."

"How do you mean?"

"Well, like she really enjoyed Sinead on account of Sinead had a real ethnic name. Irish."

"Right."

Puriefoy looked a little sheepish. "Right. And she was always asking me about my roots."

"Your family, you mean?"

"Yeah, like that genealogy shit. I read that out to Chicago, man, it is a thriving business, black folks trying hard to trace

140

themselves back just a couple generations to Mississippi, and from there all the way to the slave times. I told Mau Tim I wasn't so interested in my past as my future."

"A future that didn't include her?"

"Shit happens."

"And now you're involved with her girlfriend?"

"The fuck difference does that make?"

"I'm just wondering who broke it off, you or Mau Tim?"

No response.

"Was it because she moved on to other photographers?"

Puriefoy's molars worked inside his mouth. "This part have to go outside this room?"

"Probably not."

"That ain't good enough."

"All right. Between you and me."

"I just don't want it getting back to her family."

"Sinead's?"

"Shit, no. Mau Tim's."

"It won't."

"Okay." Puriefoy shifted his feet on the floor. "Mau Tim's shacking with me about three weeks, I'm sitting here. Right in this chair, setting up some shots, and the door there opens. I got my back to it, and I didn't hear no knock. So I turn around, and there's this little cheech standing there."

"Cheech?"

"Italian greaser. Eth-nic ster-eo-type, you know? We called that kind of dude a 'cheech' down in New York."

"So this guy comes to see you."

"Yeah. And he says to me, 'We'd consider it a good thing for you to stop seeing Tina Danucci.' Said it just like that, real polite."

"What did you say?"

"I told him I didn't know no Tina Danucci, but the last name stayed in my head, like it was a name from somewhere."

"Did your visitor point that out?"

"He said, 'Well, maybe you know her by Tina Dani or Mau Tim,' and the cheech, he really stretched it out, like 'Mau Tim' was fifty letters long. Then he said, 'Don't matter what her name is, she ain't for you.' "

"What did you say?"

"I told him to get the fuck out of my studio."

"And did he?"

A little shiver. "What he does, he pulls up his sleeves, he's wearing this long leather coat and suit, and he like shoves everything, jacket, shirt, up to here," Puriefoy pointed to the middle of his forearm, "and then the guy says, 'Let me state the message a little clearer.' And then he says, 'Hands off or hands off'—and the guy goes like this." Puriefoy chopped with each hand at the other wrist, then another little shiver. "I got the message."

"You see Mau Tim after that?"

"I told her, I was having some problems, she had to move out and I couldn't see her no more."

"Why didn't you tell her the truth?"

"Man, I believed the little cheech. I didn't want it getting back to her family that I was even talking a lot with the girl."

"How did she take it?"

"Didn't seem to bother her. And like right after that, she moved into the place in the South End."

"Did you see Mau Tim much after she moved?"

"Not at her place, but you're in the business, you're going to see each other. Plus she was Sinead's friend, lived in the same building. I talked to her some at Sinead's apartment, drinks over to the Pour House, Caiobella, like that."

"She was underage."

Puriefoy shook his head. "Mau was eighteen and change."

"For drinking, I mean."

"Aw, man, she could look any age she wanted to, most of them can, but Mau never pushed the booze thing in public. What I mean is, she'd take a drink at a party now and then, but she didn't hit the shit when she'd go out. Too many empty calories, you know?"

"What'd you talk with her about?"

"I don't know. The usual shit. Which ad agency is hot, which account just went where."

"Anything about her agency?"

"You mean like her agents?"

"Yes."

"Just the same thing I told her when I found her. 'Babe, you are the real article. You need some seasoning up here, but then you got to go to the bigs.' "

"The big leagues?"

"The Big Apple."

"Mau Tim couldn't go to the top outside New York?"

"Uh-unh. Oh, she could do okay. This dude from Dorchester, Thom McDonough? He went over to Paris, and he's doing just fine. But with her looks, Mau was like born for the City That Never Sleeps."

"Would that have meant changing her agents?"

"Yeah. Well, wouldn't *have* to, but that'd be the smart thing to do."

"You know whether she decided to take your advice?"

"No."

"Which way was she leaning?"

"Aw, man, I don't know."

"If she did leave, would you have gone with her?"

Puriefoy shifted the feet some more. "What're you saying?"

"You gave me the impression that you were from New York originally."

"So?"

"So maybe you could help her down there like you helped her up here."

"Un-unh. Mau, she was big enough now, she didn't need me no more. Besides, I believed the little cheech that came to see me, you know?"

Puriefoy made the chopping motion at his wrists again.

"Okay. You visit Sinead much over at her apartment?"

"The fuck do you care about that?"

"I was wondering about the party that night."

143

"The night Mau Tim got killed?"

"Right."

"I don't like to think about that, man."

"Force yourself, we'll get through it quicker."

"I already told the cops everything I know. Go talk to them."

"You were there, they weren't."

Puriefoy shook his head again, sounded tired. "Okay, okay. Shit, get on with it."

"Tell me what happened."

"Sinead, she's fixing a little party for Mau, then we're going out dancing after that, probably over to Citi—by Fenway Park?"

"Go on."

"So, I get there, and Sinead—girl's got no mind, you know?—she says she forgot to buy the wine, and can I go out and get some."

"She's under twenty-one, too, right?"

Puriefoy looked puzzled.

"How could she have bought the wine in the first place?"

"Oh, man, she puts on some makeup. Like I said, they all could pass for thirty, they wanted to."

"Okay. Back up a little. You first get to the building on Falmouth Street. You have a key to the front door?"

"Shit, no, man. I don't want any more to do with that building than I have to. I just ring the bell for Sinead from outside on the stoop, and she lets me in."

I said, "So the night Mau Tim was killed, you get inside Sinead's apartment . . ."

"And she says, can I go out and get some wine before Larry Shin comes by."

"Larry Shinkawa."

"Yeah. Larry Shin, he's supposed to be there already, but he's late. Sinead, she says Mau Tim's in the shower, she can hear the water coming down the pipes in the kitchen, 'Go on out and get the wine, willya?' "

"So you do?"

"Right. Takes me a while, I don't know the neighborhood,

but I find a shitbox liquor store with something decent in it, buy a couple bottles, come back."

"And?"

"And I go in and I'm in the kitchen working the corkscrew when Larry comes in."

"He rings the doorbell?"

"Right, right. So Sinead, she goes over, buzzes him in."

"Go on."

"Larry, he says, 'Mau Tim's not down yet?' And Sinead, she says, 'No, but she's out of the shower.' And then Larry, he says, 'Well, why don't we go up to surprise her, the birthday girl in her birthday suit.' "

"And then what?"

"Then I say to Larry, 'You go ahead, you want to. I'll open the wine.' "

"How come you didn't want to go up with him?"

"Aw, man. A dozen reasons. First thing, he's hosing her now, not me. Second thing, I don't like her family knowing I'm in the same building with her, let alone me seeing her buck naked after a shower."

I said, "Why didn't Sinead go up with him?"

"She thought it was shitty, busting in on her like that."

"Shinkawa had a key to get into Mau Tim's apartment?"

"I don't know." Puriefoy thought for a minute. "No, he didn't have a key, account of Larry, he come down the stairs a couple minutes later, saying he can't get in and can't get her to answer the door."

"You remember his exact words?"

"Larry Shin's?"

"Yes."

"Larry, he said something like, 'I knocked and knocked and yelled to her, but she ain't answering.' "

"So he didn't say anything about a key."

"No, not like that. You just got me thinking about keys, all the questions you're asking about them."

"Sorry. Go ahead."

"So then Sinead, she says, 'Christ, I hope nothing's weird up there. I got a key.' "

"Sinead had a key to Mau Tim's apartment?"

"Yeah."

"Why?"

"I don't know why. Water her plants, maybe."

"Couldn't the super do that?"

"Cousin Ooch? I'll tell you, I'm not sure Ooch could go to the store for bread and come back with a whole loaf."

"Go ahead."

"Where was I now?"

"Sinead said, 'I have a key.' "

"Oh, right. Right, Sinead, she says, 'I got a key, let's check, see if Mau's okay.' So she gets it from her pocketbook and we all go up there. Larry Shin hammers on the door some more, and Sinead gets the key in and turns it and the door opens, but not all the way account of the chain's on it from the inside."

"Mau Tim usually use the chain?"

Puriefoy looked at me. "How would I know, man? I stopped seeing her before she moved in there."

"Go on."

"So we can push the door open only so far, but Larry Shin, he like wedges his head in and says, 'I can see her, she's on the floor.' "

"Shinkawa did that, not Sinead."

"Right. Then he says, 'She's not moving. We got to break it down.' "

"Break the chain?"

"Right. So he tries twice and can't do it. Thought all those guys knew karate, you know? But he's just not big enough to bust through it, so I hit the door with a shoulder and the chain goes and we're in there."

"And?"

Puriefoy's voice dropped. "And Mau's on the floor, all right. Laid out, eyes half-open, face blue. She's dead, and Sinead starts screaming."

"You remember anything else?"

"Larry Shin, he said he thought he heard somebody on the fire escape—the window to it in the bedroom was open, but I didn't hear nothing. Anyway, he ran over to it, but he said he didn't see nobody."

"Did you look out the window, too?"

"Shit, no. Sinead, she's screaming at me to do something, I tell her, 'Call an ambulance,' and she says, 'How,' and I say 'Fucking shit you ever learn about anything?' and tell her 911. And then I go to work on Mau, with Larry trying to help."

"Go to work on her?"

"CPR. Took a course on it once."

"What did you do?"

"Tried to breathe for her, work the chest, you know."

"Anything?"

"No. I never done CPR outside that class, but she was gone. They say, sometimes you can bring them back, but I'm working on her, and I'm starting to see these bruises—more like little cuts around her neck—" Puriefoy stopped and shook his head. "Enough about that shit, okay?"

"Did you hear anything else?"

"No, man. Sinead was on the phone, screaming at whoever she got. Larry and I were working on Mau."

I stopped and thought it through. Pretty consistent with Fagan's version, as far as she went.

Puriefoy said, "Look, man, can I get back to work now?"

"Yeah. Just one more question."

"What?"

"The guy who came to warn you off."

"The cheech?"

"He have a toothpick in his mouth?"

Puriefoy didn't answer right away. "The fuck did you know that?"

"Ethnic stereotype."

15

THE BERRY/RYDER ADVERTISING AGENCY WAS LOCATED ON LOWER Newbury Street. The bay window in the reception area provided a panorama of the Ritz Carlton Hotel and a pie slice of Public Garden. I was watching a giddy Hispanic couple walk hand-in-hand toward the Swan Pond when the stunning receptionist told me that Larry Shinkawa could see me now.

I was guided by her to an office that just missed a view of the Garden. The furnishing was stark, a lot of chrome and white interspersed with black surfaces in lacquer or leather. A portable cassette player took up most of the windowsill. The desk consisted of a thick Plexiglas sheet laid over double filing cabinets, a snake lamp with a long neck clamped to one end of it.

Shinkawa introduced himself by coming around the desk. He was about five seven in a tailored pin-striped shirt, flowered tie, and the slacks to an Armani suit. The hair was longish and combed sideways over the head, thick but graying in streaks. He had laughing eyes behind red-rimmed aviators and a pug nose over a yearbook smile. The smile was cranked up high, like he'd been eagerly anticipating my visit all morning.

I said, "I appreciate your seeing me on such short notice, Mr. Shinkawa."

"Call me Larry, please. Or Larry Shin, if you'll be here long enough."

I must have looked at him oddly.

"You see, Mr. Cuddy—"

"John, please."

"Thanks. You see, John, when I got here, there was already a guy named Larry—Larry Ryder, one of the founders of the agency. So people had to call me Larry Shinkawa, which got shortened over time to just Larry Shin. Sit, please."

He returned to his desk. I took one of two chrome chairs with black leather slings as seat and back.

Shinkawa said, "What's this about?"

"I'm investigating Mau Tim Dani's death for an insurance company. Erica Lindqvist didn't tell you that?"

The smile distorted for just a second, then broke into a wider grin. "Shouldn't try to fool you, huh? Sure, Erica called, said a private eye might be by to see me."

In other words, trust me now because I'm finished lying.

Shinkawa toned back down to a smile. "I thought I'd just play along."

"Sort of take things as they come?"

He acted like I found him engaging. "The only way. You ever hear of *karoshi*, John?"

"No."

"It's Japanese for 'dying from overwork.' A real problem in the old country. Guys in their forties, like me, dropping like flies. The ones who get enough money or corporate bennies to join a tennis club are in the worst shape. They got high blood pressure, stress enough to make the tennis court a minefield for their hearts. Me, I take things in stride, don't let life get me down."

I cut in before hearing that he bent with the breeze. "It would help if you could tell me about Mau Tim as you knew her."

"Professionally or personally?"

"Start with professionally."

"George—George Yulin—introduced us, I think. At one of their parties at the Cactus Club, a good way for a modeling agency to get its new girls seen by ad people. Well, I had this great concept for a furrier here. We're a small agency, John, so we can put together some of the strongest print ads around for clients that haven't got the bucks or the volume to benefit from television product. I pitched the campaign to the furrier. Most concepts get rejected by the client. This one said, 'Go for it.' "

"What was the campaign?"

"A series of young models, instead of the older, 'Martha, you've raised our children and you deserve a mink' types. Only these were going to be exotic girls, not cheerleaders, follow?"

"And Mau Tim was exotic."

"Oh, John, you have no idea. Honestly. One of the few girls who never took a bad photo. Every shot a piece of art. Anyway, I met her as we were executing that campaign. She was just breaking in, and I was able to give her career a boost."

"And you started seeing her personally?"

The smile wavered a little this time. "Yes."

"How long did you see her?"

"Six, eight months I guess. It wasn't the usual."

"The usual?"

"Yeah. In this business, John, you get all sorts of opportunities. You look like you're about my age?"

"Probably."

"Well, I'll tell you, the younger ones do keep you younger. But you get tired of them after a while. They don't have any depth."

"But Mau Tim did."

"Some." Shinkawa swayed back in his desk chair. "She was interested in the sixties, for example. Made me tell her all the expressions, like 'too much' and 'far out.' Remember?"

"Most of them."

"Well, she'd change them to suit herself. Like in bed, she'd say things like 'too, too much' or 'far, far out.' Her way of showing that she understood me but could still personalize things for herself."

"Adapting to a culture she never experienced."

Shinkawa stopped for a second. "You know, that's a nice turn of phrase, John. Very nice. She was like that about my being Japanese-American, too."

"What do you mean?"

"Well, she was always asking me what it was like to grow up Asian in America. Maybe because she had a Vietnamese mother and I think an Italian—Italian-American, I mean—father."

He thought. "You never met her family, then?"

"No. No, but she was always asking about mine. Japanese customs and relationships. I wasn't born till forty-eight, but before World War II my parents lived in California. They were *Nisei*. Know what that means?"

"Born in this country of parents from Japan?"

Shinkawa gave me the "nice-turn-of-phrase" look. "Basically. My mom and dad met when they were being interned. You know about that, too?"

"Not much."

"Well, let me tell you a little then. Right after Pearl Harbor, the authorities started rounding us up. By the time they were finished, over a hundred thousand men, women, and children of Japanese descent were herded into 'relocation' camps, John. Two thirds of us were American citizens, but that didn't matter. No charges, no trials, no convictions. Everybody just lost their jobs and property and got locked away in the desert. You remember all the uproar over that Judge Bork being nominated for the Supreme Court?"

"Sure."

"Well, they went after him because of his record on civil liberties, right? Let me tell you, when I was in college, I decided to do my senior thesis on the *Nisei*. In early 1942, one of the strongest voices calling for the internment testified before a Congressional committee that we Japanese immigrants and citizens had settled intentionally in strategic areas on the West Coast, that we were racially and psychologically tied to the Emperor, and that we were just awaiting the order from Tokyo to strike treacherously at the heart of the American defense industry. You know who that voice belonged to?"

"No."

"The then attorney general of the state of California. The honorable Earl Warren, future Chief Justice of the United States Supreme Court."

"You're kidding?"

"Wish I were. I could never understand how that didn't come out more when they were going after old Borkie."

I wanted to get Shinkawa back on track. "So you told Mau Tim about your parents' situation back then?"

"Oh, yeah. Yeah, that and all kinds of other things. The kid was a sponge for it, asking me if I'd ever been to Hawaii or any other areas where Asian-Americans were like a majority."

"And?"

"And I had to tell her, 'Mau, after the war, my folks moved to the Midwest. I was born and brought up in Madison, Wisconsin, you know? All of this stuff is just history to me.' "

"She have any enemies you know of?"

"Enemies?" Shinkawa lost his smile altogether for the first time. "Why ask me that?"

"You were there that night."

"At her apartment, you mean?"

"Yes."

"Sure, but she was killed by some burglar who probably needed money for drugs and panicked."

"Even so, you mind going over things for me?"

"No." Shinkawa revived part of the smile. "No, I suppose not."

"The party was for her birthday?"

"Right."

"You know who was invited?"

"Well, originally it was just going to be Mau, Sinead, Oz Puriefoy—you know who he is?"

"Yes."

"Okay. And Quinn Cotter."

Sinead Fagan had mentioned him. "He's a model, too?"

"Right. Pretty popular in the sports lines. You saw him, you'd know him. Here . . ." Shinkawa opened a file drawer and rummaged around. "This is his comp."

Shinkawa handed me a black-and-white composite card of a tall, broad-shouldered blond in his twenties with a cleft chin, plastered hair, and vapid eyes listed as blue on the back. The photos showed him in a martial arts uniform with boards to split, swim trunks with surfboard to ride, and cross-training gear with ten-speed bike to pedal. He looked like the kind of guy who'd enjoy bungee jumping.

I handed the card back to Shinkawa. "Why didn't Cotter come to the party?"

"It's a little involved. I had an out-of-town meeting, so originally I wasn't going to be able to make the party. Then the meeting canceled, and Quinn bowed out of the party."

"Why did he bow out?"

"Because I was boffing the girl of his dreams, John."

I stopped. "Cotter was interested in Mau Tim?"

"And how. Tried to wangle a shoot with her through Erica, but his look and hers really clashed, you know?"

Not in a way I could appreciate. "So Cotter saw you as a rival?"

Shinkawa started a laugh that turned into a giggle. "No, he saw me as the guy she was more interested in. Mau thought Quinn was kind of a pea-brain, but I think that Sinead felt a little sorry for him."

"Because of him losing out on Mau to you."

"And also because another model got picked over him to work on a big running-clothes campaign we're doing this spring."

"You have anything to do with that decision?"

The big grin. "Everything. I think Quinn's kind of a pea-brain, too."

"You know how I could reach him?"

"Through the agency—wait, I might have . . ." Shinkawa went back to the drawer. "Here. This is the number and address Quinn gave me a couple of weeks ago."

"When he thought he was still in the running for the running-clothes campaign."

Just the smile.

The address was on Fisher Hill in Brookline, reading like a single-family home, not an apartment or condo. "Pretty spiffy."

"I think the guy house-sits. Good gig for a model."

"Can we get back to that Friday?"

"That . . . Oh, right. What else?"

"You decided you were going to the party when?"

"Maybe eleven that morning."

"You call somebody?"

"I left a message for Mau with Sinead. I guess that's how Quinn knew not to show."

"Sinead calling him."

"Yeah. But I don't really know that."

I said, "You talk with Mau Tim at all that day?"

"No. She'd usually be on a shoot for the morning into the afternoon."

Yulin said otherwise. "You try to call her that day?"

"No. I was seeing her that night."

"When did you get to the apartment house in the South End?"

"I stopped home to change after work, get casual because Sinead was talking about dancing afterward."

"Where's home?"

"Over on Commonwealth. I've got a condo between Dartmouth and Exeter."

"Go ahead."

"So I got to the building at seven-thirty, give or take a few minutes. I rang Mau's bell but didn't get any answer, so I figured she was already downstairs at Sinead's and tried there."

"You didn't have a key to the front door of the building?"

"No. Most of the time, Mau came over to my place."

"Okay. What happened after you rang Sinead's bell?"

"Oz—or Sinead—buzzed me in, and Mau wasn't there. Sinead was saying she just took a shower."

"Where was Puriefoy?"

"In the kitchen, opening some wine." Shinkawa looked off. "So, I guess it was Sinead who buzzed me in." He came back to me, smiling. "Hey, this is kind of cool, you know?"

"What is?"

"Reconstructing all this. Getting me to remember things."

Christ. "Then what happened?"

"Let's see. Oh, yeah. Then we talked about surprising Mau upstairs."

"In her birthday suit."

The laugh into giggle again. "Right, right. A nice turn of phrase then too, I thought. But Oz wasn't up for it, so while he did the wine and Sinead was playing with her stereo, I went upstairs."

"Then what?"

"Well, I knocked on Mau's door—No, no, I tried her door first, but it was locked."

"Was it usually unlocked?"

"No. No, usually she kept the bolt on but not the chain."

"Not the chain?"

"Uh-unh. She broke a nail on it twice and thought it was a pain."

"You have a key to that door?"

"No."

I stopped again. "Then how did you think you were going to surprise her?"

Shinkawa shrugged. "Just thought I might. Party mood, you know? You don't always think things through."

I said, "So then you knocked."

"Right. I knocked and called out to her, but I didn't hear anything back."

"Nothing at all?"

"No. No stereo, no footsteps, nothing. Then I started yelling, and I guess I must have gotten a little scared for her."

"Why?"

"Why? She wasn't answering me, and Sinead said Mau had just been in the shower. I thought maybe she slipped and hit her head or something."

"So you did what?"

"I ran downstairs and got Oz and Sinead. The three of us went back up and broke down the door."

"Was the chain on?"

"Yeah. Yeah, that's why we had to break it down. Sinead had a key for Mau's door, but the chain was on from the inside and Oz and I had to break it down. Or off, I guess. The door was still on its hinges."

Pretty consistent with Puriefoy's account. "Before you broke through, could you see or hear anything in the apartment through the chain space?"

"I didn't hear anything, the stereo and TV were off. But . . ." Shinkawa finally showed something beyond cheeriness. "I could see like her head and a shoulder, on the floor by the futon. She had a big futon for her couch. When we broke in, we tried to save her, but it was . . . too late, I guess."

"Once you were in the apartment, did you see or hear anything?"

"Yeah. I was the first one to her, and I could hear the fire escape."

"What do you mean?"

"Well, you know how a fire escape kind of, I don't know, 'clangs' when somebody's on it?"

"Yes."

"I thought I heard that, so I went into the bedroom and over to the window. But by the time I got there, the guy was gone."

"Gone?"

"Well, I looked down at the ground, and up and down the alley, and I couldn't see anybody."

"Do you remember seeing anything around the bottom of the fire escape?"

"The bottom?"

"Yes. Below where the last flight would come down."

Shinkawa closed his eyes. "It was dark, but . . . No. No, I don't think so."

"Maybe trash cans?"

"No. Definitely not. I would have seen those."

"Rake, broom?"

"No. Why?"

"Anything to pull down that last flight?"

Shinkawa shook his head. "Man, the guy was going down already. Just his weight would carry that last flight to the ground."

"Okay. You're at the window. Then what?"

"Then I went back, and everybody was yelling at once around Mau, and she looked awful, John, her face all . . . contorted, discolored. So Sinead was calling for the EMTs, and I tried to help Oz work on Mau, but I could see it wasn't going to do any good. Then I noticed the jewelry."

"The jewelry."

"Yeah. This necklace, I think, or part of one. Under the couch, kind of by Oz's feet when he kneeled down by Mau."

"But you didn't see Puriefoy do anything with it."

"No. No, like I said, the thing was just under the futon a little by his shoes, which were just about up against it."

"Anything else?"

Shinkawa stopped and adjusted his horn-rims. "I don't think so. We just waited for the ambulance, which got there just before the police, who kind of pushed us downstairs, then brought us back up after they rushed Mau off."

"You recovering all right yourself?"

Shinkawa looked at me, like he didn't quite know how I'd intended the question. "I take things easy, John, remember? Besides, I figured Mau and I were about at the end of the line."

"Why?"

"She was going to New York."

"To live?"

"Yes. The party was both birthday and bon voyage."

"Mau Tim told you that?"

"Not in so many words, but I could tell she'd been making up her mind the last few weeks."

"How?"

"She was talking about neighborhoods in Manhattan, asking my advice on modeling agencies down there, did I know anybody in them."

"And that didn't bother you?"

"Hey, it doesn't matter which agency handles a girl. I can still have her in my campaigns."

"Professionally. How about personally?"

"Mau was fun, John. A little deeper than most. But we weren't in love or anything. Life goes on, you know?"

"You share Mau Tim's decision on New York with anyone else?"

"No." The smile. "I figured that was her business, right?"

"Right." I handed him my card. "You think of anything else, let me know."

"Sure, sure." He stood up. "Can I see you out?"

"That's okay." We shook. "I'll find my way."

At the door, I turned back to him. He was watching me leave rather than lifting a phone or turning to a file.

I said, "One other thing?"

"What is it?"

"You ever had a visit from a guy in a leather coat, toothpick in his mouth?"

From the look Larry Shinkawa gave me, I was pretty sure he hadn't.

16

WALKING BACK TO THE CONDO FROM SHINKAWA'S OFFICE, I THOUGHT
about calling Quinn Cotter. Since I was having dinner that night
with Nancy, I figured it was just as easy to drive a few miles
out of my way and find Cotter's place even if he wasn't home.

Brookline lies west of Boston's student ghetto. It's a classy
town that boasts turn-of-the-century brownstones, skyscraper
condominiums, and some of the most impressive mini-estates
in the metropolitan area.

I left Route 9 and did some winding up Fisher Hill itself before
finding the address Shinkawa had given me. The street number
was etched into a stone monument, just above an orange and
black sign that said NO TRESPASSING. I let out a low whistle
as I parked the Prelude in the empty semicircular drive of a
magnificent Tudor mansion. A fieldstone first floor and four
gingerbread gables faced me. Professional landscaping, subtle
use of fencing, and what from the second-floor rear windows
would have to be a postcard view of the Chestnut Hill Reservoir
a quarter mile below and across the road.

I climbed a carefully laid flagstone path to the broad double doors at the front entrance. I couldn't find a doorbell, then discovered that a burnished tab halfway up one door made a primitive ringing noise when twisted to the right. I waited thirty seconds, then twisted again. No response.

There was a spur off the main drive that led to a separate three-car garage. I walked down the spur and used my hand to shadow the glass compartments in the garage doors. No vehicles inside except one of those swooping Suzuki motorcycles that look as though they were melded in a wind tunnel.

I went around to the back of the house. I had just passed the overhang of a blue spruce when a foot flashed out from behind it and kicked me in the stomach.

The wind jumped out of me as I doubled over but didn't go down. He'd hit me in the right place, but not terrifically hard. The foot, in a Reebok Pump basketball shoe, now came in an arc at my chin. I turned enough to dodge the force but not the impact, deciding to drop before I drew any more attention.

From the ground I practiced my breathing and looked up at a live version of the composite card from Shinkawa's office. Quinn Cotter loomed over me, his feet planted apart, one hand high and another low. The martial arts stance seemed a trifle staged, as though he'd learned it in a studio but not used it much on the street. He wore a crushed cotton rugby shirt that screamed Banana Republic and a pair of prewashed jeans that made me think of a cryptic commercial. I was disappointed to see that he hadn't even mussed his dishwater-blond hair.

Cotter said, "You ever heard of 'No Trespassing,' asshole?"

I put a hand to my jaw, wiggling it a little to be sure the numbness wasn't masking a real injury. "I have some ID in my left jacket pocket."

Cotter maintained his stance. "That better be all you come out with."

I reached in and tossed the leather holder to him. He fumbled catching it. An athletic-looking guy with poor hand-to-eye coordination, the muscles probably came from lifting weights, not playing sports.

Cotter looked at my identification, seemed confused, and tried to regain the moment by backhanding it to me. "You want to know something about the house, you have to call the management company."

"I'm here to see you, Cotter."

My knowing his name confused him more. "Me? What about?"

Putting away the holder, I said, "Look, can I get up?"

He relaxed from his stance. "Uh, sure."

I took a deep breath as I got halfway to my feet, then rose completely, brushing the spruce needles off my pants and sleeves. "How about we go inside?"

"Sure. Okay."

Cotter turned completely around, giving me his back. Whoever trained him left out the instincts.

I followed the rugby shirt to a patio with blue and white all-weather pipe furniture that cost more than my car. French doors led to a solarium room with more furniture, only nicer. We then entered what I guessed was a playroom, decked out like an elaborate sports bar. A large television screen was embedded in the facing wall. The screen was in freeze-frame, one man in an odd helmet swinging on a Tarzan vine toward another, muscle-bound guy standing on a pedestal and holding a padded riot shield.

Cotter caught me staring at the screen. *"American Gladiators."*

I said, "What?"

"American Gladiators. It's a TV show. Here."

Cotter picked up a remote device from an easy chair. The screen came back to live action. Cheers from what sounded like a studio audience for one swinger who knocked his targeted shield-bearer off the pedestal, groans for another who didn't.

I said, "This is on the level?"

"Sure. I taped it last Saturday. I'm studying to be on it."

"Studying."

"Right. I want to make the transition—from print to TV? I need to show the ad agencies what I can do. This would be a

161

great showcase, even though I couldn't really use the karate."

Cotter pronounced the word "kuh-*rah*-tay," with the same inflection some people use to make tomato "tuh-*mah*-toe."

I looked back at the screen. The odd helmets of the contestants apparently held cameras. In slow-motion replay, we got to see each shield-bearer prepare for collision as the camera swung with the contestant at him. On the ground, two guys I vaguely remembered from NFL broadcasting booths interviewed the successful contestant with much shoulder slapping and manly grinning.

I said, "This is what they do? Swing at each other?"

"That's just the Human Cannonball segment. There's also Breakthrough and Conquer, The Eliminator—"

"I'll take your word for it."

"Hold on. The chicks'll be up next."

Two female contestants, the football announcer referring to them as "contenders," were on screen. Two stolid female gladiators, named I think "Diamond" and "Lace," readied themselves for repelling boarders. I turned away from the immediate future of American culture.

"You suppose we could talk without the competition?"

"Uh, sure."

Using the remote to stop the tape and blacken the screen, Cotter dropped into a chair. One leg slung over the armrest, the other stretched out on the floor, his own arms lazing along the back and down one side of the chair. A little too perfect to be anything but a pose.

"You have any idea why I'm here?"

Cotter seemed confused again, the vapid look from his comp card. "Uh, no. Why, should I?"

It might be an act, or he might just be dense as a post. "I'm investigating the death of Mau Tim Dani."

That broke the pose. I thought I was going to have to deal with the "Kuh-*rah*-tay" Kid again.

He said, "You find the guy yet?"

"The guy who killed her?"

"Yeah, the guy who killed her. That's what you do, right? Find the killer when the cops are too stupid."

Too much time in front of the tube. "Not always. She have any enemies you know of?"

"Enemies? Mau Tim?" He seemed to try to think for a minute. "She got killed by some druggie breaking in, right?"

"We don't know that."

The idea seemed to dawn on him all at once. "You mean, like she was really murdered?"

As opposed to sort of murdered. "It's a possibility."

"Oh, man. This is too much."

The head shook, but the hair stayed put. I waited him out.

Cotter looked up at me, suddenly red-eyed. "Man, she was so beautiful, who'd want her dead?"

"Maybe somebody who was jealous of her. Or jealous of her boyfriends."

The eyes cleared. "You son of a bitch."

Cotter came out of the chair, but this time I was up at the same count. He whipped the right foot at me in a backhand motion, but not the way you should, not as a feint for another move. Stepping toward him, I parried with my right forearm, catching the leg at the calf and wrapping it tight under my right armpit.

Cotter had just enough sense of balance to stay up on his left leg. He was frustrated, pogo-sticking to maintain equilibrium against the edge of pain at his right knee.

I said, "You know, Quinn, it takes only about twenty pounds of pressure to dislocate a joint."

"I can hit you . . . ten times . . . fuckhead!"

"Yeah, but I don't see you hopping your way onto TV."

It finally sank in. "Okay. Okay, let me go."

I released his leg and stepped away. He did too, posturing until he was ten feet from me. I sat back down, and after flexing, he did too.

I tried to be conversational. "The police talked to you, right?"

"Some cop called me, asked if I saw her that day. I told him no. Then he asked where I was that day. I told him here, watching videos. He said, 'All day and all night?' and I said, 'Yeah, I like videos.' Then he said, 'Okay, thanks,' and hung up."

"That's it?"

"Huh?"

"That was it, no personal visit?"

"Uh, no. No, just the call."

I thought about Holt, sitting behind his desk, diverting his people to other cases once he found out Mau Tim Dani was Tina Danucci.

I said, "You ever go to Mau Tim's apartment building?"

"Sure."

"How often?"

Cotter looked uncomfortable. "Couple times."

"You ever in her apartment itself?"

"Uh, no."

"You were at her—"

"I was over seeing Sinead, okay? I like brought her the spare keys once, but we were just friends."

I thought about that last flight of the fire escape again. "What spare keys?"

"Lots of us leave a set at the agency, in case something comes up when we're doing a location shoot somewheres."

"And the agency had a set of Mau Tim's keys?"

"No."

"No?"

"I mean, I don't know. I'm talking about Sinead's keys."

"Sinead's."

"Yeah, like to the front door of the house and her apartment. Sinead forgot her keys one day, okay? And she called the agency from a shoot down by the waterfront, and I was at the agency, so George gave me her keys and I met her at her place to let her in."

"George Yulin gave you Sinead's keys."

An exasperated look. "Right."

"You didn't make a copy of the front door key?"

"Hell, no. Why'd I do that?"

"And you were never in Mau Tim's apartment?"

"No."

"How come?"

Cotter tensed a bit, then tried to look casual. "She didn't ask me up, okay?"

"You ever ask her out?"

"Yeah. Yeah, I asked her out. I ask a lot of the girls out. They ask me, too. Women's lib, okay?"

"But Mau Tim—"

"Look, man! Let me save you some time. Mau was a great-looking chick, okay? But she just didn't dig me. I wasn't exotic enough for her."

"Exotic?"

"Right. She went for different people, not the All-American halfback."

I wondered if other models thought of themselves as being what their business typed them. "But Sinead invited you to the party she was having for Mau Tim's birthday."

"She invited me before she found out another guy was coming. Sinead didn't want to embarrass me, okay, so she called me and said maybe it wouldn't be such a great idea for me to show up Friday night."

"And so you stayed home."

"Right."

"Watching videos."

"Right."

"Alone."

"Most of the night."

"Who was with you?"

"None of your business."

It seemed an odd place to turn turtle. I was about to try a different angle when I heard a heavy door open and close and a familiar voice call out, "Quinn? Quinn, you home?"

A little color drained from Cotter's face. "In the TV room."

As footsteps approached down what seemed a long hallway, the voice said, "Whose car is that in the drive?"

JEREMIAH HEALY

Before Cotter could answer, George Yulin appeared in the doorway, a briefcase with shoulder strap like Nancy's riding on the saddle of a tweed sports jacket today.

"His," said Cotter.

Yulin didn't say anything.

I said, "Join us."

Yulin came into the room slowly. He let the briefcase slide off his shoulder and onto the floor, watching me as he rested his rump and palms against the back of a chair. "What are you doing here?"

"My job."

"Which is?"

"Still the same. I'd appreciate your explaining to Quinn the importance of cooperating with my investigation."

Yulin looked at Cotter, who said, "George, you know this asshole?"

Yulin winced at the last word. "Mr. Cuddy is processing a claim we have arising from Mau Tim's death, Quinn. We have an obligation to cooperate with him."

Cotter stood up defiantly. "Maybe you do. I'm going for a ride."

He crossed the room and left. Very athletically.

Yulin looked down at me. "I'm sorry, John, but we're just Quinn's agents, not his parents."

"You're rooming with him?"

From down the hall came the sound of the heavy door slamming. Yulin went over to a bar. "Drink?"

"I'll pass."

He took out a tall glass and an opaque bottle. Yulin splashed liberally from the bottle into the glass, not bothering with ice or mixer. He snuffled over the drink, then downed half of it. "Single malt."

"Whiskey?"

"Right. Smooth as silk, with a bouquet you can appreciate best with a tall glass. Now, what was your question?"

"I asked you if you're rooming with Cotter."

166

"In a manner of speaking. Quinn's under contract to house-sit this place."

"He seemed a little reluctant to admit you lived here, too."

"I believe the real estate company that hired Quinn prefers . . . single occupancy."

"Who owns the house?"

"Some wealthy investor who decided to take a sabbatical. Isn't that a super idea? Just disappear for a while, travel and refresh oneself."

There was the sound of a cycle revving, just audible through the solid walls of the house. Then a high whining sound that faded quickly.

I said, "So you're kind of sub-sitting?"

Yulin looked at me, then smiled. "I see. 'Sub-sitting' instead of 'sub-letting.' Clever, John. But no. I decided to rent out my own place for a while, try living in a different environment. My own quasi-sabbatical, you might say."

"Or your own quasi-cash-shorts, I might say."

Yulin pursed his lips. "Close enough." He downed the rest of the glass and went back to the bottle.

"How tight are things for you, George?"

"Tight." He splashed the whiskey again. "Ever since the Massachusetts Miracle started turning to clay, things have looked down. Oh, we still have bookings for the campaigns that were already underway. But both Erica and I can see the dark at the end of the tunnel, at least short-term."

"Which made Mau Tim all the more important to you."

"Yes." A cautious sip this time. "Yes, frankly she'd been a savior over the last few months. You see, we service mostly the smaller agencies. Advertising agencies, I mean. The bigger ones, like Hill, Holliday, they do three, four hundred million in billings a year. But the smaller ones, they're hurt most by the downturn. They're the ones the jittery clients leave for the safer harbor of the bigger firms. Then come layoffs, and, well, fewer phone calls to modeling agencies like ours."

"How's Larry Shinkawa's firm doing?"

"Quite well, surprisingly. Berry/Ryder is riding the crest of what business there is right now."

"I understand Quinn was pretty upset about losing out on a job Shinkawa was placing through you?"

Yulin started to take another cautious sip, stopped, then took a gulp. "Who told you that?"

"How upset?"

Yulin clacked his tongue off the roof of his mouth. "Quinn is excitable. It's sincere if a bit shallow of him. But that's what comes across so well in his shoots."

"But not well enough for Shinkawa."

"John, Larry Shin is . . ." The last sip. "Larry Shin is a very shrewd man in a very tough business. He likes to make things personal and does it well enough to cover himself. Quinn was perfect for the running-wear shoot. I thought so, and Erica agreed. I'm sure even Larry thought so, but depriving Quinn of the shoot was Larry . . . tweaking Quinn with his power, tweaking him in a way that Quinn has to swallow, and knows he has to swallow, to continue to prosper in this business. Besides, as I told Quinn, Larry will probably pick him for more shoots now, just to make the point that he was only making a point the first time."

"That why you forgot to mention Cotter to me when we were in your office?"

"You asked me, I believe, about Mau Tim's 'boyfriends.' I never thought of Quinn that way."

"Seems to me he was nuts about her."

"Perhaps. But that didn't make him her 'boyfriend' in my book." Yulin gestured with the empty glass. "If you've already worked your way around to Quinn, you must be nearing the end of your investigation."

"Not quite. Quinn told me something else I didn't know."

"What was that?"

"You had a set of Sinead's keys at the agency."

"Probably still do. So?"

"I don't remember your mentioning that in your office either."

Yulin set down the glass. "I don't remember your asking me about keys, John."

"I was investigating Mau Tim being killed in her apartment. You had a key to the building, but you didn't tell me that."

"We'd heard that a burglar broke in. I didn't—and frankly, I still don't—see why keys are important. But yes, some of the models like to keep a spare set nearby, so we do have some in a petty-cash box at the agency."

"Sinead's, but not Mau Tim's."

"Correct."

There was something wrong about that, but I couldn't quite touch it. "At your office, George, you said you went home the night Mau Tim died."

"Also correct. After that ad party and some pub crawling, I came back here."

"When did you arrive?"

"Oh . . . ten? I wasn't paying much attention, and Quinn was watching video, not TV, when I got in, so I can't even peg it by what was on the screen."

"Thorough."

Yulin darkened. "What was that?"

"I said thorough. Very thorough of you to think all that through in answering a simple question."

"Yes, well, I tend to do a lot of time management, John, both for myself and my models. It's tough to leave some things at the office, you know?"

"Speaking of leaving, I found something else out this afternoon."

"I'm glad to hear it's been a productive day for you."

"It seems a lot of people think Mau Tim was about to pull the ripcord, George."

His face darkened again, and he reached for the whiskey bottle. "Ripcord?"

"She was bailing out. Moving to New York and changing agencies."

The neck of the bottle rattled against his tall glass. "You don't know that because it isn't true."

An article of faith that Yulin couldn't recant. I stood up. "Give Quinn my regards."

As I moved to the French doors, Yulin said, "John?"

"Yes?"

"We seem to have . . . We don't appear to be on the same wavelength today. My fault—the single malt, I'm afraid."

"Don't worry about it, George."

"No, seriously. If there is anything I can do to . . . facilitate this process, please let me know."

I nodded without saying anything more and made my way out.

17

"John, what happened?"

"I fell and banged my chin."

Standing in her living room and still dressed from work, Nancy reached up a hand, turning my face just a little under the light. "Looks more like assault and battery with a shod foot."

"You've got quite an eye, counselor."

"After a while. What really happened?"

"I'm not sure how much I should tell you."

Nancy cocked her head, the hair still drawn back by a silver barrette.

"I promise, Nance, I'm not doing anything over the line. It's just that it has to do with an open homicide."

"The Suffolk one from Empire?"

"Right."

Nancy frowned, the corners of her mouth knitting crosslines all the way up to the hairline. Then she nodded. In acceptance rather than agreement. "I'm going to cook us dinner."

"I was ready to take you out to eat."

"I'll be in Dallas restaurants both tomorrow night and Saturday. I'd like a meal in my own home as a send-off."

I took her chin in my hand. "You shouldn't try to live by bread alone, counselor."

"I've heard that."

"Another thing. I've been thinking about what you told me on your birthday."

"The bank robbery? The jury convicted him this morning."

"No, I meant what you showed me at the Ritz."

"What I . . . ?"

"About the sensitive spots. On the palm, the fingertips, the thumb."

"Uh-huh."

"I've come up with a few more."

"Really."

I moved my hand to the back of her open collar. "There's this one, stroking the little hairs at the nape of the neck."

Nancy closed her eyes. "So far, so good."

I moved my hand again. "Then there's the earlobe. Just a gentle, milking motion."

"Would it be rude to moo?"

I moved my hand a third time. "Then the lips. The back of the fingernail's best here."

Nancy ran the tip of her tongue along my finger.

"Unfortunately . . ." I cleared my throat. "Unfortunately, the other spots I thought of aren't yet . . . accessible."

Nancy undid her barrette, the hair tumbling down. "Make them accessible."

Nancy's hand snaked from under the sheets, turning her alarm clock so she could see its face. "Damn. I should have put the cutlets on ahead of time."

"Would have killed the mood."

She snuggled back against me. "As one of the guys at the office is fond of saying, you couldn't have killed that mood with a stick."

"Madam, such vulgarity."

"Sorry." Nancy sighed. "I really miss him."

"Renfield."

"Who else?"

"Did you check on him today?"

"I called twice. He came through the operation fine, but when I asked if I could visit, they said he was still sleeping from the anesthesia and that it was best not to wake him."

I thought back on my times in human hospitals, where they didn't seem to share the same compunction.

Nancy said, "You'll still be able to pick him up tomorrow?"

"A promise is a promise."

"They said any time after three-thirty and before six, but I really hate to think of my kitty being there any longer than he has to be."

"I'll be scratching at their door by three-thirty-one."

"Poor little guy. I had them hack off his nuts because he was spraying my furniture and his front toes because he was shredding it. Now what'll he think?"

"I'm pretty sure cats don't dwell much on motivation and consequence, Nance."

She shifted a little off the arm before it fell asleep. "Did I tell you last night that it wasn't your fault? That he was born with this problem."

"Among other things."

"God, I was so drunk."

"It takes getting used to."

"Two other times I got like that, John. Once when my mom died, and once when I found out I passed the bar exam."

"Not after the exam itself?"

"No. Oh, New England threw a party for all of us taking the Massachusetts bar. They're really good about that. The Alumni Association rents out Anthony's Pier Four, the covered patio. It's just a block from where the exam's administered, over at Commonwealth Pier."

"You mean 'The World Trade Center?'"

"Please. It was a real lift, going into that last afternoon, three more hours to go after nine hours over the two days, talking with the other New England grads about it, watching the Harvard and BU kids turn green, knowing their schools don't do anything like that for them. But I didn't get drunk. Nobody I saw did. We just milled around and decompressed, talking to the professors and administrators who came by to kind of . . . I don't know, say good-bye till the fifth-year reunion, I guess."

Nostalgia. The cat was still bothering her. "Nance?"

"Yeah?"

"Don't worry about Renfield. He's going to be fine."

"John, do me another favor?"

"What's that?"

"Stay with him?"

"Nance, I'm not going to leave him in a basket on the doorstep."

"I mean, stay here with him till I get back."

"When is that?"

"My plane touches down on Sunday at twelve noon."

"You want me here for two days?"

"Please." A little kiss on my earlobe. "I'll take a taxi from the airport."

"Nance, I can pick you up."

"No. No, it's all reimbursed. I'll get a cab and relieve you as wet nurse if you'll just stay here with him till then."

How hard could it be? "Okay."

"Oh, John, thank you." Another kiss, same place.

"I think a gentle milking motion works best there."

"Like this?"

"Just."

After a minute, I said, "Nance?"

"Ummm?"

"What did you mean by 'wet nurse?' "

"Just an expression."

Friday morning, I got a kiss good-bye as Nancy carried her garment bag out to the yellow Checker. The sun was burning brightly, cutting through the light fog we sometimes get when the water is colder than the air. Or when the air is colder than the water. Boston's not on the level of San Francisco, but we're getting there.

I decided to walk to the graveyard, drifting over to Broadway first to stop at Mrs. Feeney's for a dozen carnations.

What's it like today?

I stood up, looking out at the harbor past the foot of her hillside. "Was foggy, Beth, but it's breaking up so I can see pretty clearly."

You seem troubled, John. Is it still the cat?

"Not really." In a way I couldn't with Nancy, I went through what had happened, Mau Tim Dani becoming Tina Danucci.

So, after crippling a cat, you were sweet-talked by a mobster and beaten up by a male model.

"One way to put it."

Not exactly a week for "Dear Diary."

"It gets worse, kid."

How?

"The timing. The downstairs neighbor hears the dead woman's shower going only fifteen or twenty minutes before the body's found. Unless everybody's covering for each other, the killer had only that much margin to get into her apartment and out again."

Isn't that enough?

"Yes, but it's awfully coincidental for a burglar, and awfully close timing for something planned in advance."

What are you going to do now?

"Go back where I started. Walk through the building, try to find some holes in what I've been told."

Isn't it easier if there aren't any holes?

"Easier?"

If it wasn't planned, then maybe it was just a burglar. That way, the modeling agency gets its insurance money, and the gangsters might leave you alone and keep looking on their own, right?

"Uh-huh."

Well, wouldn't that be easier?

"All around."

A pause. *But making it easier doesn't make it right.*

"Afraid not."

Something caught my eye in the harbor. A pale hump rising above a swell, then three, then five, then . . . "I don't believe it."

What?

"I've never seen anything like this before."

John, what?

I was up to thirty-four. "Dolphins, I think. Dozens of them. Just breaking water."

I described the show for her, watching as even more of the creatures romped and veered, in pairs and squadrons, like so many synchronized swimmers. Maybe chasing fish, maybe running from something themselves, maybe just deciding to see Boston Harbor before the next onslaught of tourists in June.

"There must be over a hundred of them, Beth. I wouldn't have thought they could survive this far north."

Maybe it'll be a week for "Dear Diary" after all.

18

I LEFT THE PRELUDE A BLOCK AWAY FROM NUMBER 10 FALMOUTH and walked to the alley behind it. I looked at the fire escape, trying to find a new perspective from my talks with Sinead Fagan, Oz Puriefoy, and Larry Shinkawa. The escape still switchbacked down the rear of the building, a landing outside Mau Tim's window on the top floor, another outside the window on the second floor, a third outside a window in Fagan's elevated first-floor apartment. The last flight retracted to Sinead's landing. It still would miss the green, ribbed trash cans in the bricked space that passed for a backyard, Cousin Ooch already having moved the cans back from the alley to the building's wall. Just like he said he did the Friday two weeks before, the morning of the day Mau Tim had been killed.

I went to the rear door and knocked, noticing there was no keyhole on the exterior side. After a couple of seconds, I heard a bolt being thrown and the door creaked open, Cousin Ooch blinking out from behind it. Today he wore a bright blue cotton sweater with no shirt underneath and the same pair of droopy pants. The sweater made him look clownish, like a school principal in surfer trunks.

He said, "The family called me about you."

"Who in the family?"

The scarred face flicked right, slipping the imaginary punch, the nose sniffing twice. "What difference that make to you?"

"None, I guess."

His eyes adjusting to the light, Ooch said, "Hey, you been in a fight or what?"

"One-rounder."

"Yeah? Who with?"

"What difference that make to you?"

He thought about it. Flick, sniff/sniff. "Okay. Family said I'm supposed to take you around, show you what's what."

"Can we start down here?"

"Here? You mean, like outside here?"

"No. The basement level."

"That's just my place and the boiler room."

"I'd still like to see them. Go through everything."

Ooch thought some more, then turned. "C'mon."

Inside was a dark hall leading to a short staircase. One bulb glowed faintly at the center of the hall, two more doors off it on either side of the bulb.

Ooch pulled the back door closed behind me. There was an old dead bolt at eye level, and he used the edge of his hand to reseat the bolt into the doorjamb.

I said, "This rear door."

"Yeah?"

"It doesn't lock without the dead bolt?"

"Uh-unh."

"No key for it from the outside?"

"No key for it period. Just the bolt there."

"You usually keep it locked?"

"A course I do. Kinda question is that?"

"It was locked that night?"

"That . . . ?"

"When Mau T—when Tina was killed?"

"A course it was. I put the trash out Tuesdays and Fridays, in the A.M. Otherwise, it's locked, it stays locked."

"Thanks."

We moved down the hall and under the light. Ooch reached for the knob on the right-hand door. "This here's the boiler room."

He opened the metal door. Judging from the odor that enveloped us, it was also where the tenants put their trash before Tuesdays and Fridays. There was an unlit bulb socketed in the ceiling and dim outlines on every wall. I found the switch and got a view of old but clean oil tank, oil burner, hot water heater, even an over-and-under washer/dryer.

Flick, sniff/sniff. "I tell them not to put their garbage in here, smell gets into the laundry when they do, but nobody listens."

I nodded and turned off the light.

The other door off the hall was ajar. "This here's my place."

Ooch led me into a small foyer, closet facing us and the acrid tang of liniment all around us. To the right was the living room, to the left and through a partially closed door was the corner of a bed. I stepped to the right.

The daylight window on the Falmouth Street wall was just to the left of the little front door leading into the basement unit. The lintel was low, low enough that even Ooch at around five six would have to cringe to get under it. The window let in some sun, but not much, giving the posters on the other walls a shadowy look, like the boiler room before I'd turned on the switch.

"Those are from my collection," said Ooch, pride filling his voice.

It was pretty impressive, even if the posters weren't framed but just pinned at the corners with thumbtacks. The cardboard was yellowing on all of them, the wild-West-style tintype a little hard to read until you got used to the shape of the capital letters. Among the headliners were a few guys you'd know even without following the fight game. Rocky Marciano, Floyd Patterson, Benny Kid Paret. The ones on the undercard you'd have to be from the area or a real fan to recognize. I saw

"Carmine 'Ooch' Danucci" on only two, near the bottom of both.

"Every coupla months, I take a few down, put a few up. Like a museum does with their pictures there."

I looked a little closer at the two with Ooch's name on them. They were yellower than the rest and didn't appear to be rotated by the curator. Ooch's collection focused just on boxing but not just on Italian-American boxers. I thought about the posters in Joseph Danucci's den and wondered if this style of decoration ran in the family. I could see brother Vincent with polo players and yachtsmen in his place.

The rest of the furnishings weren't much. Couch, two mismatched chairs, low coffee table. Except for a new Zenith TV, everything looked older than the hills. There was no dining table and only a bowling alley kitchen.

I said, "Bedroom?"

The broken nose cut through the air as he indicated the back of the apartment. Bedcover tousled between a tall, solid bureau and a wobbly nightstand. Open door to the bathroom, a couple of towels on hooks. Clothes hung or heaped, maybe depending on whether they were clean or dirty. Counting the air ducts, no more than five hundred square feet of living space in the whole apartment.

Flick, sniff/sniff. "Okay?"

I wasn't sure which question he was asking me. "Nice place. Quiet."

"I like it quiet. Had enough noise in the ring there."

We left the apartment, Ooch closing the door to his place and shaking the knob to be sure it was secure. As we climbed the stairs to the first floor, he jingled some keys in his pocket, pulling them out and concentrating on them as he put his shoulder into a café-style door at the top.

"Where do you wanna go next?"

Coming into the building's first-floor foyer with him, I noticed the inner door was still propped open, the area for mailboxes and a small table just before the inner surface of the outside door.

I said, "Let's try the front door. Can you step outside, show me how the door opens?"

Ooch looked at me as though I belonged in kindergarten, but went to the front door. Just a spring lock as he turned the handle and went outside. The door closed pretty quietly.

A few seconds later, Ooch opened it with a key and came back inside. "Okay?"

"Who has keys to the front door?"

"The front door? The bum come up the fire escape."

"Who has keys?"

Ooch stopped, then began ticking off names on his fingers. "Sinead, she's got one. Tina had one. A course, the family does, too."

"The family?"

"Yeah."

"Who in the family?"

"Who? Everybody. They use the second floor sometimes."

"The empty apartment."

"Right. Well, it's got furniture and all."

"You know whether any of Sinead's or Tina's boyfriends had a key to the front door?"

Flick, sniff-sniff. "I don't know nothing about that. They did, they wasn't supposed to."

I decided to play dumb. "How about the agents at Tina's modeling agency?"

"I don't know nothing about that, neither."

"Ever see one of them here?"

"Don't know them to tell you."

I looked at the only other door off the foyer, the one I took to be Sinead Fagan's apartment. "Okay. Let's go upstairs and work our way down."

I followed Ooch up a flight of coiling balustrade. On the second floor was a door that looked identical to Sinead's. The carpet runner wasn't new but it was of good quality and still surprisingly plush.

The flight to the third floor was more enclosed, the stair shaft narrowing as it ascended. We stopped at a door that looked identical to both the other two.

Ooch said, "I'm gonna open this, but it's okay with you, I feel a little funny about going in."

"I understand."

He put a key to the lock. "After they—the cops—was finished with her, I had to go in and clean up some. There was . . . this smell, you know?"

The human body pretty much lets go at death, including the muscles that control the bowels. "How about you just stand outside here, so I can call to you if I need something."

Flick, sniff/sniff. "You got it."

Ooch opened the door, and I crossed the threshold of Mau Tim Dani's apartment.

It was bright and might have been airy if it hadn't been shut up for a week. The layout seemed to be the same as Ooch's place, but the dimensions were bigger with the absence of a boiler room and major staircase. The apartment door opened more onto the living room, with the futon sofa more centrally placed. There was a tiled fireplace, probably gas originally, and bookshelves on either side of it. One wall was sacrificed to a home entertainment center with stereo receiver, CD player, science-fiction speakers and a television/VCR hookup. A small gateleg table sat in sunshine by the bowfront window, two straight-back chairs with it, and a choir of plants on risers around it. The rug was a Dhurrie, hardwood floors polyurethaned underneath.

Moving toward the back of the apartment, I passed a wider kitchen and a squarer bath than Ooch had. The window with the fire escape was in the bedroom. The furnishings there were all ruffles and quilts, which surprised me until I remembered how close Mau Tim had been to Grandmother Amatina. I checked the quality of work on the fabrications. The slight imperfections of the lovingly handmade.

I crossed to the window itself. An old one, still with iron sash weights hung in the jamb to allow its mass to be raised. The window was closed but not locked still. I shoved it up and looked out on the fire escape. The metal seemed solid but a little rusty. Holding the bannister by the windowsill, I swung one leg onto the escape and pushed down. The ironwork gave, but only a bit. I swung the other leg out and shifted up and down on it. I got back the sound Larry Shinkawa had described. Not much and not continuous, but a clang every time I moved on the landing.

I climbed back into the bedroom, trying to picture the burglar possibility. From the ground, he somehow pulls down the first flight of fire escape and comes up to the third-floor landing. Mau Tim's just taken her shower. Sinead Fagan told me that Friday had been warm. Maybe Mau Tim has the bedroom window open. Or had it open and closed it without engaging the lock. She's somewhere in the apartment, not making any noise or making so little the TV or stereo is covering it. Then I thought back. Larry Shinkawa said the TV and stereo were off, no other sound beside the fire escape.

That probably meant Mau Tim was still in the bathroom, toweling off and being quiet. Our boy comes in through the window, place looks deserted, he starts with the jewelry box. Finds the iolite necklace, stuffs it in a pocket or bag, scopes some other pieces maybe, then . . . Wait, the necklace was broken.

I walked back into the living room and over to the futon. The pendant part of the necklace was found under one of the corners. I closed my eyes, trying to see the eight-by-ten Holt had showed me from the Homicide file. The pendant was partially under the left front corner of the couch as you sit on it, the corner nearest the front door if you're struggling with somebody who's holding the necklace.

So, the guy has the necklace in his hand in the bedroom. Mau Tim comes out of the bathroom toward the bedroom. They see each other, or he hears her or she hears him. She runs toward the front door of the apartment, he chases her . . .

Wait. Why doesn't he go back out the window and back down the fire escape? He's in the bedroom, right by it. If he's in the bedroom.

Maybe he's moved to the living room while she's still in the bathroom. He's sizing up the home entertainment center, figuring on maybe the CD player as the best candidate. Then she comes out, sees him, and heads for the door.

In other words, heads toward him and not away from him? And he still has the necklace in his hand so it can abrade her throat and break as he strangles her? And walking past the bathroom, he didn't feel the humidity from her shower or hear a telltale noise right next to the bathroom door itself?

I looked over at the front door to the apartment. The chain plate had been unscrewed from the jamb, a rectangle of bare wood in the painted molding. Then I realized that Ooch was staring at me.

Flick, sniff-sniff. "You okay?"

"I'm okay, Ooch. Why?"

"You looked, I don't know, kinda queer there, talking to yourself and walking back and forth."

"I'm okay. Thanks."

I shook my head. I wasn't okay, because I couldn't picture what happened. It's a small apartment, she had to be somewhere when the guy came in. Somewhere he couldn't see her or be aware of her, because no burglar, even an addict, is crazy enough to try a rip-off from a third-floor fire escape when somebody's in the place.

If it was a rip-off. If it was a burglar.

I went back into the bedroom. At the window, I looked out and down. The bottom, raised flight of the fire escape contrasted sharply against the background of the bricked yard. If our boy had used the green trash cans to reach and pull the last flight on his way up, Shinkawa should have seen them after our boy used the fire escape on the way down.

I walked to the front of the apartment. "Ooch, can we try the second floor now?"

"Yeah. Yeah, sure."

He locked the door behind me, then started down the stairs. At the next landing, he jingled the keys again. "Fuck, I can't never . . . There, there it is."

Ooch turned the key twice through the compass, though I didn't hear it snicking. He pushed the door open but this time went in first.

"Kinda close in here, ain't it?"

I said, "It is."

He moved into the bedroom and to the window at the fire escape, opening it without bothering to play with the lock on top. It gave me a minute to examine the lock on the apartment door. The keyhole on the outside looked the same as the one on Mau Tim's door, but on the inside, there was another keyhole, and the dead bolt operated vertically, not horizontally. On the inner surface of the metal were those screwheads you can't turn without a special tool.

From inside the apartment, I closed the door. There was no sound at the knob, and the dead bolt didn't engage. I used the knob to open and close the door again. Same.

I walked to the bedroom doorway. Ooch was taking some breaths at the window.

I said, "You can't lock that door without a key?"

He turned to me. "Huh?"

I pointed back toward where I'd come from. "Somebody inside this apartment would need a key to lock that door and a key to get out again?"

"Oh, yeah. The family, they just use this place to stay when they're in the city for whatever."

"And they lock themselves in?"

"No, no. You don't get me."

Ooch passed by and took out his keys again. "See, Claudette, Joey's wife, she was all the time forgetting her key. She's a real polite lady, she locked herself out, she don't like to come bothering me." Ooch held up an odd, pimpled key. "So my Uncle Tommy, he says to me, 'Ooch, you go see they got a lock you need a key for, let you out, too.'"

Ooch inserted the key on the interior face of the door lock and turned it twice, again without a snicking noise, then pulled the key out. "This way, she don't forget her key because she can't lock up without the thing."

I tried the door. Locked, dead bolt vertically engaged.

"Who else has a key to this place?"

"What, you mean this apartment here?"

"Right."

"All the family's got one. They don't know when they need the place, they want to be able to use it, right?"

"Does Sinead have a key?"

Ooch seemed taken back. "Sinead, she ain't family. She's a nice kid and all, but she's just a tenant."

"How about Tina?"

"Yeah. Yeah, she had one."

"Where?"

"In her apartment."

"Where in her apartment?"

"Kitchen. Drawer by the faucet there."

I looked around the second-floor unit. Modestly but functionally furnished, a notch above a suite in a good hotel.

Ooch was back at the bedroom window, me joining him there. I leaned out, looking up to Mau Tim's landing above, then down to the flight to Fagan's apartment before the raised last link. I said, "You afraid of heights, Ooch?"

"Me? No."

"Mind climbing out onto the fire escape and going up to the next floor, then down again?"

Flick, sniff/sniff. "You want me to climb up, then down?"

"Right."

He motioned for me to stand back a little. He moved agilely over the sill and went up to the third floor, just one hand on the railing. I could hear a clang with every step.

Ooch said, "Okay?"

"Fine. Now come back down again. This time, slow and light on your feet."

"Huh?"

"Come toward me slowly, light on your feet."

Ooch shook his head, but used the bannister to ease down the escape. No clanging until he hit the landing outside my window.

"Okay, now go down all the way to alley level."

"All the way?"

"Right."

He shook his head again. "You want this one fast or slow?"

"Regular speed."

"Light or heavy?"

"Regular."

"Regular." Flick, sniff/sniff.

He got to Sinead's landing fine, but then had to finesse the bottom flight, steadying himself with both hands on the bannisters as his weight counterbalanced the last link and it descended with him toward the ground. It didn't clang, though. More a grinding, squealing noise, and very loud.

At the bottom, Ooch stayed on the last rung and turned up to me. "Okay?"

Not sure it mattered anymore, I said, "You're sure those trash cans were against the wall Friday night when you checked down there?"

"What, these here?"

"Yes."

"Sure I'm sure. That it?"

"Yes. Come on back up."

Ooch stepped carefully, the last link grinding and squealing some more as it retracted into place. Coming up the flight from Sinead's apartment to the second floor, he said, "Gotta get some oil on that thing."

"You ever try this before?"

"Yeah." He climbed through the window and into the bedroom. "When my uncle asked me about being superintendent, I tried everything then. Been a coupla years, though."

A straight, simple answer. "Ooch, the door to this second-floor apartment, was it kept locked?"

"Sure."

"How about this second-floor window?"

"This here? I don't know. I'm not in here much, tell you the truth. Just to clean up, somebody's coming or just been."

"Tina's parents were coming up the day after she was killed, right?"

"Yeah." Flick, sniff/sniff. "They was coming up on Saturday, see her and have a birthday dinner Saturday night."

"So you didn't do any cleaning up for them?"

"No. I mean, yeah, I did."

"I don't follow you."

"See, I didn't know what time they was coming up on Saturday, so I was in here Friday afternoon, before I went out to the gym."

I inclined my head toward the window. "You aired the place out."

"Sure. You gotta do that, these buildings. Otherwise, they been closed up a while, they get musty like today, you know?"

"And you locked the door to this apartment when you left?"

A blank look. "A course I did. I'm the super, remember?"

"When did you close the window here?"

Flick, sniff/sniff. "Saturday."

"Saturday."

"Yeah. Saturday, it starts to rain. I remember, the windows're open on the second floor, so I come up and shut them."

"And the door to this apartment was locked then, too."

"A course it was. What's so hard to understand?"

An honest face. Roughed up some, and maybe not quite everything you'd want behind it. But enough to make me re-think a lot of things I wasn't sure I wanted to.

19

WHEN OOCH LET ME OUT OF THE SECOND-FLOOR APARTMENT, I HEARD strident rap music from downstairs and saw that Sinead Fagan's door was half-open. Ooch hurried past me and down the staircase.

At her entrance, he stopped and said, "What's going on?"

Somebody turned down the stereo. I could hear Sinead's voice before I could see her. "I'm moving the fuck out, Ooch."

Over the super's shoulder I took in the living room. Fagan in designer sweatshirt and blue jeans, her red hair in that cocklebur cut. She was dumping audiocassettes into a shopping bag. Behind her, Oz Puriefoy separated two cardboard boxes on the kitchen counter. He stopped what he was doing, but stayed by the boxes and out of the conversation.

Ooch said, "Where you gonna go, Sinead?"

"I'm moving in with Oz for a while, get my head on straight."

Ooch glanced at Puriefoy and muttered something. Then, "You mean, I'm gonna be all alone here?"

"Aw, Ooch." Sinead came toward the super, towering over him at close range as she put her hands on his shoulders, consoling a Little Leaguer who made last out. "I'm sorry, you know? But I just can't stay here after what happened to Mau."

"Tina," said Ooch, wrenching away from her without using his hands and bumping by me. "Her name was Tina."

As Ooch headed toward and down the stairs to the basement, Fagan worried her lower lip with her upper teeth. Then she remembered I was there, too. "The fuck you want?"

"Ooch was taking me on a tour of the building. Part of the investigation."

"Well, the tour's over."

"Not quite. Mind if I come in?"

"What if I do?"

I looked to Puriefoy, whose expression said he was still staying out of it.

"Your bosses at Lindqvist/Yulin need for me to finish what I started."

Fagan stopped, the way she had at the photo shoot when a question threw her. "They're not my bosses. They're my agents."

"You're moving out, what difference does it make if I take a look at your place?"

Fagan wasn't buying it. I didn't think she was so much thinking as being stubborn.

Puriefoy said, "Sinead, the man wants to look, let him look. We leave, he can just get Ooch to let him in anyways, right?"

Fagan finally stepped away from the door, stiffly motioning me into the living room. "You can't stay long. We just got started here, and we still have quite a lot to do."

Quite a lot. I shook my head.

In size, the first-floor place was between Ooch's little cave and the second-floor guest suite. The living room shared an open space with the breakfast-countered kitchen, the doorways to bedroom and bathroom on one wall.

I walked past Puriefoy to the kitchen, going around the counter to stand between refrigerator and stove. I could see the railing of the fire escape through the window. Above me, pipes crooked out of the ceiling and into the wall, painted to blend in with the surrounding planes.

"These the water pipes?"

Fagan said, "Yeah."

"Had anybody been staying on the second floor recently?"

Fagan looked at me. "The fuck would I know?"

"Footsteps overhead."

Puriefoy said, "We couldn't hardly hear you and Ooch up there just now."

"But you could hear us."

Puriefoy shrugged. "A little."

I turned back to Fagan. "So, anybody up there recently?"

"Not that I heard. Go ask the family, you want to."

"Sinead, where did Mau Tim keep the key to the second-floor unit?"

"Didn't know she had one."

"All right. You're both here. Shinkawa, too, would be nice, but let me play him. Walk me through what happened that night."

"Fuck you," said Fagan, Puriefoy keeping his own counsel.

"You can walk through it with me now, when you're already here and blowing off the morning, or the cops can pull both of you from shoots somewhere when it pleases them to do it. Your choice."

Puriefoy moved his tongue around his mouth before saying, "You running a game on us, man?"

"No game. Just a simple reenactment."

They looked at each other.

I said, "We're spending more time arguing about it than it's going to take to actually do it."

Fagan said, "Awright, awright. Let's get the fucking thing over with. Where do you want me?"

"Where you were when Puriefoy rang you from outside the building."

"When he came back with the wine?"

"No. Before that, when he first arrived that day."

Fagan looked around, closed her eyes. "I was standing by the sink there, washing celery."

I stepped out of the kitchen. "Go ahead."

"I don't got no celery in the fridge."

"Just stand at the sink."

Fagan did it. She was two feet from the fire escape through the window, a hunk of wood six inches square on the sill.

I said, "Was that window open?"

"Huh?"

"Was your kitchen window open?"

"Yeah. Nice night, I wanted a little fresh air."

"Can you show me?"

"Show you how to open a window?"

"Show me how it was that night."

Fagan turned from the sink. Heaving at the window, she niggled the hunk of wood under the frame as it came back down.

I said, "The window won't stay open on its own?"

She shook her head. "Something's wrong with the things inside the walls."

The sash cords were probably broken. "Can I try?"

Fagan let me replace her. I lifted the old window. It took a lot to move it another six inches off the sill, the sides shuddering like furniture hauled over a bare floor. I said, "How would you get out if there was a fire?"

She pointed behind me. "Door's right there."

"Okay." I looked at Puriefoy. "How about you leave the apartment and close the door. Then go outside the building, close the front door, and ring Mau Tim's bell."

Puriefoy spoke evenly. "I didn't ring Mau's bell, man. I rang Sinead's."

"Please. Just ring Mau's bell first, wait a few seconds, and then ring Sinead's."

His expression stayed neutral as he left the room, closing the apartment door behind him. Over the stereo, which wasn't on loud, I couldn't hear any noise from Puriefoy opening and closing the building's front door. Then a harsh doorbell sound, muted by distance, followed by its twin, even harsher, inside the apartment.

I said, "You really can hear the third-floor bell down here, can't you?"

Fagan said, "Like you was next to it."

"You didn't hear anybody ring Mau that day."

"No."

"What about when Shinkawa arrived?"

"Him I heard. Yeah, I remember thinking it must be Larry Shin when I heard Mau's bell."

The harsher bell inside Fagan's apartment rang again.

"Well, you want me to answer it or what?"

"Whatever you did that day when Oz rang your bell."

She left the kitchen, crossed the living room, and opened her apartment door, leaving it open as she left my sight and went into the foyer. Listening hard, I could just hear her opening the building's front door for Puriefoy. She came right back into the apartment, Puriefoy behind her.

"What did you two do next?"

Fagan started to say something, Puriefoy riding over her. "Like I told you at my studio, man. After a while, Sinead, she remembers she don't have wine, so I go out to get some."

"But didn't take a key."

"That's right."

"So you leave and Sinead, you still hear water in the pipes."

"Yeah."

"When did the water stop?"

"I dunno."

"Before Oz got back with the wine?"

"Yeah."

"How long before?"

"I dunno. A couple minutes, maybe. I remember thinking, good thing Mau's a little late."

"Why?"

"On account of me forgetting the wine, okay?"

"While Oz was gone for the wine, did you hear anybody else at the door?"

"You mean, like the front door to the building?"

"Right."

"No."

"Could Mau Tim have let someone in?"

"Not by buzzing the door. You can hear that fucking buzzer like it was next to you."

"Mau Tim's doorbell or the buzzer now?"

"Both. But the buzzer, that's like . . ." Fagan made the sound of a hundred-and-twenty-pound bumblebee.

To Puriefoy I said, "And you get back when?"

"Wasn't checking my watch."

"Fifteen minutes?"

"Fifteen, twenty, maybe. Like that."

"Same routine for the door?"

They looked at each other.

Sinead came back to me. "No. No, this time I just buzzed him in the front door—the building door—then I opened this one and went back to what I was doing."

"Which was what?"

"Picking out some tapes. I was getting tired of the crap I was playing, so I tried some Vanilla Ice."

She pointed to the stereo. "That's him on now."

Puriefoy said, "Uh-huh," like there was no accounting for Sinead's taste.

I turned to the photographer. "What did you do?"

"Brought in the wine."

"Did you close the apartment door?"

"No, man. My arms were full."

"Where did you put the wine?"

"Kitchen there."

"Open it?"

"Yeah. Corkscrew under the counter."

"Okay. When does Shinkawa arrive?"

Fagan looked to Puriefoy. "I dunno."

Puriefoy said, "Maybe two, three minutes after I got back. Larry, he rings the bell, we let him in."

"Who lets him in?"

Fagan said, "I do."

"By buzzer?"

"Yeah."

"Then what?"

I listened again to the same "birthday suit" sequence everybody had already told me.

"Sinead, what did you do after Shinkawa came running back downstairs?"

"I went to my bag and got the key Mau give me to her place."

"Do it."

"What, now?"

"Yes."

Fagan went into the kitchen and fetched the key from a handbag that looked like a leather descendant of Davy Crockett's powderhorn. "Awright?"

"You all rushed upstairs then?"

"Yeah."

"Let's go."

"What?"

"Let's go upstairs, like I'm Shinkawa and we're going up there."

Fagan said, "This is getting too weird," again the word coming out "we-id."

I said, "We're almost done. Promise."

She didn't look convinced, but Puriefoy said, "Let's get this over with, huh?" and went out to climb the stairs. I let Fagan precede me.

Even walking at just normal speed, it didn't take long to get to the third floor. At the door, I said, "Hold it. Position yourselves like you were that night."

Puriefoy said, "We can't, man."

"Why not?"

"Larry, he was in front, but you're too big for all of us to be here at once."

"Okay, simulate that."

"Say what?"

"Just make like I'm in front of you. Who did what?"

"We pounded a little, Sinead started to work the key."

Fagan said, "Then Larry took it away from me 'cause he was closer on the door."

"Then the door opens?"

"Yeah, but the chain's on, so you can't see much."

I said, "Unlock the door, but don't open it."

Fagan stopped. "Unlock . . . ?"

"Use the key in the lock, but don't open the door itself."

She did.

"Okay, now stand back a little."

I moved in front of them, turning the knob and cracking open the door. I moved it to two inches, then three, then four. At three inches I could see the corner of the futon couch, at four probably a quarter view of where Mau Tim's body would have lain.

I said, "Then you broke through the chain?"

"Oz did."

I pushed the door all the way open.

Fagan trembled. "Jesus Mary."

I said, "What is it?"

"It's just . . . it's like I was gonna see her all over again."

She turned and started downstairs.

"Sinead?"

"Fuck you. I ain't going in there."

As Fagan left us, I looked at Puriefoy. "Was there music on in here?"

"Music?"

"Or television. Anything?"

Puriefoy said, "No, nothing."

Same as Shinkawa. "How about the shower?"

"That was off, too."

"What did you all do then?"

Puriefoy said, "I don't like being here either, man. Not at all."

"What did you do?"

He walked into the apartment, but gingerly, like he wasn't

sure the floorboards had been nailed down. "I bent over by Mau, see if I could get a pulse or anything, but she was gone."

"Shinkawa?"

"Like I told you at my place, he took off for the bedroom, saying he heard something."

"You didn't go with him?"

"Shit, no. You think I'm a hero?"

Not so far. "Then what?"

"Sinead, she's screaming, and I'm trying CPR."

"Even though you thought Mau Tim was dead?"

"In the class I took, they said try it anyway."

"All right. Then what?"

"I tell Sinead, 'Call the 911,' but she's like hysterical, man. Larry, he comes back in from the bedroom and says he didn't see nothing. I tell him to help me move Mau a little so I can work on her better. Then Sinead finally goes and calls the ambulance."

"From where?"

Puriefoy pointed to a Princess phone on a shelf of the home entertainment wall. "That one there."

"The three of you stay together here all that time?"

Puriefoy said, "All what time?"

"Till the ambulance arrived."

"Uh-huh."

"Anybody leave the room for anything?"

"No."

I walked into the kitchen and pulled on the drawer nearest the faucets. Next to a pair of tongs was an odd, pimpled key like the one Ooch had used on the second-floor apartment door.

I came back into the living room. Puriefoy was squatting at the corner of the couch.

"Anything else you can tell me about what you all did?"

"Larry, he saw this piece of necklace under the futon here. I think he showed it to the cops, too."

"Beyond that."

Puriefoy stood up. "Like I been telling you, Sinead, she wasn't in great shape, and Larry and me, we was working on Mau, but with her face blue and all. . . ."

I swung my head slowly around the apartment. I didn't like what I'd already learned, but I didn't think the place had anything more to tell me.

20

AS I WAS LEAVING MAU TIM'S BUILDING, A CALICO CAT SCUTTLED
under a bush near the iron front gate. Fortunately, it reminded
me to call the vet's from a payphone and check on Renfield.
A female voice at the other end of the line impatiently confirmed
that he'd be ready for pickup any time after three-thirty and
before six. She made a point of telling me they accepted either
MasterCard or a personal check as payment. I thought that was
a bad sign. I asked her how much the bill was for. She said
they hadn't totaled it yet. I thought that was a worse sign.

The receptionist at Winant, Terwiliger, and Stevens looked
and sounded like Diana Rigg in her *Avengers* days. She asked
me if I would "care" to hang my coat in the closet. I said I
would and was led regally to an expanse of polished cherry
wood. Trusting me to use the hanger properly, she glided back
to her desk, which would have put the cockpit of a 747 to
shame. Moving toward the woman, I heard her ask the telephone if Mr. Dani could see "a" Mr. John Cuddy. She waited,

fiddling with some pink message slips, then said, "I'll advise him."

The receptionist turned to me. "Mr. Dani's secretary will be right with you. Would you care to take a seat?"

I was sitting on an unyielding silk-covered settee over an acquamarine carpet under a print of a fox hunt when a young woman came around the corner. She did not remind me of Diana Rigg. She reminded me of Whoopi Goldberg. Until she talked, at which point she reminded me of Diana Rigg, too.

"Mr. Cuddy?"

"Yes."

"I'm Rita Knox. Mr. Dani can see you in a few minutes. Would you please come with me?"

I followed the dreadlocks back through a rabbit warren of common corridors. Kangaroo-pouch enclosures of secretaries sat outside windowed offices of lawyers and windowless offices of paralegals.

At the midpoint of one corridor, Rita Knox slowed beside a closed door and looked back over her shoulder at me, swishing the braids. "Mr. Dani is on long distance. Please have a seat and let me know if I can help you with anything."

There was another silk settee, the cushions on this one also stiff as a board. Several people coming down the corridor slowed hesitatingly near the adjoining office, then walked by quickly, eyes averted from a man in his early fifties who was putting his wall plaques into a brown and green packing box. My day to catch people on the move.

When the corridor was empty, I spoke to Knox. "I don't want to impose on Vincent at a bad time. How is he holding up under the strain of his niece's death?"

The secretary shook her head. "He's doing so well, the poor man. They were quite close, but he hasn't missed a beat here."

"Did you know her?"

"No. Well, yes, but only over the telephone. I must say, every time I think of talking with her that day, it is as though a ghost crossed my grave."

I tried to keep my voice light. "You talked with her the day she died?"

"Yes." Knox took a breath, her eyes tipping me that this was a story she'd told before, a story she relished in that guilty way we all have. "She called here that afternoon, just before I left. Mr. Dani was in a meeting, so I left her message for him on the spike."

"Sorry?"

Knox held up a six-inch message spike with a brass base. "This. We still don't have a voice-mail system, so I impale his messages on it." A devious little smile, then she seemed to remember the story she was telling. "Poor girl."

I needed to be careful here. "That happened to me once in the Army. I spoke to somebody at noon, and then at dinner I heard he'd died. I kept asking myself, was there something in his voice that day that said he knew his time was coming?"

"The very same with me! I've been saying to myself, 'Was there something in her voice?' But she sounded fine. Even buoyant, like a girl her age should. So full of life and—"

At which point the office door opened and Vincent Dani stood there, the balding head lifted an inch higher than eye level, as though he were trying to sense the words that had been in the air before he interrupted us.

"Mr. Cuddy, I can give you only a few minutes."

I stood. "A few minutes should do it."

Dani looked at his secretary for a moment, then just said, "Rita, hold all my calls."

"Yessir."

His office was rectangular, but some sort of shaft for the building's structural integrity ran at a diagonal to the ceiling, creating a lean-to effect on that side of the room. The opposite surface was more standard, covered with framed prints of grouse, pheasant, and quail. At least there were no polo fields or yacht basins.

Outside his window, six other skyscrapers eclipsed most of the horizon. His view between them was a thumbprint of Boston Harbor and a hundred yards of Logan Airport runway.

Dani settled behind a cherry desk with Scandinavian lines. The credenza, desk chair, and both client chairs were of the same grained wood, the third hue in the Oriental rug beneath us picking up the cherry color. The underlying wall-to-wall carpeting that continued in from the hall was beige, as were his lowboy file cabinets and shelving. He had a personal computer on the credenza, not much of anything beyond a telephone complex and pen set on the desk.

Dani looked at me, the hair thin and the eyes sharp but the face expressionless, again the only emotional part of him his lips, which twitched a little. Dressed impeccably in another Brooks Brothers suit, this one gray with a houndstooth pattern, he gave the impression of a man who had seriously considered a hair transplant only to decide, rightly, that it would make him look silly.

"Well, Mr. Cuddy?"

"I've been out to the building. Your cousin and I did a walk-through, and I have a couple of questions."

"Ask them."

"How many people have a key to Mau Tim's apartment?"

Even his lips suggested he expected that one. "I wouldn't know. She wasn't supposed to give them out."

"To your knowledge, who has a key?"

"Certainly Cousin Ooch. Perhaps the downstairs tenant—they were good friends."

"Her agents?"

"The modeling agency? Perhaps, but I don't see why."

"Her current boyfriend?"

"If she had one. Or more than one. As I told you before, I really didn't know much about her social life."

"How about you?"

The lips danced. "Me?"

"Yes. You're a trustee of the building, right?"

"I am a trustee in a paperwork sense, yes. But Ooch would take care of all the . . . on-site matters."

"You have any keys to the building?"

A pause. "I imagine I must have a front door key some-where."

"How about the second floor?"

That stopped the lips cold. "The *sec*-ond floor?"

"Yes. The guest suite or whatever you call it."

Vincent Dani stared at me, then said, "What does that have to do with a burglary on the third floor?"

"Probably nothing."

Dani's mouth opened, but nothing came out. His silence was interrupted by a tap-tap-tap on the office door. I turned halfway to see a man lean across the threshold. His hair was that maize color blond turns to when most of us just get gray. He wore round wire spectacles and a jaunty bow tie on a white shirt so starched it rode his chest like body armor. I bet myself that his first name would be a last name.

"Vincent, terribly sorry to disturb you, but I'm just back from Washington and now off to London and I did want to con-gratulate you on joining the partnership."

The man's voice was as crisp as the starch in his shirt, the crackle of a no-nonsense, North Shore Yankee.

"Uh, oh, thank you, Whit. I appreciate your support."

"Support well deserved, Vincent, well deserved." Old Whit seemed to make the next statement for my benefit. "Contri-butions like yours cannot go unnoticed. Or unrewarded."

Dani was uncomfortable about Whit loitering in his doorway. For his part, Whit seemed to be reminded of something by his last comment. The man looked to the right outside Dani's door and then spoke more softly. "I believe this is Charlie's last day . . ."

"Thanks, Whit, I've already had the chance to wish him well."

"Right. Right then. In that case, I'll be off."

Old Whit sent a smile and a nod my way and I'm sure had forgotten about me by the time he'd taken ten steps.

Dani was coming back to me when I said, "Charlie the guy next door?"

"Uh . . . yes."

"A little young for retirement."

"He's not retiring. He's . . . leaving the partnership."

"The rest of you voted him out."

Dani's lips did another dance. "The rest of them. I didn't have anything to do with it."

"They voted you in but him out?"

"Law is a business, Mr. Cuddy. Charlie was . . . is a competent technician, but not a rain-maker. He brought it on himself, never developing any portables he could—"

"Portables?"

"Clients he could take with him to another firm. If you develop clients who come to think of you as their 'real' attorney, they'll follow you to a new firm. Since those clients would follow you, your current firm would never let you go, would want you to stay, leveraging associates and paralegals on your matters to maintain a given level of billings."

"And Charlie didn't do that?"

"No."

"And you did."

"To the extent currently expected of me."

"Like through your brother's mall development company."

"Among others."

"But his as the first among equals?"

Dani's lips tightened. "I don't suppose that's really any of your business, is it?"

I decided to take a different tack, hopefully without sinking Rita Knox. "Tell me, Mr. Dani, did Mau Tim call you the week she died?"

The lips seemed almost to fold inward, a man not wearing his false teeth. "About what?"

"About your making partner here."

"No."

"How come?"

"Because I called her."

"You did."

"Yes."

"From where?"

Dani's lips danced a third time. A lot of people don't know that the telephone company keeps track of all local calls, but I was willing to bet that Vincent Dani did.

He said, "I'm not sure."

"Not sure where you were when you called your niece about making partner here?"

"That's correct."

"Okay. When did you call her?"

"I don't recall the exact day."

"Was it the same day you were voted the partnership?"

Something inside Dani seemed to stop for a moment, a robot who'd just had his power switched off by remote control.

Then he said, "I believe I've given you all the time I can spare today." He pushed a button on the telephone complex and spoke toward it. "Rita, could you show Mr. Cuddy back to the elevators?"

21

I'VE HAD SOME ROUGH EXPERIENCES WITH VETERINARY HOSPITALS over the years. This one was sparkling clean and very busy. Two women in yellow smocks careened around behind a large reception counter, the benches in the reception area arranged obliquely, presumably to minimize the warfare between pets of different species and temperaments. The area was full, a lot of yelping and mewling and chirping in the air as I spoke to the closest woman behind the counter.

She said, "What?"

"I'm here to pick up a cat."

The woman moved to a flattened card file. "What name?"

She sounded like the impatient voice on the telephone. I said, "The owner's name is Meagher, Nancy."

"No. I need the cat's name."

"Oh. Meagher, Renfield NMI."

"NMI?"

"No Middle Initial."

I got a look like somebody put vinegar in the ice cream.

"Here he is. Just a minute." The woman picked up a phone and hit two numbers. "Donny? Julie. I need cage number seventy-three, cat, gray tiger . . . Yes, in a carry-box . . . Right."

Julie put down the phone and slapped a carboned invoice on top of the counter. "The total's at the bottom."

I looked at the bottom and said, "God in heaven."

The woman said, "What's the matter?"

"The amount of the bill."

"The cat had bilateral knee displacements."

"But this is more than the Bears spent on Gale Sayers."

When she said, "Who?," I said never mind and took out my checkbook.

Julie had just given me the pink copy of the invoice when a scuzzy-looking kid I took to be Donny appeared from behind a door. He was carrying a cardboard container that resembled a Dunkin' Donuts Munchkins box magnified five times. There were airholes an inch in diameter on the short ends of the box, and one clawless gray forepaw coming through one of the airholes, trying to bend it back.

I said, "That's him, all right."

At the sound of my voice, Renfield cried a little from inside the container. I began to think that my picking him up might not have been such a hot idea.

Donny reached behind the reception counter and handed me a little plastic lampshade and a strip of gauze bandage.

"What's this for?"

The kid said, "When you get home, you put it over the cat's head."

"Somehow I don't think he's in the mood to party."

"No, man. You put the thing over his head, small end down on his neck, then run the gauze through the slits on the thing there and pull on it a little."

"Why?"

"Keeps him from being able to pick at his stitches with his teeth."

"How can he get to the stitches through the casts?"

"Man, there aren't any casts on him. Cats are tough. He'll be fine once the anesthesia wears off."

"I thought it already wore off."

Donny was turned and halfway through the door again. "Probably has."

I hefted the box by the handle, and Renfield cried a little more. To Julie I said, "Do I need to give him anything?"

"No. Just keep an eye on him. He acts funny, give the vet a call at the number on top of the bill."

As I carried the container toward the main entrance, Renfield began crying steadily.

I parked in front of Nancy's house in South Boston. Renfield's box in one hand and my raincoat over the other arm, I used Nancy's key on the front door. I also let the Lynches know I'd be up there for a while.

In Nancy's kitchen, I tossed my raincoat on a chair. I set the Munchkins box down on the linoleum and opened the handles carefully. The cat cried and flinched when the light hit his eyes, but that wasn't the worst of it.

"Jesus, Renfield. What did they do to you, boy?"

His fur was all shaved from roughly his belly button down both rear legs and then halfway up his tail. He looked like a cross between a madly groomed poodle and a plucked chicken, especially through the legs, which were incredibly scrawny with just his skin covering them.

I lifted him out carefully, Renfield growling and trying to bite my hands, but only weakly. I laid him gently on the lineoleum. His legs were bent funny, like he was doing a deep knee bend on his side, each leg showing a line of stitches five inches long. He tried to stand up on the linoleum, flopping back down and crying.

I went into Nancy's bathroom, rifling her linen closet for the oldest towel I could find. I brought a blue one back into the kitchen, doubling it over and spreading it out. I lifted Renfield onto the towel, figuring he'd have a better chance with better friction. The cat was almost able to get to his feet, then let out a terrible yowl and flopped over again. He tried to crick his neck enough to get at the stitches, just reaching the ones closest to his hip. I tried to keep him from them, which only frustrated him more.

I realized I'd left the lampshade thing in the Prelude. I went down to the street, retrieved it and the gauze, and came back upstairs. By that time, the cat had managed to flop over to his other side, scrunching up the towel every which way. I straightened out the cloth, then tried to put the lampshade over his head.

Renfield gave me a major argument, so I took the thing off and ran the gauze through the slits in the plastic first, like a man putting on his belt before pulling on his pants. Trying it again, I got worse noise, his cottonball front paws windmilling at my hands like a first-grader in a playground fight.

I finally got the contraption over his head and secured, Renfield looking like a fantasy painting of an alien flower beast. As soon as I let go, however, he started growling and moaning, thrashing at the lampshade with paws that just skated across the hard plastic. I began to worry that he'd hurt himself, even strangle if he got it halfway off, but I couldn't see tugging the gauze belt any tighter.

That's when I got out the bill and on the phone to the vet.

I drew Julie behind the counter, who told me to hold on. Drumming my fingers through the Muzak, I finally heard a male voice with a singsong East Indian accent.

"Hello, can I help you, please?"

"My name's John Cuddy, doctor. I just picked up a friend's cat at your hospital, and he's not doing too well."

"What is the name, please?"

"Renfield."

"Renfield . . . Renfield—ah, yes. The gray tiger, bilateral knee—"

"That's him."

"What is the problem, please?"

"He's in a lot of discomfort, and he can't seem to stand up."

"That is normal, sir. Partly the anesthesia, partly the weakness in the legs, yes?"

"I also tried to put the lampshade thing on his head, but it's driving him nuts."

"Ah, the Elizabethan collar. They do not like that much, do they?"

"I couldn't say. This is my first."

"Well, I would not worry about it. The important thing is not to let him have at his stitches."

"But that's what he wants to do."

"Yes, well, there are really two sets of stitches in each leg, some inside the skin, and the ones you can see outside. If he gets only to the outside ones a little bit, you will see just a drop or two of blood which will scab over nicely. Nothing to worry about, yes?"

"Doctor, he's thrashing around so much with the lampshade on, I'm afraid he'll bust through his stitches or even hurt his neck."

"Oh, well, we cannot have that, can we? Perhaps it would be best to take the collar off his head and simply monitor him."

"Monitor him."

"Yes. Throughout the night, if possible."

"Great."

"He may imprint on you a bit, as though you are the parent and he the child. But eventually the stitches will not bother him so much."

"Is there anything I can do for him now? He really seems to be suffering."

"Unfortunately that is natural with cats. But as they are poor patients they are good convalescents. They have much better attitudes about rehabilitation than dogs, yes?"

"Am I supposed to be feeding him or what?"

"Oh, I doubt he will take any food for a while. But do offer him some, the simpler the better. Dry food over canned. And do make water available. He probably will not be able to walk very well to his dish—"

"Doctor, I'm telling you, he can't even stand up."

"—nor to his litter box, I am afraid."

Better and better. "Anything else I should watch for?"

"No. Cats have a remarkable ability to heal themselves, you will see, sir. Just be a little patient with him. And now, I really must go."

As I hung up the phone, Renfield let out a miserable yowl. Then he copiously wet himself and the towel.

About eight o'clock, I put a commercial lasagna dish from Nancy's freezer in her microwave and nuked it for seven minutes per side on low, then another five on high. Only the one towel was sacrificed to Renfield's incontinence, him seeming a lot calmer, or at least resigned, after I took the lampshade off. I cleaned his hindquarters with some paper napkins dabbed in warm water, blotting the moisture off with dry ones to keep him from getting too cold. I still decided to leave him on the washable linoleum, though, a different towel underneath him and flipped lightly over his rear legs.

When the microwave trilled at me, I zapped some frozen garlic bread and opened a bottle of red wine. I had half the wine and all the lasagna and bread, the cat turning down both food and water whenever I edged his two-sectioned dish toward him.

I tried to watch TV in the living room, but every time I left the kitchen, or more accurately, left Renfield's line of sight, he cried. Continuously. Nancy is a real fan of private investigator fiction, so I picked a Loren Estleman paperback off a shelf and settled into one of the kitchen chairs.

When the book mentioned jazz, I remembered Primo Zuppone's tape in the pocket of my raincoat. I left the kitchen long enough to put it into the stereo, then listened to both sides of Wim Mertens several times, the equivalent of two albums alternating. Thoughtful, mournful, it seemed to suit my "wet nurse" mood.

The music playing, I drank wine and read about the mean streets of Detroit until almost eleven, when I started yawning. Renfield had dropped off at some point, and I stepped over him as quietly as possible. He didn't wake up.

I was asleep for a while in Nancy's bed when I was roused by a terrible sound. Renfield. Yowling.

He'd managed to drag himself across the threshold of the kitchen, getting tangled in the towel. He cried until I disengaged him and got him back onto the kitchen floor the way I'd left him. When I turned to go to the bedroom, he started crying again.

I shook my head and went into the living room. I stacked the seat cushions from Nancy's couch like poker chips and carried them into the bedroom. I took a pillow and the blanket from her bed and stacked them on top of the cushions. Then I carried everything to the threshold of the kitchen. Renfield stopped his crying when he saw me coming.

I laid out the cushions on the floor the way they were on the couch. I put the pillow at the head of the string, nearest Renfield and just into the kitchen. Then I lay down, pulling the blanket over me. He false-started toward my face with his front paw a couple of times, like a high-spirited horse scratching the ground with a forehoof.

I extended my index finger to him. He grabbed it with the clawless paw, squeezing it reflexively. The way an infant does.

I said, "Renfield, if you ever breathe a word of this . . ."

At which point he purred once, then again, and slid back into the peace of sleep.

22

WHEN I WOKE UP SATURDAY MORNING, MY BACK FELT AS BAD AS Renfield's legs looked. Hunched up on his front ones, he did take a little water by dipping a forepaw into the dish and then licking the pads.

The phone rang as I was munching on some Frosted Flakes. When I put the receiver to my ear, the line was full of static. "Hello?"

"John, it's Nancy."

"Thought I might get a call last night."

"I tried, but there was something wrong with the circuits here. I nearly went crazy until I gave up around one A.M."

"How did your talk go?"

"Fine. How's my kitty?"

"Kind of rocky."

"Oh, John, don't torture me long-distance, okay?"

"Okay. He's having trouble getting to his feet. Shaky would be a good description. He cried a lot when I got him here, but he's evened out a bit since then."

"You stayed with him all night?"

"As promised."

"Oh, John, thank you."

"I do consider it above and beyond."

"The call of duty, you mean?"

"That's right."

"I'll plan something special for when I get back."

"Still tomorrow noon?"

"Uh-huh. Can you stay with Renfield till I get there?"

"Yes, but I didn't bring a change of clothes."

"Don't worry. For what I have planned, you won't need any clothes."

I spent most of Saturday morning in the living room, carrying Renfield in with me and laying a plastic trash bag as an exterior diaper under his towel. He seemed content to stay on the floor, sleeping.

After I finished the Estleman book, I started a Linda Barnes one that was set in Boston with a female private investigator. Halfway through that, the *Game of the Week* came on the tube, Jack Buck and Tim McCarver almost making me forget Vin Scully. Almost.

The phone rang three times, a couple of hours apart. I let Nancy's machine do its thing. The first time was just a hang-up. The second and third stopped ringing before the tape could cut into the call.

As the day progressed, so did Renfield. He took more water and even a little dry food, purring whenever I came near him. By nightfall, he was actually up and walking. Rickety, but on all fours.

Nancy had some thin pork chops in a back corner of the freezer. Shake 'n Baked, they went down with a bottle of no-vintage chardonnay, Renfield even getting enthusiastic enough to take some rice-sized scraps from the chops.

That evening I finished the Barnes book and started to get cabin fever. I turned the television back on, picking up a *Best of Nature* courtesy of Channel 2. Cheetah, shoulder muscles bristling, stalked baby antelope through high grass. Chameleons with independently roving eyes and sticky tongues slurped butterflies from twigs. Arctic foxes in a lush valley waited with infinite patience as young barnacle geese rappeled without ropes down jagged cliffs. After a week with the Danucci family, I felt for the antelopes, butterflies, and geese of the world.

Following the PBS show, I watched some network show that was so inane I at first thought *Saturday Night Live* had started two hours early. I went to bed, again on my couch cushions next to Renfield, thinking I had to stay around pets less or drink more.

"Oh, my God, John, he looks absurd!"

It was Sunday, just past noontime. After replacing the cushions on the couch, I'd snuck out for five minutes to get the Sunday papers. I'd just finished a photo ad in *Parade* magazine for Zamfir, Master of the Pan Flute. Finally understanding what Johnny Carson was always railing about, I heard a key turn in the lock.

Nancy dropped her garment bag to the kitchen floor as Renfield labored to his feet, doing one flop-over that I thought seemed faked for her benefit. She ignored me, rushing over to him and cooing and cuddling the little critter until I thought the thread from his sutures would burst.

"Nance?"

Over the shoulder she said, "Yes?"

"The vet said to be careful around the stitches."

"Poor little guy. If I'd had any idea he'd look this bad, John, I'd never have gone to the convention."

"He's going to be fine."

Nancy left her cat long enough to come give me a hug, then wrinkle her nose. "You were right about your shirt."

"It's only on its third day."

"Go."

"I thought you said I wouldn't need any clothes?"

"Don't worry about whether they match."

"How about if I pick up some Chinese or Thai?"

"Great. You have beer at the condo?"

"Yes."

"Better bring some. I think I'm out."

I said, "You're running a little low on wine, too."

"Small reward for a man who went so far above and beyond."

"They're probably making up songs about me to chant around campfires."

Nancy's eyes suddenly glistened. "John, please just go for a while, then come back."

I got serious. "Sure."

"I need some time alone with Renfield, and I know I'm going to cry and I don't want you here again for that."

"Okay. I'll be back around . . . ?"

"Five?"

"Five it is."

Another hug, this one longer despite the condition of my shirt. "Thank you, John. I mean it."

"I know."

The young black officer in front of the blue police barricade was smiling, but only barely. He'd just gotten through with a woman who seemed determined to get detour directions to North Carolina when I pulled up Berkeley Street to the intersection of Newbury and asked him what the trouble was.

He hitched a thumb toward the river and said, "Walk for Hunger. Can't cross Commonwealth for an hour or so."

Behind the barrier I could see a throng of people moving toward downtown on the Commonwealth Avenue mall. I nodded to the cop and turned left onto Newbury, lucking out with a metered space about halfway between Exeter and Fairfield. I left the Prelude and took Fairfield to Commonwealth, waiting for a lull in the parade to continue over toward Beacon.

Young men and women in yellow T-shirts and orange safety vests clapped for the marchers and acted as crossing guards against occasional cars on the street. Literally hundreds of people were going by in a steady stream. All ages and colors, many wearing white painters' hats. Lots of mothers and dads with little kids, most of them in shorts and athletic shoes but some wearing sweatshirts or sweaters against the early May air. They ate apples and pears pulled from small knapsacks, otherwise holding hands.

Most of the marchers had yellow decals, big and round, with WALK FOR HUNGER and the date on them. Others had small buttons with the same legend and background. 'Blaster radios and balloons, wheelchairs and strollers. Some folks were wilting, others almost goose-stepping with energy.

I went up to one of the crossing guards. She had sandy hair parted in the center and tied into a ponytail and looked so collegiate it hurt. I asked her how far the marchers had come.

"Twenty miles, most of them."

"You're kidding?"

"Uh-unh. Almost forty thousand people this year, and we hope to raise four million dollars for the homeless and the hungry, most of it going to Project Bread."

I thought about the last homeless person I'd known, a guy who had trained me for the marathon. I took out my wallet and handed her a twenty.

She looked at it and said, "What's that?"

"A donation."

"But I'm not like, authorized or anything."

"I'm not worried about where it'll end up. Take it."

She did. "Well, thanks. Have a nice day, huh?"

I should have remembered that the last person to say that to me was one Lieutenant Holt of Boston Homicide.

"Cuddy!"

I was about to put my key in the lock of the front door of the condo building when I heard the voice over the opening of a car door. Turning around, I saw Primo Zuppone standing at the curb, the driver's side of his Lincoln still open, one of his hands resting on top of the window frame. The leather coat lay on the leather seat behind him.

Zuppone said, "Where the fuck you been?"

I went back to the lock. "Nursing a sick friend."

His footsteps came across the sidewalk and up the stoop as I pushed on the door. He put his hand on my arm. I looked down at the hand, then up to his face, the pockmarks seeming a little inflamed.

"Cuddy, you gotta understand something."

"First take your hand off my arm."

Zuppone sent out a little breath, but let go of my arm. With an effort.

"Cuddy, you're supposed to coordinate with me."

"Not the way I remember it. You're supposed to help me, if I need help."

"Hey-ey-ey," the loose tone back, "don't you think I gotta know what you're doing, I'm supposed to help you?"

"Primo, look. I've been gone a couple of days—"

"You're telling me?"

"—and I need a shower and a change of clothes. Then we can talk."

Primo checked his watch, then looked to his car. Thinking of the phone in it, I guessed.

"Okay. Say, what, half an hour?"

"Half an hour should do it. Why?"

"Somebody wants to talk to you."

The Lincoln slalomed its way up Beacon, the cars double-parked on either side of the street, before taking a right onto the bridge across the Charles River to Cambridge and MIT. There was a solo guitar coming over the audio system.

Around his toothpick Zuppone said, "Michael Hedges."

"Somebody named Michael Hedges wants to see me?"

"No, no. Michael Hedges is the guy on this tape. Soothing, ain't it?"

It was. Until I remembered that soothing music like this was probably the last cultural experience of several people unfortunate enough to cross Tommy Danucci.

I shook it off. "By the way, I enjoyed that Mertens cassette you gave me."

"Yeah? Great. He's the best." Zuppone glanced in his mirrors. "So, where you been all this time?"

"Like I told you, doing some nursing."

"At the D.A.'s over in Southie?"

Primo could have seen my car parked in front of her house, but first he'd have to know where Nancy lived, and she had an unlisted telephone number.

I said evenly, "I hope I don't have to tell you to stay away from there."

Both hands came innocently off the wheel. "Hey-ey-ey, I never been near the place. Just called a coupla times, see if maybe I got you."

The phone calls yesterday. Meaning pretty good contacts within New England Telephone.

"Primo, can you get me the phone records on Tina's local calls?"

"What, from her apartment there, you mean?"

"Yes. For the week she was killed."

"I don't know. Documents, they're tougher to get than just numbers."

"Can you try?"

Zuppone ticktocked his head. "Sure. Sure, I can try."

"Thanks."

He gave me another look. "You're still worrying about your girlfriend. Don't. No way we'd go near a D.A., Cuddy. They're off limits, you know? The government, it don't hit us like some fucking Spic death squad, and we don't hit them or their families, don't even go around there. The Jamaicans, now, or the Dominicans, I can't speak for those fucking maniacs. They're liable to do anything to anybody. But us, you got no worries. One of us clipped a D.A. or a cop on purpose—I don't mean an accident, like thinking some undercover guy's one of ours, dropping a dime on us—but one of us clipped a government guy knowing he was government? Shit, the family'd hand the member over to the cops themselves, no questions asked."

"You wouldn't be afraid of the guy singing to get a better plea?"

Zuppone gave me a different look. "Cuddy, we hand the guy over, he's gonna be dead first."

Of course. Which reminded me. "Where are we going, Primo?"

"Mr. Danucci, he wants to see you."

"Which one?"

"Which one." Zuppone turned onto Memorial Drive, heading east back toward Boston. "The Mr. Danucci, which one."

"What about?"

Zuppone debated something, finally deciding to talk about it. "The fuck is all this shit about keys?"

"To the second floor in Mau—Tina's building?"

"All the keys, any keys. What the fuck do we care about keys, the girl was choked out by some B & E crackhead?"

"How did you know about the keys, Primo?"

"Way I know about everything. People call me, talk to me. Like you oughta be talking to me now. What the fuck difference do keys make here?"

A side of Zuppone he hadn't shown before. Edgy, finding it harder to slip into the loose mode and stay there.

"Primo, if a burglar didn't do it, somebody else did. And probably that somebody had to use a key some way."

"Let's hear why a burglar didn't do it."

"The first-floor tenant, Sinead Fagan, was in the kitchen just before Tina was killed. Fagan heard water running through the pipes there from Tina's shower."

"So what?"

"A burglar has to go up the fire escape to get in as well as down it to get out."

Zuppone nodded a few times, then turned the car onto the Longfellow Bridge back across the river. "And this Sinead, she'd see somebody going up the fire escape next to her window."

I tried not to hesitate. "You can picture it?"

"Sure I can picture it. The fire escape runs right past her kitchen there."

"Okay. Either Fagan or her boyfriend—"

"This the colored guy?"

"I understand you've met."

The toothpick rotated clockwise. "You could say that, yeah."

"So either Fagan or Puriefoy can spot somebody going up the escape. They could hear that first flight come down, too, because it makes a hell of a racket and the kitchen window was open. That leaves us with how the killer got into the building."

Zuppone looked down at his dashboard. "What about the back door to the building?"

"Can't be opened from the outside, and Ooch said he always kept it bolted from the inside."

Primo checked his mirrors. "So, maybe the guy got buzzed in the front door."

"Not by Fagan. And probably not by Tina either, she just stepped out of the shower."

"She's expecting her new boyfriend, though, right?"

This time I did hesitate. "You've been getting a lot of phone calls."

"Like I said, people talk to me. So somebody rings Tina's bell, she thinks it's the Jap, she buzzes him in."

"Only you can hear both the bell and the buzzer inside Fagan's apartment."

"From Tina's, two floors up there?"

"Yes. And Fagan and Puriefoy never heard bell or buzzer till Larry Shinkawa arrived, and they let him in."

Zuppone passed up a street that would have taken us more directly to Tommy Danucci's house in the North End. "What you're saying is, somebody had to have a key to get in the front door of the building."

"I think so."

"And a key to get into Tina's apartment?"

"Not necessarily."

"The fuck does that mean?"

"She—Tina—could have let whoever it was in her door, once she was out of the shower."

"What, she hears a knock at the door and just opens up?"

"She knew she was late to the party downstairs and figures it's just one of them coming up to find out what's taking her so long."

Zuppone rolled the pick again. "Possible."

"Also, anybody who has a key to the building door is probably somebody she'd recognize anyway."

The pick stopped. "She wasn't supposed to give out none of those keys to anybody."

"And I don't know that she did."

Zuppone hit the brakes, the Lincoln slewing into a loading zone. He slammed the gearshift into park, not bothering with the parking brake. Tearing the toothpick out of his mouth and breaking it between two fingers, he turned to me violently. "The fuck are you saying here? That ain't some fucking safe house."

"What do you mean by 'safe house'?"

"Aw, one of the . . . this friend of ours, he likes the spy novels. The way I go for the New Age music, okay? He decides we need some new places to stash a guy . . . To keep a guy or some stuff on ice for a while. In the spy books, they call those things 'safe houses.' But fucking Mother, Cuddy, only the family used that second-floor apartment. Nobody's gonna put a safe house under his own blood."

"I wouldn't think so."

"What I mean is, they don't give the keys to the building to anybody. Tina didn't give one out, and that Sinead broad didn't give one out, then only the family has any."

I didn't bring up the front door key Sinead left with the agency. Instead, I braced myself before saying, "You have keys to that building, Primo?"

All the blood drained from his cheeks, and he breathed heavily. "I'm gonna . . . I'm gonna make like I didn't hear that, okay? Because I don't wanna have to take you to Mr. Danucci without your face on."

"I think it's—"

"What you're saying here is one of the family whacked Tina? You got rocks in your fucking head?"

"You want to hear it or not?"

Zuppone breathed three more times, reining himself in, the hand shaking as he turned off the music. "I wanna hear it. Real slow, no big words."

"There are a lot of possibilities, but one keeps coming around. The killer uses a key on the front door, goes up, and gets let in by Tina or uses a key on her door, too."

Zuppone seemed about to say something, then shook his head.

"He kills her, hears Shinkawa at the apartment door, and then Shinkawa going back downstairs and coming back up with the others. The killer tries to go down the fire escape, only I don't think he gets far enough before they break through the door."

"What do you mean, far enough?"

"Shinkawa hears somebody on the escape and rushes to the window, but nobody's there below him."

I waited for Zuppone to catch up to me. "The guy that did Tina used the escape there to go down, but he ain't there when the Jap looks out?"

"Right."

"So the guy goes in Sinead's window. You said it was open, right?"

"No good. The sash weights aren't working. Nobody could lift the window high enough to slip in through it."

"So . . . what, the guy drops ten, twelve feet to the ground?"

"But then Shinkawa would have seen him or heard him running up the alley."

Zuppone squirmed against the leather upholstery. "Then how does the guy get away?"

"I think he went in the second-floor window."

Zuppone smiled confidently. "Never happen. The guy couldn't get out the second-floor door without . . ."

Zuppone chewed on it, shook his head, then kept shaking it. "Fucking Christ. That can't be it, Cuddy. That can't be how the guy got away."

"I think it is. So either he had the keys he needed, or he planned it pretty long and pretty cool and pretty tight on the timing."

"What do you mean, he planned it?"

23

TOMMY DANUCCI ASKED ME THE SAME QUESTION AT THE SAME POINT in the story as Primo Zuppone. The difference was that Danucci and I were sitting in a tiny espresso shop just off Hanover Street in the North End. Although we were the only patrons, there were five tables in all, each a circular slab of gray marble resting on a base of black wrought iron. The chair seats were round and padded like bar stools with backs, but they also sat on wrought iron bases. The bases were so heavy I nearly sprained a wrist pulling mine back.

Primo had to move Danucci's chair out and in for him, then went to the counter man who waited fervently to hear our order. Capuccino with whipped cream for Danucci, hot chocolate and no cream for me. After bringing our cups and saucers to the table, Zuppone took up some wall space, legs bent out a little.

Danucci said, "So, Mr. Detective, what do you mean, he planned it?"

"First, let's assume a burglar didn't kill Tina."

"The fuck you talking about? He stole the necklace."

"The necklace broke, somewhere in the living room, during the struggle. How do you explain that?"

"Explain it? The fucking crackhead had it in his hands and my Tina tried to take it back."

"Take it back from him?"

"Sure, sure. My Tina, she loved that piece. It was what she had from her grandmother, what I gave her after my Amatina died. Tina woulda fought for her necklace, anybody tried to take it."

I went through how unlikely that was, given where the pendant and body were found.

Danucci sipped his capuccino. "So, maybe she was wearing it, eh?"

"Wearing it?"

"You're telling me, Tina was strangled with my Amatina's necklace against her throat. Either the crackhead had it in his hand, or she was wearing it."

"Why would she be wearing it?"

Danucci shrugged. "Maybe for the party."

"I don't think so. She was just in her robe from the shower, and the party itself was supposed to be pretty casual, a little wine before people went out to celebrate."

"Maybe she was trying it on. For the dinner the next night."

"Maybe. But she was already late for the party downstairs, and she had all the next day to decide what to wear for dinner on Saturday."

Danucci looked impatient. "All right, all right. She wasn't wearing it, then. So tell me, it's not a burglar, what's your theory?"

"With Sinead in the kitchen near her open window, I don't think the killer came up the fire escape. He, or she, came through the front door of the building."

"What's this 'he or she' shit?"

"Okay. Assume it's a man, too. One possibility is that he has a key to the building, comes in, and gets up to the third floor, but has the presence of mind, and prior knowledge, to go to Tina's kitchen and take the pimpled key to the second-floor door that Tina kept in a drawer. He kills Tina, then goes out and down the fire escape, ducking into the second-floor window while Larry Shinkawa is running to the bedroom window and looking down on the fire escape. Then, using Tina's key from the drawer, the guy lets himself quietly out the second floor and down the interior stairs and out the front door of the building, replacing the key in the drawer some time later."

Danucci wagged his head. "Too complicated."

"I agree. It gets worse if we try one of the party-goers."

"Explain it to me."

"Start with Shinkawa. He could have gotten into the building if he had a key to the front door, gone upstairs, and gotten Tina to open her apartment door. He kills her, then leaves the building and rings Sinead to be let back in. He suggests to Puriefoy and Fagan that they go up to Tina's apartment, then climbs the stairs alone to knock and yell at Tina's door before coming back down to get the others."

"Simpler. What's wrong with that?"

"The chain was on Tina's door. Whoever left her apartment after killing her couldn't go out her door and leave it still chained. And Sinead would have spotted him coming down the fire escape."

Danucci shook his head again, sipping the capuccino. I hadn't touched my hot chocolate.

The old man said, "Same for the colored photographer?"

"I think so. Puriefoy could have left Sinead's apartment to go out for wine, but instead he climbs the stairs, gets Tina to let him in, and kills her. Then he actually goes out for the wine and comes back all innocent. But with the chain on, he would have to go out the bedroom window and down the fire escape past Sinead in her kitchen. Since we know Tina was taking a shower with the water running through Sinead's pipes just a few minutes earlier, it's hard to imagine either Shinkawa or Puriefoy could have timed it just so. Besides, they wouldn't have had to try."

"I don't get you."

"Tina knew both of them well enough to buzz them into the

227

building and let them into her apartment. Either one could have killed her any time he wanted without planning a split-second, *Mission Impossible* caper around the party."

The blood started to rise through Danucci's face. "I'd take it as a favor, Mr. Detective, you didn't use old television shows to talk about my granddaughter's death."

"Sorry."

Danucci pushed his cup and saucer three inches to the side. Zuppone immediately came over and asked if he wanted another. The abrupt nod and Primo was off to the counterman.

While he was gone, Danucci used a low, menacing tone to me. "So, you're saying it's family?"

"Not necessarily. It could be anybody who didn't know about the party at Sinead's that night."

"Why?"

"Because somebody who didn't know about the party wouldn't be trying to time things so closely. If the guy had a front door key and knew about the second-floor key, he could have gone to the house that night and opened the building door by coincidence when Sinead's door was closed and neither Shinkawa nor Puriefoy were coming or going."

Zuppone brought Danucci his capuccino and leaned back against the wall.

I said, "The guy then goes up to Tina's apartment, has a key to her door or she lets him in, then he puts the chain on—"

"Wait a minute. Why him with the chain?"

"Somebody had to put the chain on, and Shinkawa said Tina never used it, broke a nail on it a couple of times."

"Broke a nail?"

"Fingernail."

Danucci shook his head. "Okay, okay. The guy puts the chain on."

"And then kills her. He hears Shinkawa at the door and probably freezes, then panics and realizes from the noise that the party is coming to him. So he runs to the kitchen, gets the key to the second floor, and goes out the fire escape and then into the second-floor window."

Danucci tasted the new capuccino. "That makes a little sense, maybe." He set the cup down and watched me, then seemed to steel himself. "But you still think it's family."

"I haven't seen or heard anything that leads me to believe that anybody other than Ooch knew Tina kept the second-floor key in her kitchen drawer. And the key was back there when I checked on it Friday."

"So, you're saying the guy didn't take that key with him."

"Or he put it back before I checked the drawer, which seems tough. If we eliminate Sinead Fagan, too, because of the close timing problem and plenty of other opportunities, we're left with family, I think."

"What, because Ooch had his own key?"

"I don't follow you."

Danucci said, "What I mean is, everybody's got their own keys, Mr. Detective. I got mine, Joey's got his—Hey, Primo?"

Zuppone came off his wall. "Yes, Mr. Danucci?"

"You got a set of keys to the Falmouth property, right?"

Zuppone didn't get angry this time. "Somewheres."

Danucci came back to me. "Mr. Vincent Dani, Esquire, he's the trustee or whatever the fuck you call it, he's got a set. We all got keys, but nobody's got no reason to kill Tina. Your theory's all fulla shit there."

At that point, the door to the shop flew open and three teenagers came in, jostling and punching each other on the arms. All were male and black-haired, the sideburns cut half an inch above the ear, the rest moussed up and combed back. They each wore baggy athletic pants in different metallic colors and Air Jordan sneakers. They ordered three espressos as they yanked out chairs.

Tommy Danucci cued Zuppone with his eyebrows. Zuppone moved toward them.

"Hey-ey-ey, guys, how about you get lost for a while, huh? We got a little meeting going on."

One of the kids smirked at Primo. Raising his right hand slowly, its back toward Zuppone, the kid sent his index, middle, and ring fingers northward. "Read between the lines, zit rack."

If I hadn't been expecting it, I'm not sure I would have seen Primo's hand moving. It closed around the kid's three fingers, and I heard a snap. The bravado left the boy's face as he howled, standing up only to drop to his knees, the three fingers dangling loosely, like a glove when your fingers aren't in the sleeves.

The other two kids took one look at Primo and took off, the third kid teetering up and through the door just before it closed behind his friends. The counterman seemed particularly engrossed in a saucer he was washing.

Zuppone came back, huffing a little from excitement rather than exertion. "Sorry, Mr. Danucci."

"An insult nobody could take, Primo." Then to me, "The old days, their families would of known me and told them to be respectful. Now. . . ." A dismissive wave.

I waited him out.

Danucci cupped his hand around the new capuccino, but didn't lift it. "Like I was saying, your theory's all fulla shit. Besides, it all depends on the Jap, right?"

"On Shinkawa's hearing the fire escape, yes."

"So, maybe he's lying."

"Why?"

"The fuck do I know why? You're the detective, right?"

"He'd only be lying if he did it, and that brings us back to the timing and choosing a bad opportunity given that he knew about the party downstairs."

"Okay, okay. Let me tell you something else, so you'll know it. Maybe he's just mistaken, eh?"

"About hearing the clanging?"

"About it being that fire escape. There're—what, Primo, twenny buildings backing on that alley there?"

"Easy twenty, Mr. Danucci."

"So call it twenny, twenny-two, whatever. When the Jap goes to the window, he looks down, right?"

"That's what he told me."

"So, he looks down and maybe at the alley, too. He don't look around to the other buildings, see if somebody's on one or a pot falls over, am I right?"

Danucci had a point. "And if Shinkawa is wrong about some-body being on the fire escape . . ."

"Then it don't got to be family, which I don't see in the first place. Then the fucking crackhead did this to my Tina coulda heard the Jap at the door, then gone down the fire escape all the way to the bottom and run up the fucking alley while the Jap and everybody is coming up the stairs and busting down the door, right?"

"Except for one thing."

"What?"

"How does our burglar get into the building in the first place without going past Sinead Fagan by the kitchen window or using a key on the front door to the building?"

Danucci wiped his face with the palm of his hand. "That just means somebody we don't know about had a key to the front door. Somebody who didn't know about the party account of you and your timing thing. Find out who it was."

Which led me back to George Yulin and Erica Lindqvist. "Slightly different question?"

"Go ahead."

"How come Primo went to scare Oz Puriefoy away from dating Tina?"

Danucci's blood rose. "Dating her? The fucking monkey was living with her."

"How did you find out they were together?"

Danucci looked to Primo, but not so much to ask him to answer as just to make sure he could hear what the old man was about to say. "My daughter-in-law, she called me about it."

"Your . . . ?"

"Claudette, from down on the South Shore there. She got wind Tina was seeing a colored, and Claudette was worried Joey might do something to the guy, he found out. Besides, she—I don't know, from over in Vietnam there, she was scared stiff of them."

"Fucking right to be," said Primo casually.

"Your daughter-in-law wanted you to scare Puriefoy off."

231

"Yeah. So I asked Primo, could he stop by, pay the guy a visit, let him know what's what."

I looked at Primo, who just nodded.

Danucci said, "What difference does it make, who Primo scared off?"

"Except for Puriefoy and Sinead Fagan, I'm not sure anybody else knew your granddaughter was connected."

The old man thought about that. "So, one of the others, he didn't know my Tina was my Tina, eh?"

"Or her father's daughter. To everybody else, she's just a beautiful young model, but not otherwise dangerous."

Danucci nodded. "It's a possibility. Anything else you need to know?"

"Why didn't Primo scare off Larry Shinkawa, too?"

Danucci stared at me. "Claudette, she never told me about the Jap. Besides, he's an Oriental, more her own kind. Probably Claudette, she knows about him, she don't have no problem with him."

"And Joey?"

"The fuck do I know? He married one, right?"

Danucci offered to have Primo drive me back to my condo, but I chose to walk instead. The two miles cleared my head a little as I thought things through.

If Mau Tim was wearing the necklace to the party, or just admiring it while she waited for her hair to dry, it would explain how she had the marks from it on her throat without the "burglar" holding it in his hands. If somebody outside the family had a key to the front door of the building, and at least Yulin and Lindqvist had access to one at the agency, then somebody outside the family could have gotten in that way. If Larry Shinkawa was wrong about hearing somebody on the fire escape, then the killer could have gone down it after Shinkawa first knocked at Mau Tim's apartment door and while Fagan, Puriefoy, and Shinkawa were back at the door before they broke it down. Close timing, awfully close, but just possible.

I decided to spend Monday checking those "ifs." But it wasn't Monday yet.

"Oh, John, he can't beg anymore."

"I wasn't trying to get him to beg. The chicken just stuck to my fingers a little."

Renfield was under Nancy's glass-topped coffee table. She and I were sitting cross-legged on the floor on either side of it, enjoying the tail end of a Thai take-out I'd brought back with me. While I was gone, Nancy had changed into a white cotton safari shirt and red tennis shorts. The cat was doing noticably better in attitude, though he still moved like a newborn foal.

After I gave him another bit of white meat, Renfield tried to worm his way over my ankles. At first he purred and led with a paw the way he had the first night. Then he began to cry a little.

From the other side of the table, Nancy watched him through the glass. "Renfield, what's gotten into you?"

I said, "Beats me."

When the cat wouldn't quit crying, I put down my utensils and lifted him gently onto my lap. "Paws off the table, right?"

Renfield gave my hand a lick and purred loudly.

Nancy dropped her fork. "I don't believe this."

"Believe what?"

"When I left him at the vet's, I would have bet he'd bite your arm off. And now . . ."

I said, "I was around when he was hurting. He's just imprinted on me a little."

"Imprinted."

"That's what the vet said. It'll probably wear off."

Renfield started licking my belt buckle.

Nancy said, "Could this have anything to do with the cushions?"

"What cushions?"

She arched her head backward. "The seat cushions from the couch. They do come off, as you'll remember from the night he got hurt. After you left to get fresh clothes, I noticed they weren't arranged zipper-to-back the way I always have them.''

At the sound of the word "zipper," the cat shifted his attention southward.

I said, "Renfield trashed the living room while I was asleep in your bed. I did my best to cover for him."

The cat found the tab of my zipper, got one of his teeth through the little hole, and started to tug down on it.

I said, "Renfield, you're embarrassing me."

"He just doesn't have quite the right angle." Nancy slowly got up from her haunches. "Here, let me."

24

ON MONDAY MORNING, I DROVE NANCY TO WORK AND THEN STOPPED at the condo to shower and change. By ten o'clock I was walking through the doors of Berry/Ryder and asking the still-stunning receptionist for Larry Shinkawa.

I watched her select an inside line on the switchboard, murmur something into it, and nod to herself. She stood and beckoned.

"Larry Shin's in the conference room, but he told me to bring you by."

I said, "Thank you" to the back of her head as she led me down a hall, knocked once on a closed door, and smiled as a good-bye.

I heard, "Come on in."

Behind the door were Shinkawa and two middle-aged Caucasian males. All three were hovering over a go-fish array of photos that nearly covered a conference table.

Shinkawa lifted his horn-rims up and onto his hair, like sunglasses. "This one with the Scotch bottle, and this one with the noodles coming out of the carton." He looked at me with the yearbook smile. "John, good to see you." To the Caucasian males, he said, "Be right back, but maybe the one with just Mariel and the ice bucket, too."

The two men nearly trampled each other saying, "Same here, Larry."

Shinkawa came out and past me, speaking back over his shoulder. "Good to see you, John."

Following him down the hall, I wondered if he realized he'd said the same thing to me twice.

At his office, I took the black leather and chrome sling chair I'd used the last time, Shinkawa preferring its mate to going around behind his desk. He wore the slacks to a suit and another pin-striped shirt and expensive tie, but the collar button was undone and the sleeves turned up.

The advertising man brought the glasses back down onto his nose. "What's up?"

"I'm sorry to trouble you again."

"Hey, no trouble. We're just working on a new campaign. Planning stages for targeting the A-A community."

"The . . . ?"

"The Asian-American community. They've been doing it for years on the West Coast. You commission some market studies to get an idea of what a Japanese-American or Chinese-American looks for in booze, cars, or clothes. Then you target some of your advertising to print media the given group reads. It's done all the time with your Blacks and Hispanics."

"And now for Asian-Americans."

The big smile. "There'll be ten million of us in this country by the year 2000."

"How about Vietnamese-Americans?"

Shinkawa realigned his horn-rims. "Does this have something to do with Mau Tim?"

"I'm wondering whether she would have been used in this effort."

"Oh. Oh, probably, but not because we'd be targeting Vietnamese consumers. They're not big enough/rich enough yet. But would I have found a place for Mau in the campaign? You bet I would. This or any other campaign except for whole milk or Girl Scout cookies. Now, what can I do for you?"

"I've been out to the apartment house on Falmouth. I wonder if I could go over some of what you told me last time."

"Sure."

"You said that as you and Oz Puriefoy and Sinead Fagan came through the door of Mau Tim's apartment, you heard somebody on the fire escape?"

"Right."

"Did you actually hear a person on it?"

A confused expression. "A person?"

"Yes."

"Well, no. I mean, I didn't hear a voice or anything like that. Just sort of a . . . clang, like I told you last time."

I thought about the last, retractable flight. "Not a squealing or grinding, metal-on-metal sound?"

"No. It was . . . Gee, 'clang' really does it, John. You know, like somebody walking across a grate in the sidewalk?"

"So like somebody taking a step on the fire escape."

"Yes. Yes, in fact it was still vibrating."

I stopped. "What?"

"When I got to the window in Mau's bedroom. I stuck my head out and put my hand on the bannister of the fire escape, like to steady myself? It was still vibrating a little."

"The fire escape itself was still moving?"

"Yeah. I even remember pulling my hand back from it, like it could maybe hurt me. Stupid, I know, but it was kind of scary up there. Like stumbling into a nightmare."

"And you didn't see anybody in the yard by the garbage cans?"

"No. No place really to hide down there either, John."

"Right."

"I mean, the guy must have been quick, to get all the way down the alley and around the corner before the escape stopped moving."

I watched him. A hell of a story to commit yourself to if it weren't true.

"John, you all right?"

"Fine. You said you never met any of Mau Tim's family?"

"No." The big smile again. "Maybe I'm not the type to bring home to Mom and Dad, huh?"

"You knew her mother was Vietnamese?"

"Yes, but like I told you before, Mau was more interested in my family life than she was in talking about her own."

"Larry, her father was—is, Joseph Danucci."

The confused expression, trying to place the reference.

I said, "Her grandfather is Tommy Danucci."

The mouth came open. "The gangster?"

"The same."

"No shit?"

Like I'd just told him Tom Selleck wore a toupee.

"No shit, Larry."

"You've got to tell me, this is really on the level?"

I couldn't understand his attitude. "It is."

The laugh that turned into a giggle. "God-*damn*. I'll go to lunch for a month on this one."

"Huh?"

"The hook, John. The cachet of it. I was boffing a Mafia Princess. This is the best story I've heard in a year."

I stood to go. "Just so the Danucci family doesn't hear it."

The smile shrank only a little. "We really don't travel in the same circles."

I covered the five blocks to the Lindqvist/Yulin agency in ten minutes. As I pushed open the yellow, six-panel door to their reception area, George Yulin was just putting down the phone and standing to see who it was.

"John?"

"Right. That wasn't Larry Shinkawa by any chance?"

Yulin looked at the receiver. "No. Why, are you trying to reach him?"

"Just did. You have a couple of minutes?"

The grizzled hair looked stylishly unkempt, the eyes remembering I could bring him money. "Certainly. Certainly, come into my office."

The same hodgepodge of magazines and photos were spread around his desk and director's chairs. He cleaned one off for me, but this time sat on the edge of his desk.

Yulin said, "Have you finished your investigation?"

"Not quite. Still a few loose ends."

An uneven grin. "I hope I'm not one of them?"

Trying to mend our relationship after the scene at the house in Brookline. "When I was here the last time, you showed me a card with some phone numbers on it."

"Right. Mau Tim's casting card."

"The first number was her uncle's, you said."

"Yes."

"Do you remember if you were able to reach her there frequently?"

Yulin clearly had no idea where I was going. "Well, it has been almost a year, I think, since she started with us, and of course, at the beginning, I wouldn't have been trying to call her that often."

"You remember what times of day or night you did reach her there?"

Yulin shrugged. "Probably late afternoon, when a shoot might come in on short notice and I needed somebody I knew was free. By the time Mau started to hit, she was at Oz Puriefoy's."

"How do you know that?"

Another shrug. "Just the sense of hearing his voice more often when I was trying to reach her."

"More often than hearing her uncle's voice?"

Yulin looked at me. "Yes, I suppose so."

I took a chance. "Tell me, George, should your number have been on that card, too?"

Yulin seemed to think about how to play it, then smiled, even winked. "Once upon a time."

"Mind elaborating?"

"Well, I'm not one to brag, mind you, but occasionally some of the younger ones—not the underage ones, no, never—but the newer models appreciate an . . . older hand at the tiller?"

"You ever in Mau Tim's apartment?"

A stiffening. "The one on . . . where she was killed, you mean?"

"That's what I mean."

"Why, no. I told you that before. It was—the times we saw each other, it was at my place."

"The house in Brookline?"

"Oh, no. That was later. I mean, I was still living in my condo here in town then."

"So you never saw any keys Mau Tim had for other apartments in her building."

More stiffening. "No."

"Never used the key Sinead kept here to get in the front door of their building there?"

"Of course not."

"How about Erica?"

"Erica?"

"Yes. Did she ever use that key?"

"Not that I know of." Yulin tried to get back to conversational. "What does this have to do with anything?"

"You know who Mau Tim's uncle is, George?"

"Some lawyer in a big firm. Look, I already—"

"Know who her father is?"

Yulin started to look exasperated. "Let me take a wild guess. Her uncle's brother?"

"Because of the last name."

"Yes."

"Actually, 'Dani' is kind of a stage name. Like 'Mau Tim.' "

A deep sigh. "And therefore?"

"I understand that Mau Tim was thinking about trying her luck in New York."

Yulin seemed confused again. "I've told you, John. At least twice. We launched Mau Tim. She was loyal to us."

"Like she was loyal to Puriefoy for scouting her."

"That's different."

"Mau Tim was going to leave Boston and leave your agency, George. Five hundred thousand is a nice reverse severance package, don't you think?"

Yulin closed his eyes. Maybe counting to ten. It never helped me much.

"John, there can't possibly be any evidence involving me in Mau Tim's death. To think that my going to bed with her a few times over six months ago could have anything—"

"Mau Tim's birth name was Amatina Danucci."

That last name caught him amidships.

"Her grandfather is Tommy the Temper Danucci, George."

The mouth gaped open, and something rose in his chest. An image of Nancy after the vodka came into my mind.

"George, if I were you, I'd hie me to a bathroom."

Yulin, a hand over his mouth, lunged out and toward the porcelain facility.

"Who's throwing up?"

Erica Lindqvist spoke as I was leaving Yulin's office. Just inside the yellow door, she was stylishly turned in a sweater dress and reptilian belt. An unlined trenchcoat was over one arm, a Gucci handbag trailing from the other hand.

I said, "Your partner."

Lindqvist's voice lost the playful tone. "George doesn't usually do that on company time."

"Something I said didn't agree with him."

She tried to get the light voice back. "Should I wait to hear it till the bathroom's free?"

"I'm not sure I can stay that long."

Lindqvist reached into her bag, coming out with a small leather case. "Let's go up to my apartment, then. I know all the rooms are available there."

25

"WHY DON'T WE SIT OUT ON THE DECK?"

In her living room, Lindqvist laid the trenchcoat over the back of a barrel chair like the ones in her reception area downstairs. The handbag landed on the chair's seat. I followed the cascade of brown hair through a sliding glass door. There was a view of the Charles River over and between buildings, but mostly there was a view of the roofs of the buildings across the alley, buildings that would front on the south side of Commonwealth Avenue.

I said, "Don't you worry about your work getting too close to home?"

"My work brings me pleasure, John. Today in the form of you."

The deck was about twelve-by-twenty, redwood made smudgy by the sooty Boston air. I could see a chaise longue and two chairs, also redwood, with bright print pads and two side tables. The furniture and a gas grill pretty well filled the deck surface, which stopped only a foot or so before the edge

242

of the roof. Around that edge, the gravelly tar and flashing looked well maintained.

Lindqvist said, "I know it's a little early, but can I get you something to drink?"

"No, thanks."

She took the chaise longue, reclining to a reading position. "I take it, then, that you haven't thought much about my offer."

"Sorry?"

"You remember. A little . . . smorgasbord to go with your usual fare?"

"Thanks, but I'm still taken."

Lindqvist watched me, measuring something. "Yes, you do have that look." She shook her head and sat up straighter in the lounge. "I think I'd better hear what you said to George."

"A couple of questions first. You own this building?"

"In a manner of speaking."

"What manner would that be?"

"It's in a realty trust. You know what that is?"

"Uh-huh. What do you do, rent out the space downstairs to the agency and other tenants and the space up here to yourself?"

"That's right."

"Mind telling me where the seed money came from?"

Lindqvist gave me the measuring look again. "Quite a lot of it from that grandfather I told you about."

"Inheritance."

A nod. "Long time ago. The family always said, 'Invest in the land, Erica. The land will always provide for you.' Well, there wasn't much land under this building, but like a filet mignon, what there was is choice."

"Speaking of family, was the lawyer who set up the trust one Vincent Dani by any chance?"

"Vincent . . . He was Mau Tim's uncle?"

"That's right."

Lindqvist appeared puzzled. "Why ask me a question like that?"

"He did the trust work for the building over on Falmouth."

"Where Mau Tim was killed?"

"Right."

"John, I don't get any of this."

"You told me before that the only relative of Mau Tim that you spoke to was her uncle."

"That's right, I think. I mean, I know that's what I told you, and I'm pretty sure I'm right."

"But you never met him or anyone else in her family."

"No. Why?"

"Like I told George downstairs, Mau Tim was connected."

"Connected to what?"

"Tommy the Temper Danucci."

"Danucci? The Mafia boss?"

"Mau Tim, or Tina, was his granddaughter."

Lindqvist's eyes flitted left-right-left. "Oh, God. Oh, my God."

"You and Georgie have a half-million policy on the life of a mobster's favorite offspring."

She sagged back in the lounge chair. "But we never . . . nobody ever—what do they do, 'come around'?"

"They came around. Checked you out discreetly. Thought you looked okay for her. They took a somewhat dimmer view of Oz Puriefoy."

"Oz? Why?"

"Because he's black."

"Oh, God." Lindqvist came forward in the lounge. "What about Sinead?"

"What about her?"

"She's living with Oz. I can't afford to lose another model right now, John."

A woman who could keep her eye on the bouncing ball of business. "The family sent an enforcer around to have a talk with him. About a year ago. I don't see any threat to either of them that way."

"That's good." Lindqvist sagged back again, eyes closed. "That's a relief." Then the eyes opened. "Mau Tim's . . . relatives. Will they be looking for a piece of the policy?"

"They haven't said anything to me about it."

"Should that be a relief, too?"

"I don't know, Erica. I don't work for them. Right now, I'm just trying to work around them."

She seemed to think that over. "They're using you. To find out who killed Mau Tim."

"I'd hate to negotiate against you."

An attempt at a saucy smile. "You wouldn't feel a thing. That you didn't want to, I mean."

"You had a key to her place."

"What?"

"Mau Tim's place. You had a key to her building."

"Oh, no. I mean yes, yes to her building, but Mau Tim never—"

"But Sinead did."

"Yes." Lindqvist seemed to be trying to measure something else, maybe how much I'd found out from the other people I'd seen. "I guess the owners of her building—Oh, God, that's the family, right?"

"Right."

"I guess the owners didn't want keys being given out, but Sinead wanted to be sure that somebody nearby could get into her place if need be. So she gave us a set."

Nearby. What was wrong with Yulin's explanation at the Brookline house finally hit me. "I thought Sinead's family lives just over in Medford?"

Lindqvist's voice turned cautious. "I think that's right."

"Why didn't she give them a set of her keys?"

"For all I know she did."

Lindqvist didn't sound convincing. "You ever use your key, Erica?"

A quick "No." Very quick.

"Where are the keys kept?"

"Downstairs. In a lockbox."

"So George has access to the box as well."

A slow "Yes." Very slow.

"George ever make use of that key, as far as you know?"

"He . . . he went over to see Sinead once."

"Once."

"Yes."

"Why?"

"Why once?"

"Why at all."

"George fancies himself a . . . mentor of sorts."

"To the younger models."

"Yes."

"Male and female?"

Lindqvist gave me a frosty look this time. "Not that I know of."

"I was thinking about him living with Quinn Cotter out in Brookline."

"Oh. Oh, that's purely economics. Or economical, if you want to be specific. George was living beyond his means by quite a lot."

"Because the take from the agency isn't shared fifty-fifty?"

The frosty look. "I brought more to the agency than George did."

"Like the office space."

"And I bring more to the agency than he does. I'm the one who breaks her ass pitching accounts to lechers who can't wait to get through me to get to the girls. I'm the one who creates the market for our models. George sits and plays social director over the telephone."

"And makes house calls."

"House calls?"

"Like on Sinead Fagan."

"Yes."

"But just once."

"Yes."

"We're back to why, Erica."

Lindqvist seemed suddenly tired. "George thought there was something wrong with Sinead. Something she needed to talk out. He was wrong."

"In what way?"

"She'd already talked it out with me."

Sinead and her "quite a lots." I said, "Little sister to big sister."

Lindqvist looked very uncomfortable. "Yes."

"And when George made a pass at her?"

"I didn't say that."

"Sure you did. What did Sinead do?"

"She threw him out. He was no match for her Irish temper."

"What did Sinead tell you, Erica?"

"About George?"

"No. About what she 'needed to talk out'?"

Lindqvist looked even more uncomfortable, the eyes flitting again. "I'm not sure I can tell you that."

"I'm not sure you can get your half-million if you don't."

"So." The frosty look turned frigid. "You turn out to be a bastard after all."

When you're holding the high cards, you don't have to answer things like that.

"All right." Lindqvist dropped the attitude, twisting her hands in her lap. "Sinead had a tough time of it when she was younger."

"What kind of tough time?"

Lindqvist told me.

26

GEORGE YULIN WAS GONE BY THE TIME I GOT BACK DOWNSTAIRS, SO I had to trouble Erica Lindqvist again to find and write out the address I needed. She added the telephone number, but I decided to drive over without calling first.

"The hell do you want here?"

Oz Puriefoy looked at me from inside the front door of a wooden two-decker in Jamaica Plain. Given the open door behind him, I figured he lived on the first floor. I also could hear the tape from Sinead's moving day on a speaker system somewhere inside.

I said, "You two taking some time off?"

"We aren't on any schedule, man. What do you want?"

"I'd like to talk with your roommate."

"I think she's about had her fill of that."

"She can talk to me, or she can talk to the guy who came to see you."

"What guy?"

248

"At your studio. Leather coat and toothpick?"

Puriefoy swallowed once and swung the door wide.

"Like, I don't see why I have to talk to you anymore, awright?"

Fagan wore green stirrup pants, a little hole near the left knee. The striped cotton sweater she wore on top was too big, baggy at the waist, elbows, and wrists. Her cocklebur hair was matted here and there. With no makeup, she looked so young.

"Sinead, there are some things I need to know about Mau Tim that I don't think you've told me."

"So what makes you think I know anything to tell you now, huh?"

I waited a minute, hoping to let the silence soften her. Puriefoy had left us alone in a small room off the kitchen, the place being larger inside than it looked from the street. Fagan slumped in one of three beanbag chairs. I'd pulled a straight-back in from the kitchen and tried not to look down at her too much.

"You were her best friend, Sinead."

"So what makes you think I'd tell if I did know?"

A little progress. "I just came from Erica Lindqvist."

Fagan pouted. "So?"

"She told me what happened between you and your stepfather."

"That fucking bitch!"

The last word rose to a nerve-curdling shriek.

"Sinead—"

"The fuck right does she have to tell you shit?"

Puriefoy's head appeared in the doorway. "Hey, babe. Everything cool?"

"No, it isn't fucking cool, Oz. Get out of my face, awright?"

Puriefoy showed her both palms. "Okay, okay. Yell your heads off. The Haitians upstairs, I'm sure they understand how two white folks got to let loose from time to time."

Fagan ran the forearm of the sweater over her eyes. "Oz, just go away for a while, please?"

249

Puriefoy looked from her to me to her. "Okay. I'll go get us some ice cream for later. Rocky Road?"

I thought it sounded appropriate, but Fagan just nodded in a "whatever" way and dropped her head.

She waited until the apartment door closed. Then she waited a little longer, picking at the fabric of her pants near the knee hole. "Erica shouldn't have told you that shit."

"She didn't tell me much. Just enough to know I ought to hear it from you."

"Why?" The face came up, tears welling at each corner of her eyes. I suddenly remembered how truly young Sinead Fagan was, a woman's body wrapped around a teenager's mind and emotions.

"Because you told Mau Tim about it, too."

I didn't know that for sure until Fagan dropped her head again and said, "So what?"

I let out a breath. "Sinead, look. I'm sorry I had to interrupt your shoot, and I'm sorry I made you go through finding the body again. But I'm grasping at straws here, trying to make sense of what happened. What could have happened."

A shake of the head.

"Sinead?"

She drew her knees up to her chest, embracing them the way a track star does on a cold day.

"Sinead, I'm trying to find out who killed your friend."

"My life's got nothing to do with that. My stepfather's gone. He went to California like three, four years ago."

"Please. I promise you it won't go any further than this room."

A laugh. Sarcastic, cutting. "Yeah, that's a good line. Real fucking good. You get that from Erica?"

"No."

" 'Cause that's the same fucking thing she said to me when I told her about it."

"I forced it out of Erica, Sinead. Nobody'll force it out of me."

"Sure."

"Sinead, I promise."

Fagan looked up at me. "Awright. Awright, I'll tell you what I told Mau, okay?"

"Okay."

"No . . . details. Just what we were talking about."

I sat back and tried to relax.

Fagan took another swipe at her eyes with the sleeve of the sweater. "Mau and me were sitting around her place one night, and we were thinking about maybe getting a video, you know, except it was raining, almost snowing. So she starts working the remote and finds a channel showing this Ted Danson movie called *Something About Amelia*. Well, like the title rang a bell somewheres, but I couldn't remember why and Mau always thought Ted Danson was so boss on *Cheers*, so she says, let's watch it. And I says okay, and then two minutes later I remember it's about this guy, this father, who's fucking his daughter. Like fucking her, and the wife, the mother, doesn't even know.

"So I tell Mau to turn the thing off. And she says, but I think Ted Danson is just so boss, and I get up and take the remote away from her and turn the fucking thing off. And she says, what's the matter? And I tell Mau how my mom's new husband always used to hit on me. Always around when I was trying to take a shower or get dressed for something. And how one night, he . . . he didn't just hit on me, awright? And how the fucker kept coming back, like one night a week, trying to get more. And Mau, she's watching me, with those great eyes of hers? And she's listening to me tell her about my step' and what I did to get even, why he had to go out to California and all."

Fagan seemed to run out of steam. I chanced a question. "What did you do to get even?"

She looked up at me absently, then just shrugged, a little girl realizing the worst was over. "My step', my mom told me he was supposed to get this big promotion at work. She was always like that, always paying more attention to what was going on at work with him instead of at home with me. So, anyway, I got the fucker good. What I did was, I called up his boss and told him my step' was a baby-raper."

Jesus Christ.

"It got my step's fucking ass in the fucking sling and even my mom had to throw him out. And of course he didn't just lose the promotion. He lost his job, too. That's why he had to go out to the coast like that."

"And you told Mau about all this?"

"Yeah."

"When?"

The little girl shrug. "I dunno."

"You said before it was almost snowing out."

"Right. It was like, I dunno, a couple months ago."

"A couple of months."

"Yeah. That's why it can't have nothing to do with her being dead, see?"

"Did Mau Tim ever say anything to you about it?"

"No."

"Nothing?"

"No. Well, just that night."

"That night?"

"The night I told her about my step'."

"What did she say?"

"Something like . . . The fuck was it? Oh, yeah, Mau says, 'That'd never work with far-far'."

"What?"

"Her eyes got all weird and she says something like, 'Too bad. That'd never work with far-far.' "

I thought back to who had said something like that to me. Larry Shinkawa, as Mau Tim's play on the sixties expression "far out."

"What did she mean, Sinead?"

Fagan sniffled once. "Fuck am I supposed to know?"

27

ON THE DRIVE BACK TO THE CONDO, I TRIED TO FIGURE OUT WHAT "far-far" could stand for. Maybe a pet name, like "Mau Tim" itself when the girl was growing up. I found the number Joseph Danucci had given me and dialed it.

"Hello?" said Claudette Danucci's voice.

"Mrs. Danucci, this is John Cuddy."

"Oh. Oh, yes."

"I have kind of a strange question to ask."

"Please?"

"Does the expression 'far-far' mean anything to you?"

A pause. "It is America word?"

"I'm not sure. I thought it might have been a nickname or a pet name your daughter used for something or someone."

"Please, can you spell?"

"I think it would be F-A-R—F-A-R."

Another pause. "No. I do not remember her say this word."

"Could it be Vietnamese?"

253

"Vietnam word?"

"Yes."

"No. In Vietnam, we not have the 'F' letter. Only the 'Ph' letter, and 'phar-phar' mean nothing."

"How about Italian?"

"I do not know."

"Is your husband there?"

"No. But he not speak Italy words very much. I can call Primo?"

"I have his home number. I'll try him."

"No. Primo is in his car. He just leave here. I can call, ask him."

"Okay. I'll call you back later if I need to."

"Mr. Cuddy, you know who kill my daughter?"

"No, Mrs. Danucci, I don't."

She didn't say anything more, but it did take her a good five seconds to break the connection.

I pushed the buttons for directory assistance, getting the general numbers of four local universities. At each, I asked for the Linguistics department. The first school didn't have one, the second didn't answer. The third wasn't much more help.

"Linguistics." A female voice, snooty.

"Hello, I wonder if you can help me?"

"With whom do you wish to speak?"

"Well, I'm not sure. I need to know if a word is from a foreign language and what it means."

A glacial sigh. "Sir, I'm afraid we cannot be of help."

"I thought Linguistics stood for the study of languages."

"Then you are mistaken. We study language, singular and in the abstract, if you will. We are not some sort of universal translation table. Good day."

I hung up before the dial tone came on and tried number four.

"Linguistics Department, Roy speaking." A cheery voice.

I told him the same thing I told number three.

"Gee, I'm sorry but I don't think anybody here like knows *all* the languages. But there is someplace I can send you."

"Where?"

The librarian at the reserve desk on the second floor curved her hand to the right. "The section closest to the copy machine, the shelves on both sides. In alphabetical order."

I edged past a high school student in a football varsity jacket who looked like he was using both a copy machine and the Boston Public Library itself for the first time. I found the dictionaries and decided to start with Italian/English, carrying it to the nearest work table in the center of the room. I went through it slowly, trying every phonetic spelling I could think of for "far-far."

Between pages, my mind drifted to Sinead Fagan's story about her stepfather. To "Tina Danucci" moving in with her Uncle Vincent for a while, changing not just her first name but her last as well. To her uncle's chosen surname, a perversion of what a bride might do. Then I thought about Mau Tim Dani and New York. Oz Puriefoy advising her to move there, Claudette Danucci afraid she'd decided to go, Larry Shinkawa sure of it. A young woman making a clean break with everything from Boston, personal as well as professional. Burning bridges with a passion.

Then I focused on Vincent Dani himself. Making partner in his office tower, Mau Tim finding out about it and calling him from her apartment late in the afternoon of the day she died, when he was in a meeting. The lawyer maybe calling her back, listening to Mau Tim's version of what Sinead had done to her stepfather, seeing his partnership fly out the window.

After five minutes, I'd exhausted the Italian dictionary and pushed it to the corner of the table.

I got up, went back to the shelves, and started at the A's. I took down six or seven books and carried them back to my work space. Forty minutes more. Nothing.

Over the next few hours, I lost count of how many trips I

made, each time coming back with as many volumes as I could manage. Some of them were unintelligible, the language involved not using our alphabet. Those I took back to the shelves, becoming aware that I was getting some strange stares. I kept at it, though, thumbing through the pages, trying theme and variations on far-far. Zip.

By suppertime, I was down to the S books and thinking about a different approach when I reached the Swedish/English entry.

It didn't do much for my appetite, but there it was. The English translation of the Swedish phrase *"farfar."* Unless it was a complete coincidence.

I took the English word and went back through the dictionaries on my table. It was eerie, finding Mau Tim's pet word for Oz Puriefoy in the Dutch and another of her expressions with Larry Shinkawa in the Hawaiian. Even her "first boyfriend" in the Gaelic, striking my forehead with the heel of my harping hand on that one. So clear, once you had the English-version key.

Then I felt cold. Claudette Danucci had said her daughter looked things up in the Vietnamese dictionary, and everyone had commented on the dead woman's curiosity about other cultures. Now knowing why that curiosity might have been an obsession, I pictured Mau Tim Dani in my chair at the library, using the English word to go through the books. Just as I was then.

I sat there, the volumes piled up around me, forgetting to eat dinner.

Primo Zuppone was out of the Lincoln before I could get to the driver's side. The car was backed into the narrow driveway, and he was standing in front of the door with the aluminum awning as I walked toward it.

"I gotta frisk you."

Zuppone's voice didn't sound right. Strained, like he was imitating himself.

I raised my arms even though I wasn't carrying. "He told you I was coming by?"

Zuppone broke off the pat-down, his eyes getting wide.

"He told you to frisk me, but not to come up with me, right?"

Zuppone's eyes got wider, the toothpick doing a jitterbug as he finished with my ankles.

I said, "Claudette reached you and when you didn't know the answer to her question, you asked him what 'far-far' meant."

Zuppone spit out the toothpick and stepped back, letting me go in the door and up the stairs alone.

28

"So, Mr. Detective, you'll join me in some wine?"

"I don't think so."

Tommy the Temper Danucci and I were alone in his magnificent dining room. Standing at the head of the table, he was dressed in brown slacks and a brown flannel shirt with a red and green tartan pattern. The model of a modestly retired man, trying very hard to adopt an attitude of normality toward the current guest.

Danucci gestured over the decanter and two chalices to the other end of the table. I sat down, elbows on the linen cloth.

He sank slowly into his throne chair, twelve feet away. "So, you know."

I nodded.

"Tell me how, eh?"

"The timing that night at the building on Falmouth. It was all wrong because it was so tight. Too tight unless it was planned by a professional."

"Which I told you it wasn't."

I nodded again. "If the killing wasn't planned by a professional, then it was a burglar gone panicked or a crime of passion."

Danucci's blood started to rise past his throat. "And I couldn't get you to buy the B and E."

"The fire escape problem. Larry Shinkawa doesn't hear the last flight grind and squeal. Instead, he both hears the clanging noise of somebody on it and feels it still vibrating when he gets to it. That means it wasn't some other fire escape, it was this one, and it also means the killer got only as far as the second-floor landing."

"Where only the family had a key to get out of the apartment and down the inside stairs."

"Unless the killer used and replaced Tina's spare key for the second-floor door."

Danucci leaned forward, very carefully pouring himself some wine from the decanter. He swirled the chalice, inhaling before sipping from it. "How did you figure it was me?"

"I didn't."

"Eh?"

"I thought it was your son."

"My son was in Philly."

"I meant Vincent."

"Vincent." A dismissive wave from the hand that wasn't holding the chalice. "You shoulda known it wasn't Mr. Vincent Dani, Esquire. That first night with me here, you knew. You said it, remember?"

"Brains and ambition, but no heart."

"Right. No heart, no . . . passion." Danucci set the chalice down firmly. "I never told this to no one. Not my confessor, not Primo, not nobody."

I tried to stay as still as I could.

"I lost my Amatina. That Claudette and Tina, they nursed her as good as they could, as any million-dollar doctor could, but I lost her. Then I had the heart attack, and they nursed me, too. For a while there, I was weak and outta my head, then I got a little stronger but still not right, still a little outta my head. And one night, Tina, she comes into my room in her father's house. Comes in to check on me."

Danucci looked up at one of his religious paintings, a hazy Madonna. "It musta been the light from outside, through the windows. The light playing tricks on me, but I coulda sworn . . . I could swear today it was my Amatina's eyes, looking down at me, asking if I was okay, if there was anything she could do. I . . . reached up for her, and took her into my bed, and . . . That was it. She didn't fight back or resist or nothing. Then she was gone. But she come back, two nights more. And by then I knew. Knew it wasn't my Amatina. But I couldn't . . . I couldn't . . ."

The abrupt nod, scooping the chalice up again and this time drinking in a gulp.

Danucci put the chalice down but didn't refill it. "She never said a thing, Tina. Nothing. Then I got better and got back here, and still nothing. She was always polite to me, the family get-togethers. Always a hug and a kiss. I figured she . . . forgave me. That she understood that what happened, it was out of weakness, not . . ."

"You set her up in the apartment."

The eyes blazed. "What're you saying, you fucking cock-sucker? You saying I set my own blood up in that apartment to be a whore for me?"

"No. I'm saying she decided to stay in the apartment house, and probably had to ask you to do it."

"It was her mother."

"Claudette?"

"She was afraid for Tina, being in the city, living with the colored photographer. So I got Primo to scare him off, then gave Joey the idea Tina should have the place on Falmouth, where Ooch could look after her."

"And Sinead Fagan?"

"The Irish girl, Tina was friends with her. Wanted her to be in the building, too, less than market rent. I got lots of buildings, lots of properties. Didn't cost me much."

I thought about it, Mau Tim getting her revenge indirectly, receiving from her grandfather without confronting him. "What set Tina off?"

"You don't know?"

"Her mother's phone call that Friday."

"You do know. You cocksucker, you don't toy with Tommy Danucci!"

"I'm not toying. I'm guessing."

The old man lowered himself a notch. "Yeah. Well, I pick up the phone when it rings, and it's Tina. And she says, 'Mom told me, you got picked to be president of the Order of the Cross.' And I'm thinking, this is great, this is terrific, my granddaughter, she cares enough about me, she calls to congratulate me. So I say, 'Yeah, it's something I wanted since your grandmother died.' And then she hits me with it. 'Well, I don't think any religious thing is gonna want you to be their president after I tell them you're a baby-raper.' "

Danucci used the empty chalice as a prop. "I tell you, Mr. Detective, I hold the phone away from me, just like this. I hold it away account of I know it must be wrong, it's gotta be defective, I didn't hear anything like that come out of it. Then I pull it back and I say, 'Tina, Amatina, what're you saying?' And she says she's going to a party that night, she's gonna try it out on her friends before she tells her mother and father about it the next night at dinner. Tina says she wants to make real sure she's got it down right before she calls the Order and tells them."

"You told me Tina talked about the party when she called you."

"I figured, you're a detective, you can get the company records on her phone there. They'd show the call to me, I had to have an explanation for it."

"But you didn't know the party was going to be in her building."

"No. No, she didn't say that over the phone. So, I hang up, what am I supposed to do, eh? You tell me. I pace back and forth here, maybe two, three minutes. I can feel my heart, racing. Primo, he's out shopping for me, but I can't bring him into it, anyway. Can't let him know. . . . So I grab my keys to the place on Falmouth, I got them all on a ring. I go out, walk up to Hanover, find a cab. A colored, just dropping off a fare for one of the restaurants, he don't know me from a hole in the ground. I tell him to take me to the corner by the building. He's driving, I'm thinking, what can I say to her?

"I get to the front door of the building, I let myself in with my key to it. I go past the apartment door on the first floor, and I hear this music. But it's not real loud or nothing, so I figure the Irish girl's just got it on for company. It don't never occur to me, she's having the party for Tina there."

Danucci refilled the chalice from the decanter. "I get up the stairs to the third floor. The door—I can just hear the shower on, then turned off. I use the key, slip inside her apartment. I can hear her moving around in the bathroom, I don't figure she can hear me. I musta put the chain on like I do here, I don't remember. Five, ten minutes I'm standing there like a jerk before Tina's out of the bathroom. She's in her robe, six feet away from me, and she says, "What are you doing here? Get the fuck out!"

The old man shook his head. "To me, she said that. I say to her, 'What do you mean, get out?' She says, 'It's my apartment. Get the fuck out.' I say, 'Your apartment? I own the whole building. This is my property.' She says, 'You can have your property. I'm late for my party.' And I say, 'Tina, Amatina, we gotta talk here.' And she says, 'Uh-unh, too late to talk, far-far.'"

Danucci looked over at me, both hands cupping the chalice. "That word, far-far, I never heard it before. Then I say, 'We gotta talk, Tina.' And she goes, 'I'm gonna do my talking to everybody who'll listen.' And I say, 'After all I done for you? After all I give you, this is what I get?' And she runs away from me into the bedroom. I start after her, but she's already back, throwing the necklace, my Amatina's necklace, at me. I go to catch it, she's bumping me, pushing me out to her living room and the door, saying, 'Take back your fucking necklace, I'm going to New York, out of your life, out of this whole life.' I say, 'New York? Tina, what're you talking about?' But she just says 'Take back your fucking necklace,' and then starts yelling a whole bunch a things at me, words I didn't understand. All I know is, I see her face in front of me, all screwed up, and crazy and I . . . I . . .''

His hands tightened around the chalice, the knuckles turning white. "I strangled her. Before I realized what I was doing, I choked the life out of my own blood."

Very quietly, I said, "Is that when the pendant broke off the necklace?"

A dismissive wave, then the abrupt nod. "I suppose. All I know is, I opened my hands and she just fell away from me. I could feel my heart, I had to sit, think about it. Try to decide what to do.

"Then there's the Jap, knocking at the door, getting louder, sounding nervous. I hear him run back down the stairs, and I get up, figure, go to the bedroom, take some more jewelry, make it look like a B and E. But I just about get in there, I got some earrings and stuff in my hand, when I hear a whole crowd at the door, voices yelling and pounding on the door, and I got to get out. So I jam everything in my pockets and go through the window. I'm on the fire escape when I hear the door open and smack against the chain. I go down as fast as I can but I hear the chain give and somebody running. The second-floor window's open, so I get in there, try to catch my breath. And I can hear everybody, I don't know how many it is, running around upstairs, yelling. So I get to the door, find the little key on my ring, and slip myself into the hall. And it's quiet enough there, except for the voices upstairs through the open door. And I go down the stairs and out. I walk a couple, three blocks before my heart says I gotta take a cab. So I do, back to like Hanover and Richmond.

"And then," Danucci seemed to deflate a little. "I walked back here."

I waited for him to recover a bit.

The old man pushed the chalice three inches away, but Primo

wasn't there to take it. "So, you figured it was family, but it wasn't Mr. Vincent Dani, Esquire. How'd you know it was me?"

"Two things other than the timing. One, the words Tina used with you she used with other people, always being careful to ask them first about their backgrounds, to be sure they wouldn't know what the words meant."

"What they meant?"

"It was her way of dealing with what happened, I think. One young guy who was interested in her told me he wasn't exotic enough for her. What he should have said was he wasn't old enough for her. That's what she did. She saw older men like George Yulin at the agency, Oz Puriefoy the photographer, and Larry Shinkawa the ad exec. Maybe she got the idea from Erica Lindqvist, talking about her family from Sweden. Tina used *seanair* with Yulin to describe her first boyfriend, *groot vader* as a pet name for Puriefoy, *tutu* and *far-far* with Shinkawa."

Danucci's mouth worked but at first nothing came out. "Those were . . . Tina yelled those things at me. What do they mean?"

"In different languages, 'grandfather.' "

The old mobster looked down at the chalice. "Mother of God."

I gave him a minute. "The other reason I knew it was you was something that didn't make sense until I knew what those words meant."

Danucci looked at me squarely. "My Amatina's necklace."

"I couldn't figure why it didn't just get left at the scene. Or why it wasn't turning up somewhere, on the street or in a trash can."

The old man rose slowly. He turned away from me and shuffled toward the tall china cabinet. Opening the door, he brought his hands shoulder-high and lifted down the big rosewood box. Turning back, he carried it to the table like a butler with the family silver. He opened the lid, reaching in and coming out with the iolite necklace.

He held it in his hand like a rosary, slowly turning it so the light from the chandelier could sparkle off the violet stones. "I couldn't leave my Amatina's necklace behind. For some fucking cop to scoff up."

"That why you didn't set up somebody else for the fall?"

Danucci spoke more to the necklace than to me. "I thought about it. Before you came into the picture, I thought about planting this on one of the people from the modeling thing who knew her. But then I'd lose my Amatina's necklace to the cops for a long time, maybe even the rest of my life. 'Evidence,' they'd say, just wanting to stick it to old Tommy the Temper as much as they could. I still haven't got back the pendant part there. Cocksuckers.

"Then I thought about suiciding somebody, like maybe the colored photographer or the Jap. I can get a couple friends of mine to arrange things with maybe a note. But I couldn't do that without my friends thinking, 'The fuck is Tommy having me set this one up for?' "

Danucci tore himself away from the necklace, giving me a look as empty as a shark to a bleeding fish. "When I realized that first night how smart you was, I even thought about having you hit, Mr. Detective." Back to the necklace. "Only I couldn't do that, either. My Joey, he never woulda thought it was an accident or some scumbag from another one of your cases. He's got a lotta heart, my Joey. He woulda known something was queer, that something got set up by somebody knew how, and he woulda never rested till he found out the straight skinny."

The ultimate irony. Tommy Danucci, the man who'd ordered a hundred deaths, not daring to order the hundred and first. A victim of his own resources.

The old gangster reluctantly laid the necklace on the linen tablecloth. "So, what's the deal, eh?"

"The deal was that if I found out who killed Tina, I'd come to you first."

Danucci watched me. "And you done that, so what's the new deal? What do you want from me?"

"Nothing."

"What's with nothing?"

"You asked me to come here first, I did. That's it."

"What are you talking about? You can't go to the cops, you wouldn't live three hours—"

"I'm not going to the cops. I'm going to your daughter-in-law."

"My . . . ? Claudette?"

"Right."

"Why?"

"Because I promised her."

"What?"

"I promised her. If I found out who killed her daughter, I'd tell her."

Danucci seemed not to breathe. He watched me, canting his head twice, the spotlight eyes boring into me. "You're serious, Mr. Detective."

"I am."

"A matter of honor."

"I don't know."

Another moment, then the abrupt nod. He reached back into the rosewood box with both hands and drew out two long-barreled, chromed revolvers by the handles. Danucci kept one trained on me while he flipped the other in his hand, then lofted it down the table toward me, the linen slowing it as the gun bunched the cloth a foot from my right hand.

The old man said, "Let's you and me play a little game of Guts, eh?"

I tried not to look at the weapon, keeping my eyes on Danucci, figuring that would give me the last warning I'd get. "I don't think so."

"Why is that?"

"I'm a little unsure of the way mine might be loaded."

A disappointed scowl. "You're a man of honor, Mr. Detective. So am I. Don't matter what you think about what happened between my Tina and me. I wouldn't give you an unloaded piece."

"I also don't particularly want to be known to your family as the man who shot you."

266

"So, maybe that ain't gonna happen, eh? Maybe Lady Luck, she'll smile on me."

If I'd seen the game of Guts coming, maybe I would have thought it through, would have seen through it. Instead, when Tommy Danucci suddenly leveled at my chest, barked "One," and pulled the trigger, I reached for the gun in front of me. When he said "Two," and pulled it again, the snap/ching of the hammer on an empty chamber made me level the heavy old piece on him. When "Three" produced flash and bang from his muzzle and a thump at my lapel, I reflexively fired three times, the way I'd been taught in the Army. The chrome andiron jumped in my hand and roared in that room, far louder than the report from his weapon.

The impact of my slugs lifted Danucci up and back, into and displacing the throne chair but not knocking it over. He drew in a huge breath, and I was to him as his lungs let it out. Behind me, feet thundered on the stairs toward the mahogany front door.

Tommy the Temper looked up at me and fingered the little burn mark on my lapel, the blood burbling through the holes in his shirt. "Before Primo gets in here . . . how's about you put a real bullet in my gun . . . so I don't look like such a jerk, eh?"

I didn't have anything smart to say back to him. Not that he could have heard it if I did.

29

THERE WAS NO NEW AGE MUSIC FLOATING THROUGH THE LINCOLN as we rode south on Route 3.

After he came through the mahogany door, Zuppone had kept a Beretta automatic pointed at me in Tommy Danucci's dining room as he made six or seven telephone calls in rapid succession. We waited about five minutes after the last one before three street soldiers in varying sizes and uniforms arrived. Primo spent a full minute kneeling before the body of Tommy Danucci in the throne chair. Then he checked both of the old chromed pistols. I could see three more live rounds drop from the gun Danucci had given me, one more blank from the one he'd fired.

Zuppone shook his head, as if to clear it, then made another telephone call, not seeming to care about me overhearing it. Finally, Primo left a soldier named Bootsy with Danucci's body in the dining room. One of the other two carried the rosewood case, with both pistols and the necklace, down the stairs to the car. The third soldier kept something in his coat pocket aimed at me, the only words spoken being "Give me a reason."

At the Lincoln, Zuppone got behind the wheel, turning with his Beretta on me as I was shoved into the back seat, passenger's side. Then the guy with the rosewood case got in the front passenger's side, putting the case between his shoes. I was told to lie on the floor of the backseat while my guard got into the backseat behind Primo and pressed the business end of his drawn weapon behind my left ear. I stayed there all the way to Joseph Danucci's house.

Zuppone left the two soldiers at the car in the driveway. He marched me in through the kitchen again, the rosewood case under one arm. Claudette Danucci was coming halfway down the hall to meet us as Primo pushed me past her and into the den.

Joseph Danucci sat in his desk chair like a heroin addict badly into the second day off the needle. Vincent Dani stood when I came into the room. Zuppone tried to close the door behind us, but Claudette managed to wedge her way into the room.

Her husband got up, his voice a rasp going against the grain. "Claudette, stay out of this."

"No."

"Goddammit, this is family business!"

"And I am family."

Claudette sat down on the edge of one of the leather chairs, folding her hands deliberately in her lap.

Joseph Danucci seethed, blinking in a ragged cadence. Then he seemed to remember me.

"I get a telephone call from Primo, I don't believe what I hear."

"I heard his side of it. What he said was true."

Danucci sent the words out one at a time, dictating to a slow scribe. "You killed my father."

"I did."

The color shot upward through his face, every vein throbbing. "And you got the gall to admit it? Before his sons?"

"I want you to hear it. All of it."

"Oh, we're gonna hear it, all right. And then we're gonna hear you make some other kinds of noises."

"I want you to hear it because I don't want to be looking over my shoulder the rest of my life."

"Won't be so long you should worry about it."

I said, "Can Primo open the case, show you what's in it?"

Danucci noticed the object under Zuppone's arm for the first time. "My mother's jewelry box?"

His attention on the box, Danucci seemed to lose a little of the rage.

Vincent Dani took advantage of the moment. "Primo, why don't you put the case on the desk and show us."

Zuppone still waited for the sign from Danucci. It came in the form of his dead father's abrupt nod as he sat back down.

Primo lowered the case to the desktop carefully. He opened it, then took out the two revolvers.

Joseph Danucci said, "What the fuck? I haven't seen those . . ."

Some distant memory worked at him. Worked over him.

Vincent Dani looked at me. "What happened?"

"Your father asked me to come to him first if I found out who killed Tina. I did, and he treated me to a game of Guts."

Tonelessly, Joseph Danucci said, "Guts."

Vincent said, "Why would Pop play Guts with you?"

"Because he knew I'd figured out that he'd killed Tina."

Zuppone sucked in half the air in the room and charged for Joseph Danucci just as Danucci showed his teeth and came out of his chair at me. Primo cushioned the collision with his chest, then waltzed Danucci back to the chair, saying "Hey-ey-ey, Boss. Boss, easy, huh? Easy."

Danucci flailed past him, only to be confronted by his wife, who had stood and crossed to them. Claudette Danucci clouted her husband across the cheek as hard as I've ever seen a man hit by a woman. Zuppone, sure of the advantage and being as gentle as possible, dragged him back, finally letting him go ten feet from me. Danucci rubbed his cheek, staring at his wife.

Claudette Danucci said, "We listen to this man." She turned to me. "What you tell us?"

"Look in the case again."

Claudette went to the desk, the top of the case still up. She first looked in, then haltingly put her hand in, picking up the necklace like it was a sleeping snake. Her good eye squinted at it, the glass one lolling for the first time in its socket as the eyelid worked on its own.

She said, "How? How can this be?"

"Your father-in-law had the necklace. All the time."

"You're a fucking dead liar, Cuddy."

I looked at Joseph Danucci. "What do you think, I found the necklace on somebody else and took it to your father's house? Then planted it on him to cover myself for shooting Tommy Danucci? When he knew I wasn't carrying, when the gun he gave me had six live rounds in it and his a couple of blanks?"

The son plowed his hair with crabbed fingers. "Primo?"

Zuppone nodded. "I believe him on that, Boss."

Danucci's hand left his hair and began to rake at the back of his neck.

Vincent Dani said, "Why would my father kill his grand-daughter?"

I looked at the lawyer. "Because she was going to expose him."

Joseph Danucci's head came up. "Expose him? For what?"

I got ready in case Primo wasn't. "When your father was recuperating from his heart attack, here in this house, he mistook your daughter for his wife and went to bed with her."

Zuppone was too jolted to move quickly enough. Joseph Danucci was on me before I got all the way up. Spluttering and gasping, he landed a wild left before I was able to get him into a clinch. I held on until I felt Primo clamp on his biceps and pull him off me and back to the other chair.

Danucci's voice was cracking as his legs kicked out for me. "Cocksucker! You fucking, lying, cocksucking bastard. We're gonna keep you alive for *days* for that! You're gonna crawl to us, beg us to kill you."

Vincent Dani, in a very low voice, said, "It's true."

Everything stopped, everyone in the room turned to him.

In a monotone directed at the carpet, Dani said, "Six years ago, a little after Pop went back home to his house, Tina came to me. At my office. She said . . . she said a friend of hers at school had a problem with . . . an uncle. She said this uncle had done some things to her friend, and was there anything a lawyer could do about it? I told her . . . I told her not likely. That if it had stopped, it would just be more trouble for her friend than it would be worth." Dani looked up at all of us. "It was good advice. That sort of matter rapidly becomes a can of worms once—"

But Claudette's hand, the one with the necklace in it, was already following through, cutting the words off his lips and a layer of skin off his cheek. "You know these things! You know my daughter tell you these things and you keep silent?"

Dani touched his cheek, gawking at the blood on his fingers. "Claudette—"

She stomped to her husband. "Look at me."

He didn't.

She shook the necklace in front of his face. "Look at me."

Danucci, mouth open, breathing badly, raised his head.

"My husband, this man live." She pointed to me. "This man tell us who kill our child. Your father still live, I kill him for my daughter. You kill this man, and I kill you."

Danucci grunted something.

"You kill this man, I kill you, my husband. I kill you with your food or I kill you in your sleep. But I kill you."

Claudette Danucci wheeled and stood in front of me, the lid of the glass eye quivering at half-mast. "Thank you."

She moved, at first quickly, then at a normal gait, out the door and toward the kitchen.

Vincent Dani had found a handkerchief and was holding it to his cheek. His brother was slowly getting his lungs used to regular volumes again. Zuppone stood just behind Danucci's chair, the hands on the back of the seat but close enough to the shoulders to push him back down.

The voice from the chair sounded like a man with strep throat. "Primo?"

"Yes, Boss?"

"The fuck do we do here?"

The situation man said, "First we call Bootsy back at your father's house, get him to do the clean-up. Then we call Doctor T, get him to do the death certificate, saying he was the attending physician and your father's heart gave out. Then we get Richie and Paul over at the funeral home there, do their thing quick."

Danucci looked at me as though I were dirty dishes the morning after a party. "What about him?"

Zuppone said, "He dates a D.A., Boss. We clip him, we got more trouble, maybe all this about . . . Tina comes out. We let him live, he don't got no reason to tell nobody. Right, Cuddy?"

"All the insurance company needs is me saying the people at the modeling agency didn't have anything to do with it. I can tell the company that without getting into any of what we talked about tonight."

Danucci said, "Primo, you see to that?"

"Sure, Boss."

Danucci came back to me. He gave his father's abrupt nod, his voice steadier. "Get the fuck out of my sight."

Zuppone was walking me toward the kitchen when I heard it. A sound somewhere between nails being driven and glass being broken.

We entered the kitchen. Claudette Danucci was crying, trying to center what was left of the iolite necklace on one of the tiles in her countertop. She glanced at us with the good eye, then used a forearm to mop sweat and tears from her face as she raised a heavy skillet in that hand and smashed down again on the gems in the necklace, tiny shards skittering across the tiles, some of which were broken from earlier blows.

We left her like that, hammering to dust the necklace that was the color of her dead daughter's eyes.

In the driveway outside the kitchen door, Zuppone told the two soldiers that Joseph Danucci just got word that his father had died of a heart attack. The soldiers, both of whom had seen me with the old man's riddled body, exchanged looks and nodded and said they were sorry to hear it. Primo told them to stay with the Danuccis in case they needed anything that night. As we drove toward Boston, he put a tape into the slot on the dashboard and settled in to piano and violin.

I waited ten miles before saying, "Thanks for backing me in there."

Zuppone kept his eyes on the road. A minute later he said, "I wasn't backing you. I was looking out for them."

That was it. Just the music and the tires slapping the junctions in the pavement as we dodged potholes on the way toward the bright lights.

When we got off the Expressway, Primo drove up Kneeland to where it becomes Stuart, then down Charles to Beacon. He stopped the Lincoln at the corner of Arlington, five blocks from my condominium building.

"Okay you get out here?"

I looked around but didn't see anything or anybody except a couple walking some kind of hairless terrier down the ramp from the river. The dog looked like a rat on a rope.

"I think I can find my way."

Zuppone spit his toothpick out the window and reached for a new one. "I'm gonna be busy next couple of days, taking care of things."

"Probably a good idea nobody sees us together anyway, given tonight."

Primo seemed to savor the fresh piece of wood in his mouth. "You gonna need any help with the insurance thing there?"

"I maybe have an idea on that. Can I call you about it?"

"Make it from a pay phone, huh?"

"I will."

Zuppone said, "It was a good thing you didn't punch back after Joey landed that left."

"He had a right to be upset. Besides, I didn't want to press my luck."

"Luck." The half-laugh. "Cuddy, after what I seen tonight, when it comes to luck, you must shit shamrocks."

30

THREE DAYS LATER, A TAXI WAS TAKING US FROM NEW YORK'S PENN Station uptown. Our cabbie sat on those woven beads that are supposed to allow circulated air to keep you cooler in summer and warmer in winter. Cooler would be good, the temperature being in the high seventies.

Around 45th Street, Primo Zuppone leaned forward. Through the Plexiglas he said to the driver, "Go a little farther north, okay? Drop us at Rockefeller Plaza."

"Whatever you say, mon."

We got out there, the flags of the nations slacking high above our heads as canned music wafted up from below.

Zuppone said to me, "Come on. Take a look at this."

About a hundred people stood around in the heat looking down toward the ice surface. A young woman in leotards and a short skirt, graceful as a ballerina, was doing a figure skating drill. The woman was magic, and she knew it.

Zuppone said, "One time I'm down here, I remember seeing this. Incredible, ain't it, this time of year?"

"We had the ice in Boston, kids'd be playing pick-up hockey on it."

Primo started to walk east toward Fifth Avenue. "Cuddy, you got to look for the art in life."

We passed a mime in a black scuba wet suit. He wore a Greek mask and was doing his routine to a boombox blaring the theme from *The Exorcist*.

I said, "Art is everywhere."

We turned south onto Fifth catercorner from St. Patrick's Cathedral, the two spires striving heavenward above three massive entrances. On the steps, tourists clicked their cameras, construction workers sunned themselves, and the homeless shook large soda cups containing salted change.

Zuppone and I did a couple of blocks on Fifth. Past a slim Hispanic woman giving some Japanese schoolgirls directions. Past a Korean grocer helping an elderly couple pick out two nectarines. Past a brawny black man driving a delivery van with a pink stuffed animal tied to the grille.

I found the address I wanted just where I remembered it, between forty-eighth and forty-seventh, in the jewelry district. On the first floors of the surrounding buildings, bunkers with porthole windows displayed all sorts of set gems against felt backgrounds. Despite the heat, grave men in black frock coats and matching hats moved quickly along the sidewalk, heavy sample cases clutched tightly in their hands. Behind them, graver men wore ill-fitting sports jackets, bulges over hips or under arms. The men in black were Orthodox diamond merchants with ringlets of sideburns and shaved necks, the others their bodyguards with short hair and no necks.

Primo said, "I get tired of what I'm doing, looks like plenty of work down here."

We entered the lobby, the directory telling us Empire still had the whole building. Winningham, Bradley K., was listed on fourteen.

The elevator opened onto a carefully cultivated reception area. Beautiful potted plants, probably professionally maintained, canopied over a beveled desk. The woman behind it held herself like a pre-Hippie Barnard graduate. She asked if she could help us.

"Brad Winningham, please. I know it's his first day back, but he said he wanted to see us as soon as possible."

Barnard let me finish. "Will Mr. Winningham know what this is regarding?"

"Just tell him John Cuddy is here with an associate."

She looked at Primo, who smiled senilely.

"Just a moment." The receptionist lifted a receiver, tapped a button, and paraphrased my words to someone else.

A minute later, another woman about the same age came down the hall. "I'm afraid Mr. Winningham's schedule is full for the day." She sounded like the voice I'd heard when I telephoned Winningham's office the prior week. "Perhaps if you—"

Zuppone said, "Thanks, we can find him," and set off up the corridor she'd come down.

The second woman said, "Wait! What are you doing?"

I told her, "Believe me, this won't take long," and followed Primo as the women spoke urgently to each other behind us.

When I caught up to Zuppone in a branching suite, he was standing outside a door with Winningham's nameplate next to it.

I said, "We have maybe three minutes before some kind of security gets here."

Primo knocked once and went in.

Winningham looked up from behind a desk with neat stacks of opened mail on it and a couple of visitor's chairs in front of it. My first impression of him was that not much had changed since I'd seen him last. But then, a nice tan can fool you. When he opened his mouth, I notice the bottom front teeth were a little cruddy, the lines around his mouth digging deeper into the cheeks and toward the ears. He still had a great preppy haircut, though, most of the strands more brown than gray.

"What the—Cuddy?"

"Your secretary gave us the impression you were flat out, so why don't we just get to it."

Winningham stood up, shooting his cuffs even though he wasn't wearing a suit jacket, trying to seize control. "John Francis Cuddy. The 'John F. Danucci' message. Hilarious."

Hilarious. Four syllables. Some things never change.

Winningham turned to Zuppone. "And who might you be?"

Primo moved forward comfortably, taking a chair and making a ritual out of fitting a toothpick into his mouth. "Let's just say I'm a guy who don't need no introduction."

Zuppone let that go around the room a bit before adding, "The Danucci family, they ain't crazy about you fucking around here, Bradley."

The tan faded, the flesh beneath it a tad doughy. "What . . . What do you . . . ?"

I said, "We want to have a little talk with you, Brad. Without benefit of tape-recording or other memorialization."

At that point, Winningham's secretary and two guys in rent-a-cop outfits and sidearms came into the room behind us.

She said, "Mr. Winningham, these men just barged past me—"

"I know, Louise."

"Do you want them removed?"

It was still Louise who spoke. The guards, after a quick study of Primo and me, didn't seem all that keen. Winningham looked like a man having trouble toting up the score.

Zuppone said, "We could always talk later, Bradley."

Primo didn't make any attempt to move, and there was no doubt that Winningham had a bad feeling about what "later" might mean.

"No. Er, Louise, that will be all."

The rent-a-cops exhaled, but the secretary didn't seem so sure. "Mr. Winning—"

"No, really, Louise. It's all right."

She showed her disapproval but left with the uniforms, closing the door behind her.

Winningham tried a recovery. "Very well, Cuddy, why don't you take a seat so we can—"

Zuppone said, "Sit down, Bradley."

Winningham wiped his hands on his thighs and sat. I took the chair next to Primo.

Zuppone said, "Cuddy?"

I waited until Winningham looked over at me. "Brad, I think you really stepped in it this time."

"What—"

I held up my hand. "You get a claim. You recognize the changed name. You think, 'Hey, be jolly fun, Cuddy chasing his tail, thinking he was doing a favor for old Harry Mullen. Maybe Cuddy gets his tit in the wringer with a mob family.' That would really—what did you call it, Brad? 'Effectuate reparations'?"

Primo said, "That what you called it, Bradley?"

Winningham shook a little.

"Well," I said, "we have a problem, Brad. The family is less than amused by your sense of humor. They think the death of one of their children is kind of a sore subject for practical jokes."

Primo said, "Listen to the man, Bradley."

Every time Zuppone spoke, it took a few words of mine before Winningham could look from Primo back to me.

"Brad, the time with that casualty claim, just before you edged me out of a job? That's nothing compared to this. When that happened, I thought about maybe putting on a sandwich board and standing out on the sidewalk with a cowbell, letting the passing public know what you'd pulled. But then it was just between you and me, Brad. Now, the oil's aboiling."

Zuppone said, "You ever see anything boiled in oil, Bradley?"

Winningham's Adam's apple bobbed for the knot in his tie.

Time to throw the lifesaver. "So, here's what we're going to do, Brad. Brad?"

Winningham came back to me.

"First, we're going to sign off on the death claim on Mau Tim Dani. Paid in full after concluding investigation."

He said, "I can do that. Tomorrow, there's—"

Primo said, "Today, Bradley."

Winningham nodded.

I said, "Second, we're going to maintain Harry Mullen as Head of Claims Investigation/Boston for—"

Winningham's eyes bugged. "I can't restore—"

Zuppone said, "Bradley, Bradley. You interrupt, you might miss something important."

Winningham just stared at him.

I said, "You've got the chips to do it, Brad. Over the course of a career, a man like you squirrels away a lot of chips. Haul them out and play them, Brad. See to it that everybody who matters agrees that closing the investigation office in Boston would be a real mistake. See to it that Harry is taken care of with the job he's got for as long as he wants it."

"You don't understand. There's no way I—"

Primo made a sizzling sound through his teeth. The sound of something being cooked.

Winningham looked at him and then to me. Then he nodded again.

I stood up. "That ought to do it, Brad. I'll send my bill through Harry. See ya 'round the quad, huh?"

Out on Fifth, Zuppone flicked the toothpick into the gutter at the curb. The traffic was flowing pretty smoothly, lots of taxis just cruising.

I said, "Want to head back?"

Primo reached into a pocket. "Little while now, I'm gonna be pretty hungry."

"There'll be a café car on the train."

Zuppone made a face, then stuck a fresh toothpick in it. "Tell you what, I know a good restaurant." He pointed downtown. "On Mott Street by Hester."

"Stay over, you mean?"

"Yeah. We go to a hotel for the night, or we can crash with some friends of mine, we need to."

"I like the hotel better."

"Sure, sure."

"Primo?"

"Yeah?"

"What kind of restaurant is this?"

The toothpick moved from one corner to the other. "What kind."

Zuppone turned from me with the half-laugh and raised his hand to hail a cab.